SLADE'S MARAUDER

by

Steven Cade

BOOK CLUB ASSOCIATES   LONDON

This edition published 1980 by
Book Club Associates
by arrangement with Souvenir Press Ltd

For Shane and Dorothy Duff

Printed in Great Britain by
Richard Clay (The Chaucer Press) Ltd
Bungay, Suffolk

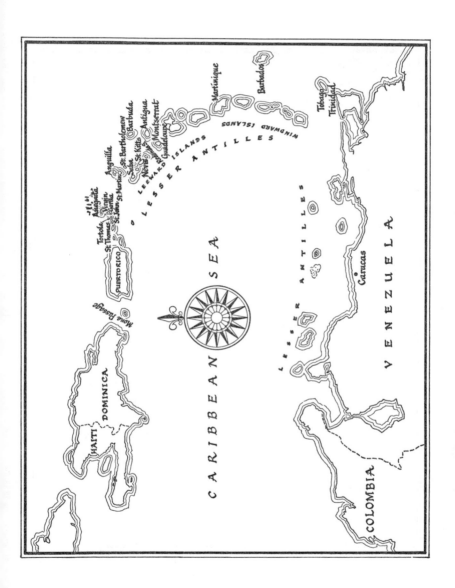

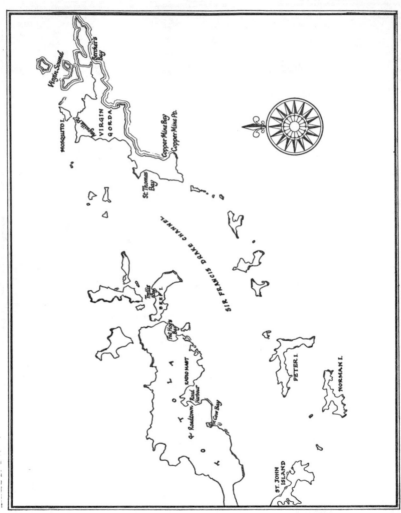

September 3rd 1939.

'The German Navy can do little more than show it can die courageously'—Grand Admiral Erich Raeder, Commander in Chief, Kriegsmarine.

'Between November 1939 and October 1943 German marauders destroyed, damaged or captured a total of 890,000 tons of shipping'—Bundesarchiv, Militärarchiv.

1

The sun had not yet tipped the balance of night into day across the Caribbean, but colours were flowing down from the east like carnival streamers. A mist hung over the sea, caught in pastel shades of pink and glowing purple, breaking now and then to reveal dark lagoons etched with phosphorescent blue. It was a ghostly dawn and the ship that came gliding out of the fading night enhanced the image of a twilight world, its diesels throbbing like a distant drum, its slab-sided hull dark and silent, showing no lights or sign of life.

On the bridge dark shapes stood motionlessly behind the glass, beyond them an eerie helmsman glowed in reflected green light from the compass. Faces with the palor of death gazed ahead where, briefly, another ship appeared and was as quickly gone into a blanket of mist. But its effect was immediate. The captain turned and spoke urgently in German and in the bowels of the ship muted bells began to ring.

'Range two thousand,' said the first officer, gazing through his binoculars. 'Steady on two-four-zero, all engines one third.'

'Stand by to collapse bulwarks. Ready with ensign.' The captain replaced the plug in the voice tube and looked out across the foredeck. Seamen were moving to the deckhousing, preparing to pull the forward section away. And along the hull of the freighter collapsible steel plates were being unfastened, ready to swing down and expose the four single 21 inch torpedo tubes.

The gunnery officer turned in his seat at the rear of the bridge, earphones around his neck. 'Forward guns manned and have range, sir.'

9

Captain Erich Kroehner nodded and lifted his glasses. His heavy, square-jawed features conveyed no sign of tension. His voice was quiet, but firm; his gaze direct without being intense. Yet the ship ahead, its lights glowing through the purple mist, would soon become his first kill as the master of the German marauder *Tamerande*.

Erich Kroehner was forty-nine, his black hair flecked with grey and his face lined and weathered by a lifetime at sea. He was the son of a merchant captain and had already made his first officer's ticket when World War 1 broke out and presented him with a new career in the Kaiserliche Marine. He rose to be one of the youngest commanders in the Kaiser's navy, but with the German surrender in 1918 found himself without a ship or a future. He married a girl from Bremen who produced two sons he saw sporadically over the years, for he soon returned to the Merchant Navy and served as first officer on a freighter operating in the Far East out of Singapore. In 1932 he became captain of his first merchantman and sailed the Pacific until 1938 when he returned to Bremen where his ship, the *Tamerande*, was scheduled for a lengthy refit.

Over the years his wife had become a plump, matronly woman who doted on her two sons and had little in common with the tanned, squarely built man she had seen for a total of two years during the nineteen years of their marriage. Her eldest son, Karl, was eighteen and studying medicine at Hamburg University whilst his brother, Otto, was a rising member of the Hitler Youth and the apple of his mother's eye. Erich felt only a mild regret that he neither liked or understood any of them, least of all Otto who strutted around the house with a swastika on his arm and a baleful contempt for anyone out of uniform.

Early in 1939 Captain Kroehner was summoned to the Seekriegsleitung in Berlin where Admiral Schniewind, chief of the Naval Operations Staff, informed him that the *Tamerande* would no longer be available for service in the Pacific. It had been requisitioned by the kriegsmarine and would undergo a secret refit by Deschimag Werke of Bremen. The captain took the news calmly, his three months in Germany having been sufficient to see and understand the massive preparations for war. The navy, he knew, would be the most vulnerable service, for the Treaty of Versailles had limited Germany to a handful of warships and a total strength of only fifteen thousand men. And yet the *Tamerande* was no fighting ship and the old fashioned, slab-sided freighter was too large and clumsy as a supply vessel.

He requested a meeting with Grand Admiral Erich Raeder and was flattered when it was granted immediately. He duly arrived at Berlin's Tirpitzufer and was shown into the oak-panelled office of the Commander in Chief. An hour later he left with the rank of Lieutenant Commander and orders to supervise the conversion of *Tamerande* into a disguised marauder, one of thirteen ships which would be operated by the Special Intelligence Division of the Seekriegsleitung. When Britain and France declared war on Germany on September 3rd 1939, Captain Kroehner was on the bridge of the *Tamerande*, clearing the Straits of Denmark bound for the North Sea, and from there across the Atlantic.

'Starboard tubes ready to fire. Range one thousand.' The First Officer, Wolf Tellmann, held the microphone cupped in his hand, looking across it to the captain.

Kroehner gazed through his binoculars at the glowing ship in the mist, wishing he could see its name and class. It still seemed impossible to believe that the deck which throbbed beneath his feet, the bridge which had been the focal point of so much contentment over the years, was now to become an instrument of death. He hesitated, knowing that Tellmann was growing impatient, but trying to remember who it was who had said: 'In a war of ideas, only people die.'

'Captain?'

He lowered the glasses and swung round, nodding briskly.

Tellmann's eyes gleamed. 'Torpedoes. Fire one, fire two, fire three.'

There was no sound. They continued to plough steadily through the gentle sea, concealed by mist which coiled around them like a shroud.

'Break the ensign,' said the captain, his words measured and grave.

'War colours,' said Tellmann briskly.

'All guns standing by,' said the gunnery officer.

Kroehner nodded, closing his eyes, counting the last seconds. There was a dull concussion, then a red glow in the mist. 'Commence firing.'

'Commence fire, all batteries,' snapped the gunnery officer.

Steel panels slid aside in the forward funnel of the freighter and a second later a 75 millimetre gun opened fire. Along the starboard side of the ship sections of bulwarks collapsed outwards on hinges, revealing heavy 5.9 inch guns which had seen service a quarter of a century ago. They opened fire, their shells screaming over the narrow stretch of sea as the second torpedo took the vessel amidships. There was a tremendous explosion which sent a ball of fire into the sky, sweeping aside the mist so that for a moment the ship was clearly visible.

Captain Kroehner gripped the steel rim of the bridge so hard that his knuckles gleamed like ivory. The ship that was already coming apart with gouts of flame was a liner, its decks festooned with bunting and lights. Even as he watched it heeled, spilling a torrent of water from a swimming pool on the promenade deck. Another explosion shook the vessel, but it was impossible to tell whether it was the last torpedo or some fuel tank which had ignited. The upper deck erupted into the sky on a column of fire, then black smoke rolled out in oily clouds. The last thing they saw before smoke and mist enveloped the stricken vessel was the main deck dipping into the sea as the liner began to capsize, its stern already lifting clear of the water as it began to slide beneath the waves.

There was silence on the bridge of the *Tamerande*. The

mist closed around them, the rising sun tinging it with reds and golds. Behind them there was a last concussion, a shock-wave that went through the deck beneath them. The ship swayed, then steadied, ploughing on.

2

The *Tinkerbelle* once plied the coast of North America all the way from Vancouver Island to Acapulco, delivering grain and fruit to San Francisco or steel from the mills of Oregon to the industrial complexes of Los Angeles and San Diego. She was a blunt-nosed 3,000-tonner with narrow decks and a stubby bridge that sat squarely amidships above a saloon deck carefully designed to attract the more discerning passenger. Staterooms were veneered in walnut and sandalwood, with murals of angels and distant rosy mountains. The main saloon was full of mahogany and deep hide chairs which glowed redly in the light of brass oil lamps.

In the Twenties the combination of freight and passengers proved to be successful and *Tinkerbelle* established a reputation for efficient and comfortable service, but as the automobile gained in popularity and the depression of the Thirties began to bite, the owners saw the need for larger bulk carriers and the elegant vessel was sold. The new owner was a shipping company in Caracas which had built up a precarious business serving that wide sweep of islands in the Caribbean from the West Indies to the Windward Islands. Soaring inflation and plunging freight rates soon wiped out their slim profit margins and in 1935 the vessel was withdrawn from service and laid up. A year later the company went into bankruptcy and the *Tinkerbelle* was taken over by the creditors, who succeeded in leasing it to Captain Lincoln P. Slade.

The leasing agent was later informed that he met Linc Slade on the only day he was ever known to have been sober in the afternoon, and that the only reason he still had his

Master's ticket was because his previous employers were fighting a desperate battle with their insurers who were trying to prove negligence on the part of the captain. Certainly Slade lost no time in putting to sea, beginning a celebration cruise of the islands which was still going on four years later.

The agents responsible for collecting the meagre return due to them under the lease spent much of the time impounding the vessel at ports which usually refused to recognise their authority. To be fair to the captain there were occasions when he was able and willing to pay what he owed, but it would also be fair to say that he spent more time and energy evading payment than he did in looking for business. He had never made any attempt to operate the ship as a commercial enterprise, preferring to run it as a kind of mobile home that occasionally carried cargo to pay the bills.

The *Tinkerbelle* was crewed by a motley collection of Puerto Ricans who were the only seamen prepared to sail with a captain given to falling off the bridge at regular intervals and a chief engineer who suffered from DTs and had to be locked in the forward hold from time to time. To say it was a happy ship would be to grossly understate the facts. It was the closest thing to floating nirvana that Linc Slade would ever know, and the Puerto Ricans were content to forego regular pay packets in exchange for minimum work and unlimited supplies of rum and gin. Occasionally, when they were down to the last crate and the cook was serving salted sailfish, the ship would go into overdrive and spend a month collecting and delivering cargo, but once it was fully provisioned lethargy would descend once more and they would resume their cruise of the islands.

These were idyllic days when Captain Slade would doze beneath the awning on the forward deck, a jug at his elbow and the deck vibrating comfortably beneath his feet. And when vision blurred and coherent thought became impossible, there was always First Officer Culpepper to straddle the bridge with his bible tucked firmly under his arm and a psalm on his lips to suit the day.

The captain and his mate were two men in complete contrast. Whereas Linc Slade was tall and bony with a shock of hair bleached almost white above a face that looked as if it had been put together for Hallowe'en, the first officer was small and plump with smooth features and curling black hair. He looked younger than his thirty-three years and could have taken his pick of larger vessels, but Culpepper had a mission in life and the *Tinkerbelle*'s endless island cruise gave him the time and opportunity to carry the gospels to the un-enlightened islanders. These people, for all their carefree smiles, were clearly in need of the kind of discipline that only Christianity could provide. The fact that his captain was also in need of the Good Book was another reason for staying with the ship, although his early hopes of converting Slade to a life of temperance and prayer had long since given way to a more realistic acceptance of the fact that this could only be achieved by something approaching Divine Intervention.

Captain Slade was as much a mystery to Culpepper as anyone else in the Caribbean, appearing as he did out of nowhere to haunt the waterfront bars of Caracas for a month before hearing of the *Tinkerbelle*. There were rumours that his ship had floundered in the South China Sea – overladen and undermanned according to some – but Slade had never confirmed or denied the stories. He never spoke of the past, even in his most loquacious moments when he was into his third bottle of gin and rapidly approaching the stupor stage.

All that could be gleaned from his papers was that he had been born in Baltimore in 1891 and served his apprenticeship on the sailing barges that plied the eastern coast of the United States from Boston to the Florida Keys. In 1910 he had been a midshipman with the White Star Line, but in spite of the prestige of serving with one of the world's major shipping companies he had left within two years to join a broken down fleet of cargo vessels based in Singapore. After that the information in his papers was sparse and of dubious origin. He took his third officer's ticket on a Greek freighter out of Bombay, his second on a Liberian vessel that sank the following year, and finally became master of a small freighter based in Hong Kong.

Culpepper had no idea at what point during his climb up the ladder of command he took to the bottle, or what distant event made it necessary to blind reason with alcohol and replace it with primitive passions that even today took him to the depths of depravity on half the islands of the Caribbean. It was enough that Lincoln Slade was a sinner of epic proportions striding through a world that seemed tailored for debauchery; where every island yielded a throng of nubile women who seemed incapable of shame; where every village responded with delight to the drunken orgies of the *Tinkerbelle*.

On these occasions Culpepper could only seek solace in the bible, praying for guidance and hoping for the miracle that would one day show the captain and his crew the error of their ways. But in the meantime it was like sailing with Satan's right hand man; a voyage where each day was a challenge, each night a burden that only the bible could help him to bear. His great fear was that in time he would come to accept the excesses of Slade and the crew; that he would come to accept the drinking and gambling and even those unmentionable acts which echoed through the forecastle whenever they were anchored off some friendly island. Perhaps one day he would even come to terms with their forays in the Virgin Islands where a visit from the *Tinkerbelle* was always an excuse for festivities and a subsequent increase in the birth rate nine months later. It was as though Slade and his crew were obsessed with the idea of destroying any claim the inhabitants might have to calling themselves Virgin Islanders.

Fortunately a week at one of the islands invariably meant a month's recuperation among the Leeward Islands followed

17

by a month's work to replenish fuel and provisions. Nevertheless, the cycle worried Culpepper who could see that the population of the Virgin Islands was getting paler by the year. At this rate, he estimated, they would have created a new race in less than twenty years.

By the winter of 1939 the *Tinkerbelle* bore little resemblance to the elegant vessel that once plied the wealthy ports of America's Pacific seaboard. The decks were rutted and stained, the paintwork barely worthy of the name, and rust festered from the leaking funnel to the creaking plates of the hull. The chief engineer, Harry McVay spent more and more time taking the old engines apart and cursing with drunken fury as pistons failed or another jet of steam meant another day lagging the boiler pipes. When it all became too much for him he would retire with a crate of whisky and not emerge until he had to be carried screaming to his cell in the bow. On those occasions they would alter course for the nearest island and while away a week or so until he got back to work in the engine room, his eyes like open sores and his skin the texture of crumpled lead.

Slade had neither the money nor the inclination to put the ship into dry dock for the refit it badly needed, and as the weeks wore into December Culpepper began to feel that the cruise of the *Tinkerbelle* was finally coming to an end. He spent long periods in his neat cabin, reading the bible and praying for some miracle that would inject a new spirit of determination into the captain and crew. He was convinced that only this could save the ship from coming apart at the seams, probably when he was the only sober man on board.

Culpepper's prayers were answered on the 19th day of December, 1939, but in a manner which convinced him even more that God did, indeed, work in strange and mysterious ways.

3

Captain Slade awoke with his mouth tasting like the bottom of a very busy birdcage and his eyeballs feeling as though they didn't fit the sockets any more. He forced open a lid, wincing as a shaft of sunlight lashed the optical nerve and began beating a drum in the back of his skull. Somebody groaned in agony. He recognized the voice as his own.

'Jesus, Culpepper,' he whispered, identifying the plump figure in sparkling whites, 'what the fuck are you trying to do? Just crucify me and be done with it!'

'I'm sorry, Captain, but you have to come up on the bridge.'

'I couldn't come up on my left knee. My liver is in spasm and if I nod my head it's going to fall off, so do me a favour and just . . . just piss off for a day or two.'

He closed the eye. The relief was almost worth the pain.

'Captain Slade, I have to insist that you take command of your ship.'

'Oh, Jesus, we're not going to have another bleeding sermon are we?'

He spoke painfully between his teeth. There was no reply, but something resembling a sob reached him. He frowned and opened his eyes, looking up at the first officer with growing astonishment. Culpepper was clutching the bible in both hands, his tanned features strangely contorted. With growing horror Slade realized that his first officer was crying, then with the thought came the awareness that the ship was not moving. The engines were silent.

He forced himself onto the side of his bunk, grappling with his trousers whilst trying to guess what calamity had befallen them. 'Are we still afloat?' he asked finally.

Culpepper managed a shaky nod.

Slade tottered to the chair and pulled on the stained grey T-shirt. It should have been washed weeks ago, but there was a hole about the size of a fist in its side and one more pounding by the cook was all it needed. He slipped on a pair of battered sandals and reached for the bottle of gin, shuddering in anticipation.

'Sir, I don't think you ought to.'

'Oh shit, Culpepper, when are you going to learn?'

There was a repetition of the sound that was remarkably like a sob. He glowered at him, noting the tears on the man's cheeks and quite baffled by the phenomenon.

'Look, Culpepper, if McVay has finally hanged himself you don't need to get all screwed up about it. If ever a man deserved to go by his own hand it's that whisky-sodden engineer of ours.'

He poured half a tumbler of gin and took a long drink, revolted by the taste but bolstered by the rawness of the spirit. He took a long wheezing breath, clamped a battered cap on his head and started for the door, pausing there to drink the rest of the gin and place the glass on the shelf where he automatically reached for it whenever he entered the cabin. Culpepper, who was clinging to his bible as though he would drown without it, began to follow.

'Is it McVay?'

Culpepper shook his head. 'He's on deck. It's something that you have to see, Captain.'

Slade shook his head and wished he hadn't, then went through the door and along the passage to the companionway. When he stepped out on deck the first thing that struck him was the revolting odour. At first he thought that someone had been gutting fish on the deck again and not cleaning the mess away, but the absence of any fishy elements in the smell made him look around for another source. The foredeck was very still and silent, but crewmen were lining the rails on both sides and there was something in their attitudes that brought the first spasm of alarm. He walked towards them, the smell growing stronger with each step, his brain beginning to relate it to other things so that when he reached the rail he had begun to steel himself for the shock. It didn't help at all.

The ship was lying in a sea of bodies. As far as the eye could see were men, women and children. They floated face up or face down, already bloated by the sun into caricatures of human beings. Seagulls circled overhead, diving now and then with dreadful intent. Slade felt his stomach turn and closed his eyes, trying to pinch the smell from his nostrils.

'It's the air in their bodies that keeps them afloat,' said a voice beside him. It was the galley hand who doubled as sick bay attendant. 'That and the sea being calm like this.'

'How in God's name did this . . . ?'

Tommy, a Puerto Rican who served as third mate, turned and pointed to the body of what had once been a young woman. His face was yellow, glistening with perspiration. 'Gunshot wound in that one. And there's a little lad over there who's had an arm blown away.'

'Oh, Jesus!' said Slade, hunching over the rail, forcing his eyes to move from body to body. There were children, many children, in pyjamas and nightgowns that must have been frilly and perfumed with talcum not so long ago. Some of the men had uniforms that had been white until blood stained them and buttons tore away as the bodies inside grew too large. He staggered back from the rail, bending and retching. When he straightened Culpepper handed him a mug of water. He nodded and gulped it down, understanding now why the first officer had been in tears.

'What can we do, sir?' asked Culpepper, his voice filled with despair.

'Lower two boats,' said Slade. 'You take one, I'll take the other. Every man to wear something over his mouth and nose, and we'll need knives. A lot of knives.'

They looked at him with growing horror. He glared back, wishing he could cry too.

21

'They must be given a Christian burial, Captain,' said Culpepper.

'We couldn't get them on board, not half of them. If we did what the hell could we do then? We're not equipped for anything like this. Nobody is. And there'll be disease. Those bodies have been roasting in the sun so long some of them are ready to explode. Think about it, Culpepper.'

The first officer nodded with wooden features and moved away towards the boats. Tommy went with him, looking afraid. Slade returned to the rail, gazing at the bodies that bobbed gently in the turquoise sea. What kind of hideous monster did this? he asked himself. What kind of evil mind could conceive death on this scale, in this manner?

The two longboats were lowered from their davits and six men went down the ropes into each of them. They all wore masks of cheesecloth from a bolt the cook kept in the galley, and the pieces had been soaked in a solution of antiseptic that was unpleasant to breathe but at least protected them from bacteria and the odour of death and decay. Nobody spoke as they moved slowly away from the ship and began with the first body. It was the young woman, an ugly wound in her shoulder. Slade lifted the sharp kitchen knife over the bloated stomach, staring at the men around him.

'This is the only thing we can do. If we had help, or a bigger ship with plenty of tarpaulin, then it might have been possible to do more. But we cannot leave them to rot, to be picked at by the birds. The only thing we can do is this.'

He plunged the knife down, trying not to listen to the rush of gas and fluids that spurted from the body. A moment later it began to sink, stiffly, the arms and legs at odd angles, turning slowly as it went. They moved on, the men bending out from the side of the boat, plunging knives and spikes into the bodies. The humid air held the heavy gases like a cloud so that after a while they could barely breathe, their minds bending under the strain as body after body was punctured and laid to rest. Men whimpered, others vomited over the

22

side. And all of them saw a vision of hell that would be with them for the rest of their days.

They found the survivors on a piece of broken lifeboat that was floating in a circle of wreckage. They were about a quarter of a mile from the *Tinkerbelle*, dealing with the last of the bodies on this side. Tommy was in the bow, leaning out to reach three women huddled on the piece of wreckage, their legs trailing limply in the water.

'Wait, Tommy,' said Slade, moving forward. 'They're not bloated like the rest.'

They came alongside and pulled the first of the women into the water. She stirred, her arms moving weakly. The men cheered and two went over the side, lifting the women into the boat. They were all alive, one of them even opening her eyes to thank them. Somehow it eased the horror of the past hour, made them feel that the terrible things they had been forced to do had accomplished something worth while.

Back on the *Tinkerbelle* the captain got under way, making a wide sweep of the area in the hope of finding more survivors, before finally accepting the fact that there were none to be found. He handed over to Culpepper who had said nothing since he came on board, his eyes haunted by the ordeal. For the first time that anyone could remember he had drunk a glass of brandy, but even this had done nothing to change his ashen pallor.

Slade made his way to the saloon deck where Tommy and the sick bay hand, an elderly Puerto Rican called Santiano, were doing their best to revive the three women. The one who had recovered consciousness was lying in a stateroom, her head propped up on two pillows. She smiled wanly at the captain as he entered, a half empty bowl of soup beside her. He sat down and held a spoonful to her mouth. She sipped it, her eyes curious as they took in his unkempt hair and clothes.

'Are you really the captain?' she asked in a weak but pleasantly husky voice.

'Linc Slade, ma'am,' he said, suddenly conscious of the

23

stubble of beard. 'Is there anything else that you'd like?'

'The soup is fine, thank you. How many survivors did you find?'

He tried to ignore the question, spooning more soup into her whilst searching for some other topic. She gripped his wrist with surprisingly strong fingers, her deep brown eyes searching. His mouth tightened. 'Just two more, ma'am. They'll be alright.'

'But . . .' Tears came into her eyes and she shook her head, refusing to believe him. 'But there were hundreds of people on board, Captain. It was the SS *Cormorant* on its Christmas cruise. There were over three hundred passengers and heaven knows how many crew.'

'There may have been more survivors who got away in the boats,' Slade told her, although he knew this could not be true. If there had been any lifeboats they would have stayed with the swimmers, trying to help. He suddenly realized that many of the bloated bodies must have died at the same time, perhaps all of them, from shock, otherwise they would have swallowed water and probably sunk.

'Was there an explosion?' he asked.

She nodded, her eyes clouding with fear. 'A terrible one. It blew everyone into the sea. And there were flames, and so much smoke. I was coughing terribly and must have passed out.'

'Just as well you did,' Slade said gently. It was beginning to make sense, now. Many people would have gone down with the ship, or tried to swim away from the scene and perhaps drowned. But the mass of bodies they had found probably died from shock or asphyxiation at the time of the explosion.

'I saw the ship that did it,' she said suddenly. 'We had rushed out onto the promenade deck after the first explosion. That was by the stern, a torpedo I think, and then there were lots of smaller explosions. We were by the rail, looking through the mist, when it swirled away for a moment and there was a big freighter painted black with no

24

lights at all. And yet, although it looked like a freighter, guns were firing all along its side. I remember watching a big flash from its funnel and hearing the scream of a shell over our heads. Then Helen, she's one of the women you saved, suddenly screamed and pointed at the sea. It was a torpedo coming right below our feet.'

'You're lucky,' Slade said.

She nodded, depression settling over her as she thought of all those who had not been. 'I had some good friends on that ship.'

'We're not going to think about that,' Slade said firmly. 'Finish your soup and then sleep.'

'I'm all right.' There were tears in her eyes again.

'You know, I haven't learned your name yet?'

'Oh,' she looked apologetic. 'I'm sorry. It's Diana. Diana Curtis.'

'You call me Captain Slade or Linc. I'd feel more at home with Linc.'

He found himself shuffling his feet and fumbling with the hole in his vest. She looked at it and grimaced.

'You must be tired yourself, Captain. I suppose you got all torn and dirty helping us in the water.'

Slade managed a shameless nod and said: 'I'd better get changed.' He paused, looking puzzled. 'Are you sure you're right about the ship? I mean, it could have been some kind of pirate outfit or drunken smugglers. But a freighter firing torpedoes? Who would do anything like that?'

'The Germans,' she said bitterly.

'Germans? Why should they?'

'The war I suppose.'

'What war?'

She looked at him in astonishment. 'Captain, Britain and France are at war with Germany.'

'Oh.' He felt stupid, recalling vaguely something he had heard months ago about the invasion of Poland. 'But that's not here.'

'No,' she agreed. 'But the British do own quite a few of

these islands. Anyway, it had to be a disguised German warship. All those guns and torpedoes.'

'I suppose you're right.'

He left her finishing the soup, the beginnings of colour returning to her small-boned features. He crossed the saloon, noticing the litter and empty bottles for the first time in years, and went along the companionway to his cabin. The bottle of gin was on the shelf beside the door and he took it without thinking, crossing to the deep leather chair beside the chart table where he sat and poured half a tumbler, sprinkling a few drops of angustora bitters to give it a pink glow. He took a long drink and leaned back, closing his eyes, resting the glass on his chest.

The horror of the morning had begun to recede to manageable proportions. The stench, the revoltingly distended bodies of people who had been happily enjoying a Caribbean cruise, the grotesque duty he and his men had been forced to perform; all of it was now contained within the helpless rage that he felt. The sea had a way of levelling those who sailed on her, but the barbarous act which had resulted in death for so many innocent people could have no purpose beyond a brutal need for destruction. The SS Cormorant could never have been mistaken for a ship of war, or even a freighter carrying supplies, and no man of the sea could have failed to know the kind of passengers such a liner would be carrying.

He took another drink of the gin, the alcohol beginning to hollow the mind, blurring the ghastly images. He thought of the captain of that ship, wondering what kind of man could hold such a command. A madman, he decided. No matter what act of war he was engaged in, to strike down a helpless passenger liner could only be the work of a madman. And he would still be here. He leaned forward, hunching over the chart table with its stained and well-rubbed chart of the Antilles. The traces of a hundred plots were there, the wandering courses of the Tinkerbelle among the islands.

There was a tap on the door and he straightened, telling the caller to enter. It was Culpepper, his eyes deep in their sockets, his features sallow like old wax. Slade reached for the gin and topped up his glass, waving the bottle at the chart.

'The bastard's out there somewhere.'

'I know.'

Culpepper sat down, wincing as the captain took a long gulp of his drink, then coughed, spraying the already gin-laden air.

'Do you have any brandy?' he asked.

Slade looked at him in astonishment. 'You? Brandy?'

'I've been sick. Perhaps it would help.'

'Try the medicine cabinet.' He waved at the cupboard above his bunk.

Culpepper found a bottle that was half full and returned to the chart, pouring a small measure into a glass. He sipped it, his mouth compressed, as though forcing down a particularly revolting medicine.

'We'll have to notify somebody,' he said finally.

'You know our transmitter has been useless for more than a year.'

'I thought we could put into one of the islands. We'd make Martinique by morning.'

Slade ignored him, hunching over the chart, staring intently at the islands. 'The bastard's got to be in there. Somewhere.'

'Captain, it's our duty to warn shipping as soon as possible.'

'All right, Culpepper. So we put into Martinique and what the hell do they do? There isn't a gunboat this side of the Florida Straits and if it's a German the Americans are going to think twice before getting into the war.'

'Shipping can be warned.'

'Right. They'll broadcast on the general waveband and guess who'll be listening.' He slapped the chart, spilling gin across it. 'All we do is warn the bastard.'

Culpepper gave him an exasperated look. 'We have to do something, Captain.'

'Damned right we do. We go find him.'

They looked at each other in silence. The room creaked around them, the distant throb of the engines vibrating beneath their feet. The first officer drank the rest of his brandy and closed his eyes, grimacing. He remained that way until Slade began to think he had suffered a seizure. Suddenly the eyes popped open and he said hoarsely: 'If we find him he'll sink us.'

'Culpepper, you're a disappointment to me. All these years you've been walking around my ship telling me what a drunken lazy bum I am.' The first officer opened his mouth to protest but Slade stopped him with a gesture. 'You've waved that bible of yours every bloody chance you got and now, when you've looked into hell and smelled the devil himself, all you can do is worry about your own salvation.'

'I was merely stating a fact, Captain,' Culpepper replied primly. 'Even if we could find this German, the exercise would be pointless.'

'Jesus! You're a pacifist as well.'

'God is a pacifist,' replied Culpepper sharply.

'An eye for an eye?'

'Vengeance is mine, sayeth the Lord.'

'Culpepper, that doesn't sound like pacifism.'

'It means that God will take care of the German in His own time.'

'Oh yeah? Maybe he needs help?'

'Captain Slade, we are unarmed, barely seaworthy, and totally undisciplined. What can we possibly do?'

'Sink the bastard.'

The First Officer's thin mouth twisted with contempt and he rose to his feet, his cheeks flushed with the effects of the brandy. The ship surged beneath them and he staggered, clutching the edge of the chart table, glaring at the captain who grinned back with delight.

'You better sober up, Culpepper. We're going to be busy.'

'I am not drunk. I have never been drunk in my life. If anyone needs to sober up, Captain, it is you. And once that happens you will realize that your little fantasy belongs where it came from . . . in that bottle of gin.'

'Are you refusing to carry out my orders, Mr Culpepper?' Slade growled.

The first officer stiffened, controlling his anger with an effort. 'No sir. But if you persist in this affair then I must ask to be replaced.'

'Request granted.' Slade grinned suddenly. 'As soon as we get back to Caracas.'

'You can't do that. My articles clearly state that. . . .'

'They don't count any more,' said Slade, beaming at him. 'This ship is now in a state of war and as such its officers and men are on active service and outside the rules of Maritime Law.'

Culpepper's eyes bulged. 'That is absolute nonsense. There is no such amendment, even if we were at war . . which we're not.'

Slade drank the rest of his gin and moved unsteadily to his battered cap with its tarnished ribbon of braid. He placed it on his head at a jaunty angle before turning back with a stern expression. 'You can make an entry in the log, Mr Culpepper. I am declaring war on that Kraut bastard right now. You may instruct the crew to break out the arms and prepare them for use.'

'Oh they'll prepare them alright,' Culpepper replied with grim satisfaction. 'And when they find out what you've got in mind they will probably blow your head off.'

'They're a good bunch. They'll back me to the hilt.'

'Captain, they're scum. There isn't a man on board with the slightest vestige of honour or duty. Half the time they're so drunk they don't even know they're on a ship, they think this is a floating bar with funnels!'

'That's a bit unfair, Culpepper.' Slade discovered that the bottle of gin was empty and began to root around for a replacement. 'We wouldn't get very far without them, even if they do take a drink now and then.'

'Now and then! Do you know how many gallons of rum they go through . . . a day!'

'I think they use it for cooking.'

Culpepper gazed at him in despair. 'They use it for everything. I even saw one man soaking his feet in it. They're rummies. All of them. If that German ever fired a shot at us they'd run for the boats . . .' Culpepper paused, looking sad. 'No. I tell a lie. If it was after sundown running would be out of the question. They'd crawl. Some of them would even float!'

Slade had found a fresh bottle standing in the centre of his shower cubicle. It was dusty. He looked at it, trying to remember why he had put it there. The first officer waited, fuming. Slade remembered. 'Time I had a shower,' he said, pulling the cork and taking a reflective drink. 'Must be all of . . .' He frowned and took another drink.

'Oh, God!' said Culpepper.

'This is no time for prayers, Mister. I want every man assembled on the foredeck in five minutes.'

'Captain, they won't go for it. They'll mutiny. They'll set us both adrift in a lifeboat.'

Slade squinted at his worried features through the neck of the bottle. He looked like a dyspeptic gargoyle. After a moment he nodded reluctantly. 'All right, we'll do it another way. We'll have a boat drill, every man on station.' He grinned. 'Except you.'

'What's that going to accomplish?'

'Discipline. While they're on deck you go into the galley and mess deck, collect all the crates of booze and put them in the old strong room. From now on this will be a dry ship.'

Culpepper blinked, then searched his pockets for the bible he normally carried. He felt the need to touch it, to murmur some short prayer. 'A dry ship?'

'Until we get the Kraut.'

'Captain,' Culpepper whispered, an expression of pure joy coming into his face. 'I feel as though I am in the presence of the Lord. For years I have prayed for this day, never believing . . . never having the faith to . . .'

Emotion overcame him and he began to sink to his knees. Slade grabbed his elbow and pulled him upright again. 'Go to it, Mr Culpepper. I want us on a course for Montserrat before noon.'

'Aye aye, Captain.' Culpepper leapt for the door, pausing there to say : 'And don't worry about me, sir. I'm with you every step of the way.'

When the door had closed Slade sat and took a long pull from the bottle of gin. He felt pleasantly at one with the world, the warmth of the gin blending with the glow of satisfaction. Whilst he didn't entirely agree with Culpepper's assessment of his crew, there was certainly an element of truth in his words. In fact, he admitted, when you really thought about it you couldn't get much sense out of any of them after dark. Even the man on watch had been found slumped over the helm on more than one occasion although to be fair, Slade told himself, they always managed to set it on full port rudder so that they spent the night going round in circles.

He felt a twinge of doubt when he remembered McVay, the chief engineer. He hadn't been sober since they left Caracas, except for the time they ran out of booze and credit. It had been two weeks before they could haul a cargo of freight and buy fresh supplies, and in that time the gnarled old Scotsman had become a ranting, raving lunatic attacking anyone who came into his engine room. He was finally caught in a cargo net and locked in the forward hold where he screamed for hours each night, claiming that he was being attacked by green lizards and giant butterflies. It had been a harrowing experience and they were all relieved when he reverted back to his old self – some five minutes after gulping down a bottle of Johnny Walker.

He would have to go easy on McVay, Slade decided. They

couldn't afford to lose their chief engineer in a moment of crisis. He would have to ration his supplies, just enough to keep the green lizards at bay. He decided to drink to that and belched with satisfaction. No bastard Kraut was going to spoil their little piece of paradise. They would find him, sink him, then resume their normal routine. He tipped the bottle back, noting with a mild surprise that it was already half empty. Or was it half full? He chuckled at the thought.

The call to boat stations was three blasts on the siren, but they made do with two because McVay complained bitterly about the drop in pressure and threatened to shut down altogether. The crew assembled in groups on the foredeck, many of them barely able to focus on the captain. The harrowing experience of the morning had resulted in an early pilgrimage to the galley where the jugs of white rum had been passed around, washing away the taste of death little by little until the world was once again a pleasant place to be. The abrupt summons to boat stations was an irritating interruption to what was beginning to look like an interesting day. They answered the call out of curiosity rather than duty, gathering in puzzled groups in front of their captain who swayed before them in his stained whites and tattered cap, looking more like an unsuccessful beachcomber than the master of the *Tinkerbelle*.

'Men,' began Slade, taking a deep breath to clear his head. 'You all witnessed that abomination of the high seas this morning, so I don't need to dwell on the gory details. I want to talk about the bastard who did it. A Kraut bastard! A German marauder disguised as a peaceful freighter out to sink anything he can find in the Caribbean.'

He paused, watching their faces flush with anger, letting them turn to each other and exchange curses. He raised his hands, regaining their attention. 'What it means, men, is that the war in Europe is here with us now. We know what it looks like, know what it smells like, know what it means to those poor bastards on the *Cormorant*. And I think you all know what it is we have to do.'

Everyone looked at everyone else. Clearly they had no idea what it was they had to do. Tommy, the Puerto Rican who served as Third Mate without actually receiving officer status, shuffled his feet and stepped forward, scratching his head.

'What's that, Cap'n?'

'Find him,' growled Slade, letting his disappointment show. 'We're going to find that bastard Kraut.'

The cook whose name was Felipe, began to shake his hand as though he had just let go of something hot. He was small, wizened like a prune, with permanently bloodshot eyes. To see him in the galley in the early hours was to witness the miracle of the walking dead. 'What we goin' to do when we find him, Cap'n?' he said, his voice creaking with alarm.

'That's tactics,' said Slade, as though they were entering the realm of pure maths. 'First we find him, pin him down, look him over and see what we've got.'

Miguel Panacero, the tubby bosun who could out-drink any man on board and looked as though he was trying to grow into a barrel, gave a lop-sided grin to the men around him and waved a pudgy hand. 'Cap'n, we got no reason to go looking for this German. We got ourselves a neutral ship.'

'So what the hell was the *Cormorant*?' snarled Slade. 'What the hell were all those passengers doing on board? Cleaning guns? Polishing torpedoes? What kind of a fat-arsed fairy are you, Panacero?'

'I didn't sign on to go hunting no warships,' said the bosun stubbornly.

'You didn't sign on at all,' snapped Slade. 'Come to think of it, none of you did. A bottle of rum and a day's pay, that's what you got.'

The expressions before him grew mournful. The men began to shuffle their feet, thinking longingly of the jugs in the galley. Tommy gestured at the men who had begun to mutter, cutting them off like a conductor about to start the first movement. He turned to the captain, forcing a broad grin, placing the thumb and forefinger of his right hand against his forehead as though searching for the answer that eluded him.

'Cap'n,' he began. 'This is a small ship. A good one, but small and old. How can we find a big German raider, and if we do, what do we say? Go 'way, bastard Kraut?'

Slade glared at him, but the Third Mate, acting and unpaid, stared innocently back. 'What happened to your balls, Tommy?' he said, then turned his gaze on the rest of them. 'What happened to the cojones, eh? You've been guzzling rum for so long they're hanging down there like pickled onions. I don't mind telling you men that I've been getting worried for some time. I can remember the days when we'd put into one of the small islands, especially those Virgin Islands, and every man on board would be sporting a hard-on before we hit the beach. And when we left there wasn't a woman under the age of thirty who didn't have a smile on her face.'

He paused and spat deliberately, letting his mouth curl with contempt. The crew began to study the deck with growing concentration. 'But those days have gone. When we call at an island now the women don't even bother to comb their hair. The cooking fires don't burn the minute we hove in sight; the mothers don't hide their virgin daughters; the fathers don't start digging up the flagons of coconut juice. You know why? Because it's a non-event, that's why. You don't even know which leg it's hanging down any more.'

Two deckhands beside Tommy were exchanging shame-faced looks and nodding their heads. Others were studying the cloudless sky as though expecting rain. Slade's contempt hung over them like a shroud.

Tommy's smile had turned into a sickly grimace, his features pale and uncertain. 'Some of us still have a good time, Cap'n,' he muttered, looking as though he didn't know where to put his hands. 'It's not so long since we started that riot on Tortola.'

34

'That was last summer. And it wasn't a riot, it was an expression of sheer frustration on the part of the islanders who had been waiting more than a year for a bit of action. Jesus, you guys. I can remember the days when every woman in the Lesser and Greater Antilles got the hot flushes just thinking about the *Tinkerbelle*. You know what they call us now?'

They waited, dreading his scorn. He pushed his cap on the back of his head and let his hand fall limply from the wrist. 'The Fairy Queen. That's what they call the *Tinkerbelle*. The fucking Fairy Queen!'

An angry murmur rose from the crew. They stared straight ahead, mouths thin, eyes burning in the sun. The only exception was the bosun who had never made any secret of his preference for a jug of rum. His cackling laugh was the last straw. The mutters became a babble of protest, a wave of anger that beat at the captain who gazed back without compassion. He waited until their expressions were ugly, savouring their fury, then lifted his hands to silence them.

'All right, you don't like it, but now we've got a chance to set the record straight. This bastard Kraut has got to be found, and the ship that does it, the crew that sorts him out, will earn the gratitude of every islander in the Caribbean. They'll be fighting for the privilege of having us drop anchor, and our credit will be good as long as we sail these waters. Now who's with me?'

The roar of assent vibrated in the hot noon air, rising up from the ship and scattering the circling seagulls overhead. Slade beamed at them proudly and then gave them the bad news. 'We're going on the wagon, men. Until we find the Kraut, the bar's closed.'

He turned on his heel and left them before they were able to absorb the full horror of his words. When it finally penetrated their euphoria he was gone and they could only look helplessly at each other, wondering how they could be party to such a decision. How such words could even be uttered.

'He doesn't mean it,' said the bosun, his eyes like rotten walnuts. 'He knows we'd never wear it.'

'That's why Mister Culpepper wasn't here,' said Tommy in an empty voice. 'The sodding parson's been shutting the bar.'

They began to move, at first in a determined group towards the companionway, but deteriorating rapidly into a frantic stampede as each man tried to remember where he had left his last jug. Few of them noticed the figure watching from the bridge. If they had they would have known from Culpepper's benign smile that the *Tinkerbelle* was dry and its first officer was happy for the first time in years.

4

The German marauder moved across the smooth surface of the sea like a dark grey ghost, the muffled throb of its engines blending with the gurgle of water along its hull. Half a mile ahead, its navigation lights gleaming like new stars, was the French freighter *St Nazaire* bound for Guadeloupe from Puerto Rico.

On the bridge of the *Tamerande* the captain sat in the leather-backed command seat, his face gaunt in the reflected green from the compass light. The gunnery officer was already giving range and load instructions in his slightly nasal voice, making calculations on the calibrated plotter before him. The first officer, Tellmann, moved from the armoured glass screens along the bridge to the captain.

'We're making about one knot on him, sir.'

'Then we should be in position in fifteen minutes?'

'Yes, sir.'

Tellmann waited, searching the commander's features. He could swear that not a muscle had moved in over an hour. It was like gazing upon an old copper mask, the eyes deep holes that swallowed the light.

'Do we follow standard procedure, sir?' Tellmann asked quietly.

'Of course,' replied the captain. 'You will hoist the flag signal "OL", "LNU" and "LUL". If there is no response we will fire port and starboard torpedoes at three thousand yards.'

Tellmann hesitated, desperately trying to read the metal mask before him. The flag signals were the international order to 'heave to or I will open fire' and 'you are prohibited from radioing', but who could see them in the dark? He cleared his throat, wishing he dared ask if they could break radio silence. The attack on the liner two days ago had weighed heavily on them all, but the captain had given no indication of his own emotions. His entry in the log had been a cold and formal statement of fact: 'The SS *Cormorant* attacked and sunk at 0625 hours, December 18th. 1939. No survivors.'

The captain stirred, aware of his uncertainty, and spoke gently in a voice too low for the helmsman to overhear. 'We cannot break radio silence, Mister Tellmann. Until our presence is known we must maintain maximum security. You are certain that the ship ahead is the Frenchman *St Nazaire?*'

'Yes, sir. We have monitored two transmissions during the night. He is bound for Guadeloupe.'

'Then he is a target.'

'Yes, sir,' Tellmann replied crisply, starting to turn away.

'Mister Tellmann,' said the captain, his voice barely a whisper. 'It is not our wish that we should be the brutal instruments of war, but it still remains our duty to fulfil the purpose of this ship.'

'I understand, sir. Thank you.'

Tellmann moved back to the heavy glass screen, raising his binoculars and holding them on the freighter ahead. He was surprised that the captain had felt compelled to explain actions which they all understood were necessary, and yet his words had gone a long way to dispelling his own doubts. It had been bad luck to sink the *Cormorant*, he thought. Had they seen it clearly he was sure the captain would never have given the order to attack. Now it was the turn of the freighter ahead.

He sighed and bent to the voice tube. 'Engine room. Increase one third.' He felt the shudder in the deck as the tempo of the engines changed. There was no other sound. The ship had been on silent running for the past hour, all lights extinguished above and below decks.

The voice of the gunnery officer came through the speaker

above his head : 'Target bearing oh-five-zero. Set all tubes for three thousand, one degree angle on the bow.'

Tellmann checked the bearing, watching the lights of the freighter ahead drift closer. There was still no indication that they were aware of the ship behind them. The duty officer was probably in his cabin with only the helmsman on the bridge. He began to think of the rest of the crew, asleep in their bunks dreaming of wives and girl-friends. Tellmann pushed the images aside, bending to the rangefinder and focusing on the red and green masthead lights.

'Range four thousand,' he said softly. 'Stand by all tubes.'

'Forward guns ready. Prepare to collapse shelter deck.' The nasal voice of the gunnery officer quickened with the tension.

Captain Kroehner stirred, rose from his chair and moved to stand beside the first officer. The armour-plated glass reflected their images back at them. Hard, grim faces with empty eyes.

'Do you wish to give the order, sir?' asked Tellmann.

'For the record, Mr Tellmann. Just for the record.'

'Range three thousand five hundred.'

'Thirty seconds.'

'Forward guns confirm.'

'Number One battery, ready.'

'Number Two battery, ready.'

'Thirty-seven millimetre ready.'

'Range three thousand two hundred.'

Tellmann was staring intently through the rangefinder. The captain looked at the lights ahead. He could make out the long low silhouette of the vessel, setting an angle of forty-five degrees to their own course. The position could not be better for attack, even the sea was flat and calm. He closed his eyes.

'Range three thousand,' said Tellmann.

'Fire torpedoes,' said the captain.

'Enttarnen,' snapped the gunnery officer, using the single word which meant 'drop all disguises.'

On the foredeck the front wall of the deckhouse crashed down, revealing the long barrels of the two 5.9 inch guns. Along the sides of the ship hull sections hinged upwards, bulwarks crashed down. In the foreward funnel a hatch opened and the stubby barrel of the 75 millimetre machine gun jetted out. From the four torpedo tubes the silver metal fish leapt out, hissing into the water and streaking towards the freighter ahead. The spinning propellers agitated the plankton to produce blue phosphorescent tails which grew steadily in the night.

'Remarkable,' said Tellmann, watching the pale blue lines converge on the freighter. 'They're luminous.'

He watched until the blue trails faded into the night, then transferred his gaze to the navigation lights ahead. The gunnery officer was counting seconds, his voice empty of all emotion. When he reached the last second, Captain Kroehner opened his eyes.

The night erupted into crimson fire. The first torpedo took the freighter just above the stern, blasting open the engine room and fuel tanks. The second and third were square amidships, the explosions so close together that they were indistinguishable. The last torpedo took the ship in the foreward hold, ripping open a massive section of the hull and igniting a cargo of paint the ship was carrying. A great fountain of fire roared up into the sky as concussion after concussion shook the vessel, slewing it round whilst the sea poured through gaping wounds in its hull. Within seconds it had canted over, still turning, the long flat deck belching smoke and flames from a dozen points. And then, so quickly they barely had time to assess the damage, the ship heeled over and slipped beneath the waves. All that was left was a cloud of smoke and steam, a foaming sea that spewed up wreckage.

No one spoke on the bridge. Even the gunnery officer was silent. They passed over the area that still seethed and gurgled, a widening circle of debris and oil. If there were any bodies they were hidden in the darkness.

'Engines full ahead,' said Tellmann quietly. 'Gun crews stand down.'

Captain Kroehner returned to his chair, his face lined and weary. The gunnery officer ordered the deck crew to replace the disguise sections, then crossed to the captain.

'A clean kill, sir,' he said, making no attempt to conceal the pride in his voice.

'Yes,' replied Kroehner. 'It was all of that. A very clean kill indeed.'

Afterwards, in his cabin, he drank an extra large glass of schnapps and wrote in the log: 'The French freighter *St Nazaire* was attacked and sunk at 0230 hours on December 20th 1939. The vessel was struck by four torpedoes and sank immediately with all hands.'

5

Slade worked the bolt of the battered .303 Enfield and threw it at Tommy with a grimace of disgust.

'Is that the best you can do?'

'It hasn't been used in years, Captain.'

Slade glared at him. 'All weapons are supposed to be kept oiled and ready for use.'

'Like the lifeboat winches?' asked Culpepper in an accusing voice.

Slade ignored the question and picked up a 9mm Luger that seemed reasonably serviceable. All together they had unearthed four weapons. Two rifles, the Luger and a .38 revolver with a badly cracked butt that had been bound with copper wire now green with rust. He passed the revolver to Culpepper and placed the Luger on the night table beside his bunk.

'How about ammunition?'

'Ten rounds for the Luger, five for the revolver and half a box of .303 for the rifles,' said Tommy.

'Oh that's great! With that kind of firepower we're damned near invincible!'

Culpepper held the revolver between thumb and forefinger, his mouth pinched with distaste. 'I really don't have any use for this, Captain. I'm sure one of the crew would make better . . .'

'Don't give me a hard time, Culpepper,' snarled Slade. 'You take the revolver and have it with you on the bridge at all times.'

'But I couldn't possibly shoot anyone with it.'

'Then wave it at them, play tunes on it, pick your Godamn nose with it . . . but when that bastard Kraut starts shooting at us, Mister Culpepper, you will bloody well shoot back!'

Culpepper stiffened angrily, but refrained from making a reply. Slade swung round on Tommy and barked out instructions to get the rifles cleaned up and placed on the bridge. He collected them and backed to the door, his eyes wide and nervous as the captain began to pace the cabin, cursing savagely. Tommy had never seen him like this before. The only time he ever lost his temper was when he ran out of gin, or when he fell out of his hammock on the after deck.

'We can't fight no German raider with these, Captain,' he said, and then wished he had kept his mouth shut.

'You're right, Tommy. We've got to have something more. Now what have we got plenty of that's lethal? Rum. That's what we've got.' He beamed at the third mate. 'We'll empty all the bottles into a barrel and mix it up with some of that white spirit we use for cleaning, add maybe a gallon or two of diesel and then fill up the bottles with the stuff. Add a bit of wadding, put a match to it, and we've got one hundred per cent proof incendiaries. Get to it.'

'Aw, Cap'n, not the rum.'

'You think maybe bullets are better?'

Tommy swallowed and nodded miserably. 'I think maybe we should give them a try, Captain.'

After Tommy had left Slade sat down at the chart table and glared at the islands. 'He's right, Culpepper,' he said after a moment. 'We've got to have something heavier than a .303.'

'Sir, you can't be serious about this. We're no match for a German warship. We're not even a match for its liberty boat!'

'We've got eyes, engines underneath us, and we know these islands better than any other ship in the Caribbean. We can find it, identify it and . . .'

'And what, sir?'

Slade began to pace the room again, his features dark and deeply lined. He was like a tiger looking for someone to maul. He stopped in front of Culpepper after half a dozen circuits of the cabin, his steel grey eyes cold and determined in spite of the red rims and watery sockets. For one weak moment Culpepper wished he had left a bottle or two of gin in the cabin, but he was immediately ashamed of the thought.

'You said you were with me, Culpepper.'

'I am, sir, but we've got to be sensible about it.'

'Were those bodies sensible? Were all those bloated women and children behaving in a reasonable manner? What the hell do you need? A couple more like that?'

'No, but we're not a fighting ship, Captain.'

Slade clenched his fists and strove to control the frustrated anger that had been boiling inside him since morning. The headache that had been with him for most of the day was getting worse, and his mouth felt hot enough to pop corn. He needed a drink. More than anything he needed a long cool glass of gin clinking on ice with just a touch of tonic water. He felt a wave of guilt followed immediately by despair as he began to comprehend the magnitude of his self-enforced abstinence.

Culpepper watched the anguish in the captain's face and assumed it was over his inability to fight the German. He felt remorse and shame, realizing that he had never understood the forces that drove Slade. Here was a man of courage and selfless determination so appalled by the brutal murders he had seen that he was prepared to lay down his life. The knowledge made him feel small and humble, filling him with a bitter sense of inadequacy.

'Captain Slade,' said Culpepper, almost overcome with emotion. 'We will find that German. With God's help, and your strength, we will find him.'

After he had left Slade sat on his bunk and tried to understand what had made Culpepper change his mind. He sighed

44

and gave up, then began to search the cabin in the hope of finding a bottle. He was deep in a locker, surrounded by mouldy socks and sweaters, when there was a tap on the door. It opened to reveal two very large brown eyes and a boyish figure in jeans and a patched blue shirt. He had just felt the outline of a bottle at the bottom of the locker and although he couldn't place the figure in the door, his mind was already doing somersaults of joy.

'Go away,' he said, pulling out yellowed shirts and a grey tunic that had once been white.

'I just wanted a word, Captain.'

'Look, for Christ's sake, if I'm busy I'm busy.' He snapped unearthing the bottle which was half full. 'Now be a good lad and piss off, will you.'

'I am not a lad, Captain.'

He turned, peering at the figure. The hair was black, cut short, but the skin was much paler than the rest of his crew. He looked at the shirt, getting slowly to his feet, admitting grudgingly that unless he had a couple of pigeons in there the lad was quite right . . . a lad he was not.

'Do you always talk to your crew like that?' asked Diana Curtis, sounding reproachful.

He shrugged and crossed to the chart table, glancing at her more closely as he passed. He recognised her finally, but there had been quite a transformation since he had last seen her. 'Miss Curtis, isn't it?'

She nodded, watching him put the bottle on the chart table and start looking around the room with an urgent expression. 'I thought you'd like to know that the other two ladies you rescued are feeling much better now. They'd like to thank you personally.'

'No need,' he said, going into the shower cubicle and coming out with a baffled expression.

'Is anything wrong?'

'The bastard's even taken my glasses,' he said savagely.

Her cheeks went red. 'I thought we established that I am not one of your crew, Captain?'

He gave her a puzzled look.

'Your language,' she said in a crisply laundered voice.

'Oh. Ah, yes. Well, ma'am, this is very much a man's world here. In fact, apart from the occasional . . .' He stopped, realizing he was on dangerous ground again. She waited and he grinned inanely. 'Fact is, we're not used to women on board the *Tinkerbelle*.'

'The what?'

He sighed. 'The name of my ship, ma'am, is the *Tinker-belle*.' He watched her amusement, wishing his headache would go away so that he could fight back.

'Doesn't sound a very masculine world, Captain,' she said.

'We don't name our ships, we just sail them. As a matter of fact the name has caused more fights than I care to remember.'

'I'm sure.' She smiled and the effect was distinctly pleasant. 'But if you wouldn't mind choosing your words more carefully.'

'I'll do my best,' he promised, looking longingly at the bottle of gin. 'Now what can I do for you?'

'We wanted to know how soon you would be putting us ashore? There are people we have to contact.'

'Ashore?' He wondered if she would be shocked if he took a swig from the bottle.

She gazed at him patiently. 'On one of the islands.'

'Oh, well, it's not quite that simple.'

'I don't understand?'

'We're not bound for a port at the moment. Naturally we'll be passing an island pretty soon and if there's time, and an opportunity, we'll lower the launch and run you ashore. But right now I can't tell you when that will be.'

'But, Captain, we must be put ashore. People will be worrying about us. Mrs Hartford-Jones has lost her husband on the *Cormorant*. My friend, Miss Jameson, has a brother in Caracas.'

'Well I can see those are powerful reasons, Miss Curtis,'

he said with heavy sarcasm, 'but right now we're engaged on a very important mission.'

Her mouth tightened and her eyes took on an icy gleam. 'I'm sorry, Captain Slade, but I really must insist.'

He reached for the bottle of gin, then froze as footsteps approached his cabin door. He groaned, knowing who they belonged to. 'I think you'd better go, Miss Curtis.'

'I have no intention of leaving, Captain,' she declared firmly.

The door burst open and a short, thickset man with tousled hair and ears that would have looked better on a jug stormed into the room. His arms were thick, hairy and streaked with oil, and his overalls looked as though they had been soaked overnight in the bilges. He positively reeked of diesel and oil and yesterday's whisky, a combination that put the finishing touches to Slade's stomach. He made a brief, futile gesture towards the girl, but it was a waste of time.

'That fucking bible-punching bastard has gone too far this time! He's down in my engine room giving me a load of shit about confiscating my whisky on your orders!'

Slade hadn't the courage to look at Miss Curtis. He stared at the engineer with desperate eyes, making small motions with his head towards the girl. McVay frowned and glanced at her, then back with a puzzled expression.

'Well, Linc?' he demanded in a grating voice. 'What the fuck is going on?'

'May I introduce Miss Diana Curtis,' Slade said, making frantic signals. 'Miss Curtis, Mister Harold McVay, our chief engineer.'

She seemed rooted to the floor, her features frozen with shock. McVay turned with some surprise, glancing at her shirt long enough to bring the colour back into her cheeks, before sticking out an oily hand and grinning amiably.

'A pleasure to meet you, Miss Curtis. For a moment I was thinking you were a new deckhand.'

'Obviously!' she said icily, ignoring his hand.

47

'Of course if you had a bit more up front it wouldn't be so difficult to tell,' he said cheerfully, 'though I don't suppose you can now do much about that.'

Her cheeks flamed red and she turned to Slade with a furious expression. He managed a shaky smile, convinced he couldn't last another minute without a drink. She glanced back at McVay, measuring each word with contempt: 'I always believed that Scotsmen had manners . . . until today.'

McVay scratched his chin with an oily forefinger and gave the matter some thought. 'They invariably do, Miss,' he acknowledged finally. 'But on occasions we're inclined to be a wee bit blunt. Take the present situation, for instance. The captain here has taken it upon himself to steal my supply of whisky knowing full well that the engine room of this ship is no place for a sober man.'

'I'm sure Captain Slade knows what he is doing,' she said coldly.

'I doubt it,' McVay replied calmly. 'If he doesn't reverse his decision, I will reverse the direction of this ship.'

'Harry, will you just calm down.'

'Then get Culpepper out of my engine room. He's finally gone round the twist, ranting on about the ship going on the wagon. I always knew he'd crack one day. Any man who can't fight, won't drink and doesn't . . .'

'Harry!'

McVay grinned savagely and went on: 'And doesn't appreciate the finer qualities of the fairer sex has just got to be missing a few marbles. He's even saying that the reason behind it all is that you've decided to go after this German marauder.'

Diana looked quickly at Slade, her eyes widening. 'Is that true?'

Slade groaned and headed for the medicine cabinet. 'Will you all get out of here. I've got a head like Vesuvius.'

'Maybe a drink would help, Cap'n?' suggested McVay maliciously.

'Captain, you must think I'm terribly selfish. There was I insisting that you put us ashore while you were hunting the monster who sank our ship.'

She gazed at him radiantly, but he was too busy searching for the bottle of aspirin. It wasn't there. He glared at the medicine cabinet. Surely Culpepper hadn't confiscated those as well. The speaker tube beside his bunk whistled, grating on his nerve ends like a steel file on broken glass. He took it with a shaking hand and pulled out the plug.

'Slade.'

'The bridge, Cap'n. There's a freighter ahead.'

'What are you? The coastguard!'

'Just thought you'd be interested,' said Tommy in an injured voice. 'It's flying a Panamanian flag. I can't make out its name yet, but it's not one of the normal islanders. Too big for one thing.'

'I'll be right up. And get those rifles loaded.'

Slade slammed the tube back into its socket and started towards the door. McVay stepped in front of him, his eyes small and angry.

'What about Culpepper?'

'Harry, will you get down to the engine room. I might be needing all the speed you've got.'

'Not one bloody rev unless Culpepper gets his hands off my whisky.'

Slade glared at him. McVay glared back. 'Alright you bad-tempered Scottish git! Tell Culpepper to report to the bridge.'

He was half-way through the door when he remembered the girl. She was watching, eyes big and filled with something that reminded him of a spaniel he'd once had. 'Get your friends into life jackets, please, and stay in your cabins.'

'Yes, Captain,' she murmured softly.

He ran for the bridge, his head throbbing with every step. Tommy was studying the approaching freighter through binoculars, passing them to him as he arrived. A young

Puerto Rican called Lasco was on the helm, his skin a dirty grey stretched tight around the mouth.

Panacero, the bosun, was loading cartridges into the rifles, shaking his head with every round.

Slade got the ship into focus, steadying on the bow. The name was obscured by rust or dirt so he gave up trying to read it and began to study the lines of the vessel. It was tall, broad on the beam with derrick booms fore and aft. A single funnel carried a blue band with a white diamond, but they were not colours he knew. He scanned the deck and bulwarks, looking for openings or hidden guns, but there was nothing to see. An officer in whites appeared on the wing of the bridge, looking back at him through binoculars. He cursed beneath his breath, feeling his stomach tighten as two crewmen appeared and crossed the deck to the port lifeboat.

'Who's on radio duty?' he snapped.

Tommy looked uncomfortable. 'Well, er . . . It's three o'clock, captain.'

'So?'

'Siesta,' he said weakly. 'We always have siesta!'

'Jesus!' He shook his fist at him. 'Get everybody on deck. Panacero, get up there in the bow and when I give the signal start blasting away at the bastard's bridge.'

Panacero went pale. 'But Captain . . .'

'Don't argue. Two of the crew are messing with a lifeboat. For all we know there could be a bloody great cannon underneath it. Now get up there.'

Panacero went with leaden feet, muttering something about being too old to fight and too young to die. Slade lifted the binoculars again, watching the ship eating up the distance between them. It appeared to be making a good fifteen knots, which in itself was suspicious. The two crewmen were barely visible, crouching down beside the lifeboat. He swung his glasses to the starboard side and felt his stomach turn as he picked out two more crewmen beside the other lifeboat.

Culpepper climbed onto the bridge, breathing heavily. His face blanched when he saw the freighter and he stood with hands clasped together, as though in prayer.

'Where the hell's your gun?' Slade bellowed.

'I put it in my cabin,' he answered, his eyes fixed on the approaching ship. 'Surely you're not planning to open fire on that?'

'If it fires on us, we will fire back,' Slade said firmly. 'And any man who chickens out will be charged with mutiny!'

Tommy had entered the bridge and stood behind the helmsman like a nervous ghost. All their eyes were on the freighter which was now less than two thousand yards away. Slade lifted the binoculars, cursing when he had to refocus. When the image cleared he was looking at the officer on the wing of the bridge. He was signalling urgently to the men on the foredeck.

'I think the officer is waving to us,' said Culpepper.

Slade gazed at him with utter contempt. 'That is not a wave, that is a signal. Tell the engine room I want full power, then stand by the helm. The minute the bastard opens fire I want us hard to port.'

Culpepper bit his lip and crossed to the voice tube. Slade caught sight of Tommy and bellowed instructions to get out on the port wing with the other rifle. He looked sick, but collected the rifle and went outside. Panacero was kneeling in the bow, his rifle resting on the rail. The two ships were almost abreast, less than a thousand yards of water between them.

Diana entered the bridge, moving up behind the captain as he trained his binoculars on the passing freighter. He could read the name on its bow at last. 'Sea Venture'. He moved his glasses along the deck, finding the crewmen beside the lifeboat. They had cans of paint in their hands and were quite busy.

'That's not the ship, Captain,' said Diana. 'The one that sank us had a different funnel.'

Tommy chose that moment to wave to Panacero, pointing at the vessel. He had also seen the crewmen painting the lifeboat and was trying to draw the bosun's attention to it. Panacero nodded, gritted his teeth, and opened fire on the bridge of the *Sea Venture*.

'Oh, shit!' said Slade.

'Full speed ahead,' Culpepper shouted hysterically. 'Helm hard to port.'

The *Tinkerbelle* began to turn sluggishly towards the freighter whilst its first officer, who was just accepting a mug of tea from the steward, dived for cover as a bullet screamed off the steel coaming an inch from his hand. The fact that Panacero came within a hundred yards of him was purely accidental, but the effect on the officers and crew of the *Sea Venture* was dramatic. It immediately went to full power, turning away from the *Tinkerbelle* whilst the engine room fed heavy oil to the diesels producing a thick black smoke which billowed out behind it to envelope its pursuer.

Slade was trying to throttle Culpepper who was going glassy-eyed and sagging at the knees, whilst Tommy was desperately trying to reach Panacero who was firing blindly into the dense smoke as it rolled over the *Tinkerbelle*.

'Hard to starboard. All engines stop,' snarled Slade.

'I wish you crazy bastards would make your minds up,' howled McVay through the voice tube.

Hermanez Torres charged blindly onto the smoke-filled bridge, colliding with the helmsman and rebounding into Culpepper who was still gasping for breath and went down like a ninepin. Hermanez ignored him, pushing on through the smoke to the captain.

'Captain Slade,' he shouted. 'Captain Slade there's an urgent message on the radio.'

Slade glared at him. 'Don't bother me now, Torres.'

'But, Captain, this is important. There is a freighter called *Sea Venture* and it is being attacked by the German marauder at this very minute!'

Slade looked at him with such ferocity that Hermanez felt

physically ill. 'You Puerto Rican prick!' said the captain. 'They're talking about us!'

He turned away from him and found Diana Curtis beside him. Her cheeks were smeared with smoke and tears, but there was no mistaking the revulsion in her eyes.

'Captain Slade,' she said in a choking voice. 'I think you are the most revolting man I have ever, ever known!'

She turned and ran from the bridge. Slade gazed after her with a baffled expression. 'What did I say?' He asked no one in particular. Someone was clawing at his knees and he looked down to find Culpepper.

'Oh Christ, Culpepper,' he said wearily. 'This is no time to start saying your prayers.'

6

As the sun began to burnish the sea with a coppery glow the *Tinkerbelle* was north of Montserrat, its lush green hills wreathed in mist that caught the dying rays so that whole sections of forest seemed to be on fire. They turned east into Redonda Sound with the volcanic island of Nevis on the horizon to port, its barren slopes in sharp contrast to the tree-clad slopes of St Cristopher some ten miles beyond. It was still too far to pick out the beaches of white coral sand, the deep blue bays so clear and still behind protective reefs, the stately palms that leaned out and beckoned with both fruit and shade.

Culpepper sighed and turned back to the chart, plotting a course that would take them north from the Sound towards the small group of islands around St Bartholomew. The sea was quiet, deepening to purple now as the light began to fade. The only sign of life since their ill-fated encounter with the *Sea Venture* had been a squadron of dolphins playing tag with their bow for most of the afternoon, but even they had left as the air began to cool and wisps of golden cirrus high above suggested there would be a chill in the air once darkness fell. He gave the helmsman the course change, then went out onto the wing and took a bearing on the rocky knoll that was Redonda, checking out of habit rather than caution. The sky was a majestic canvas of reds and golds and he watched the colours mix and change, breathing the velvet air and wondering if, finally, this tranquil world of theirs was to be infected by the madness which was gripping Europe in the winter of 1939.

It seemed impossible to believe that the ugliness of war

could intrude here, destroy the calm and beauty of the Caribbean, involve them in its brutality. And yet, in less than a day, it had stained their lives so that they would never again be quite the same. He wondered about Slade brooding over the marauder in his cabin. Although the bodies that had floated like strange sea carrion had shocked them all, with Slade it seemed to go deeper. It was as though the sight had wrenched him out of the idyllic existence he had been enjoying all these years, turning his paradise into a nightmare world that could only be destroyed by ridding the Caribbean of the ship that had caused it.

Culpepper frowned at the thought, wondering at the captain's rage. It was in such contrast to his normal behaviour – though admittedly he was rarely sober enough to behave normally – that the incident alone hardly seemed sufficient. Slade's background had always been a mystery, even those who had known him when he sailed his previous ship along the South American coast had never discovered where his career began, or even how he became a master. He never talked about the past, nor did he refer to family or vessels on which he had sailed. And yet Culpepper was the first to admit he had considerable ability when he put his mind to it. There had been times, when they were in difficulties or faced with a dangerous situation, when he would snap out orders and con the bridge with such competence that it could only have been learned with a major shipping line. Yet he never spoke of those days, never recounted stories of his early years at sea. It was as though the past was blocked out, a book forever closed because, perhaps, it was too painful to open.

It was not a new idea to Culpepper. Over the years he had become convinced that Slade was hiding from something, either images of events or people. But now he wondered if those events did not have a parallel in the horrifying scenes of that morning. It would explain the captain's irrational obsession with hunting a hunter who would surely destroy them all the moment they came face to face.

55

The train of thought was disturbed by the whistle of the engine room tube. He went inside the bridge and pulled out the plug.

'Culpepper.'

'Would that be one of the whisky-stealin' Culpeppers, or one of the bible-punching Culpeppers from Boston?'

Culpepper grimaced. McVay was drunk again. 'It's the First Officer, Mr McVay. What can I do for you?'

'Well now, Mister First Officer, I'll tell you what you can do for me . . . that's apart from jumping overboard, or keeping your nasty little eyes off my medi . . . medit . . . medicinals. You can tell that wee man in the galley we laughingly call a shnook . . . excuse me, I should shay a cook. You can tell the fat little bastard that if I don't get my bowl of slop he calls stew in five minutes I'm going to come up there and fill his panties with it. Now have you got that, Mishter Firsht Offisher.'

'I'll have him send down soup and coffee, Mr McVay. Drink the coffee, then the soup. We all need clear heads tonight.'

'And what the fuck is that supposed to mean?'

Culpepper winced. 'It means that it's six o'clock, Mr McVay, and you are drunk. The only difference between today and any other day, is that everyone else is sober. Especially the captain. If he finds out that you're drunk, he's going to come down there and play coconuts with your so-called medicine. Now have you got that, Mr McVay?'

He put the plug in before the Scotsman could bellow an answer.

On the mess deck most of the crew were sitting in disconsolate groups, the bowls of chilli beans and spiced meatballs hardly touched. Apart from the helmsman and two boilermen in the engine room, the entire complement of the *Tinkerbelle* was there. They had been discussing their plight with growing dejection for the past hour and had come to the conclusion that either the captain was having a nervous breakdown, or they were experiencing group hallucination.

Felipe the cook entered and glared at the uneaten food. 'You pigs,' he said. 'You Godamn pig-faced pigs.'

They looked at the wizened little man whose only virtue was that he could stand temperatures of a hundred and twenty degrees and whistle. His ability as a cook had been open to much debate over the years and it had generally been agreed that if he had been a fish instead of a cook he would surely have drowned. But Felipe had pride and the crew had grown wise, so rather than risk duty in the galley they had learned to eat the food and smile. It had not been easy, but the jugs of rum were a help. Without the rum their taste buds had begun to function again and stomachs normally well-insulated turned over in protest.

'I spent all afternoon cooking the food,' he went on in a shrill voice, 'and you throw it back in my face like shit.'

'I've got to hand it to you, Felipe,' said Panacero gravely. 'You're as smart as hell. We've all been sitting here for the past hour trying to decide what to call this stuff, and you just walk right in and put a name to it. Shit.'

There were the beginnings of sniggers around the room and spirits began to rise as Felipe drew himself up to his full five feet, his eyes bulging.

'I've got a knife I've been sharpening for a man like you, Panacero. It's long and thin and I'm going to put it right up your arse.'

'Well let's face it, that's about as high as you can reach!'

Pasqual, a deckhand built like a teak chest, almost choked. Felipe whirled on him, dancing with rage.

'So it's funny, eh? Felipe's a big joke. Well you pigs can cook your own food. I finish. The next place we hit I find myself a real ship. A ship with a crew of men . . . not a floating house for pigs.'

Tommy rose and tried to put a friendly arm around him. 'Don't take it so hard, Felipe.'

'I don't take it at all, you pigs. From now on I cook only for the ladies and the officers. The ladies! Now they know good food. You know what they say about my meatballs? Eh?'

They solemnly shook their heads.

'They say they are special. Very special. The Miss Curtis, she says that never, never has she tasted anything like them.'

'Was that before or after they threw up?' enquired Panacero.

'After!' screamed Felipe. 'After they have eaten them all.'

He gazed at them with contempt and then marched angrily towards his galley. At the door he paused and looked back, his eyes gleaming maliciously. 'And don't none of you pigs come asking me for rum. I have no rum for you!'

'You think he meant it?' Santiano asked after he had left. 'About having rum, I mean?'

'He's bluffing,' said Panacero, but without conviction.

'He could have some stashed away,' said Barbeza, a tall, taciturn deckhand with greying hair and heavy, morose features. He was a two-jug man, inclined to go berserk on his third, and the unaccustomed state of sobriety was decidedly unpleasant.

'Culpepper would find it,' said Tommy. 'He's been praying for an excuse ever since he carried his bible on board.'

'You think it's going to last then?' Santiano asked, his sallow features glistening with the thought.

'The captain will be the first to go,' declared Panacero. 'I'll take bets on it.'

'What odds?' asked Torres quickly.

Panacero ignored him, developing the idea with growing fervour. 'To start with he's a gin man, and that stuff rots your liver a lot faster than rum. I'll bet that he can't function more than twelve hours without a drink and by tomorrow he'll have forgotten all about this German marauder. The only thing he'll be able to think about is getting hold of a drink.'

'I don't know,' said Tommy. 'He's tough as old leather. He won't give up that easily.'

'Who said it would be easy?' Panacero asked. 'Every chance we get we're going to remind him. Every time any man speaks to the captain he mentions drink, booze, gin.

We'll get a crate of those empties from the hold, fill them with water, then every chance we get leave one lying around. He'll crack.'

'He's got to crack,' said Barbeza. 'Can you imagine how *we're* going to feel by tomorrow?'

* * *

In the number two stateroom, once known rather grandly as the Pacific Suite, Diana Curtis was trying to rouse Mrs Hartford-Jones from the face-to-the-wall depression she had been in for most of the day. Neither she, nor Susan Jamieson beside her, really believed that Mrs Hartford-Jones wanted to die for she had fought with the strength of two men to get onto the piece of wreckage to stay alive.

'Mrs Hartford-Jones,' said Diana, 'if only you would put these clothes on and go up on deck. You'll feel much better then.'

'Really?' said a muffled voice. 'I suppose gazing upon my Henry's grave will make me feel very cheerful.'

Susan Jamieson rolled her eyes up to the ceiling and sighed. She was a small, freckle-faced girl of eighteen who had only recently left England to spend a holiday with her brother in Venezuela. The Caribbean cruise had been a last minute decision when her brother had found it necessary to visit a rubber plantation in the hills, and as Diana had been going anyway it solved the problem nicely. She had long, fair hair and striking blue eyes that had a tendency to stop men in their tracks.

'Would you like us to leave you?' she asked the older woman sweetly.

'Do whatever you wish,' she said heavily, as though they had just offered euthanasia. 'It doesn't matter.'

'We're all very lucky to be alive,' began Diana, trying a new approach.

Mrs Hartford-Jones sat up suddenly, clutching the sheet to her chin. 'Lucky? Lucky! Have you any idea how hopeless my life has become. I spent years helping Henry to find success. Boston, San Francisco, Montreal, Mexico, and finally Venezuela. At last it was all beginning to happen for us. We would have been able to buy a house next year, perhaps even a villa on the coast. And now . . .' Her face crumpled and she pushed the corner of the sheet into her mouth.

'But you're alive,' said Diana. 'That's what matters.'

'Not to me. All that matters to me is that my Henry is dead and I . . . I can't go on without him.'

They were silent as she sobbed, rending the sheet in her wiry hands, choking on despair. After a while she gazed at them with reddened eyes, her face hardening with anger. 'If I was a man I'd never rest until I had found that monstrous German who sank an unarmed ship. I'd find him and . . . and . . .'

She began to twist the sheet again, her eyes bulging with the intensity of her anger. The two girls watched, hypnotised by the hands as they wrestled with the thin cotton until it was knotted with hate.

'That's what the captain intends to do,' Diana said finally, dragging her eyes from the sheet. 'He's looking for the marauder now.'

'I beg your pardon?' said Mrs Hartford-Jones, releasing the sheet as though it was a snake. 'You can't be serious?'

'She's hardly going to joke about a thing like that,' replied Susan.

'You mean he's actually chasing the German navy now?' she asked incredulously.

'He's actually doing that,' Diana answered.

'With us on board?'

The girls nodded. Mrs Hartford-Jones rose from the bunk in the mangled sheet and gestured imperiously for the clothes she had been provided with. They consisted of a pair of dungarees and a T-shirt.

'We will see about that,' she said. 'I have no intention of being subjected to any further acts of war. The captain cannot possibly expect us to risk our lives again. It's quite intolerable.'

The trousers hung loose around her lean buttocks and the T-shirt emphasised her bony frame, although managing to flatter her small breasts and narrow waist. She rolled the dungarees up to her knees, as though she had been doing it all her life, then marched out of the cabin without another word.

'Is she real?' giggled Susan.

'Like a dragon,' replied Diana. 'I wonder what she'll do to Captain Slade?'

*　　*　　*

Culpepper was watching the last of the sun fall into the sea in crimson splendour, smelling the sweetness of the air as its moisture cooled and brought out the full scents of the day. It was a time for prayer, his favourite hour when he would walk the deck, bible open at random, reciting it in the mind with only the occasional glance to refresh his memory. He smiled and murmured: 'And your eyes shall be opened and ye shall be Gods.'

'I beg your pardon?'

He swung round and found himself looking at a most unusual woman. Apart from the fact that she was standing in her bare feet with a pair of bleached dungarees rolled up to her knees, she had strangely compelling features and piercing grey eyes. Her hair was brown, a suggestion of grey at the sides, and her chin jutted sharply from a pale, thin neck. It was not a face to be trifled with, he decided.

'I'm sorry,' he said. 'I was just quoting something.'

'Genesis?'

'Well, yes.' He looked away, finding it difficult to look into her eyes for long. 'It's that sort of evening.'

'For some, perhaps,' she snapped. 'For some it can be quite frightening.'

61

'Ma'am, there is nothing for you to be afraid of here,' he said quickly.

'I didn't say *I* was afraid. I was thinking of two poor girls who are close to hysteria at the thought of once again becoming the target of those brutal Germans. How a man can quote the bible and yet embark upon such a course, taking with him three helpless women who wish only peace and goodwill, is quite beyond me.'

'Ah, well you see that decision was taken by the captain.'

'Oh,' she said, looking at him more closely. 'You're not he?'

'No, ma'am. First Officer Culpepper.'

'I see.' Some of the chill went out of her gaze and even a hint of warmth appeared as she noted his nervousness. 'In that case I had better talk to the captain.'

'He's in his cabin,' replied Culpepper, then hesitated with an anxious expression. 'But . . . if you'll forgive my saying so, ma'am, this is not the best of times to discuss the matter.'

'Indeed?' Her eyebrow rose imperiously. 'May I ask why?'

'He's a trifle out of sorts. A rather difficult day and, frankly, he can be somewhat short-tempered.'

'At least we have that in common,' she said waspishly. 'Nevertheless the man needs to be told that I do not intend to be hurled into the front line of battle on his whim.'

'I couldn't agree more, ma'am. In fact, I would even go so far as to say that no one as charming as yourself should even be on board such a vessel as this.'

When Mrs Hartford-Jones smiled it transformed her rather sharp features into softer, rounder curves that made Culpepper think instinctively of Bathsheba. The mother of Solomon must have been just such a woman, he thought. Strong-willed yet warm and benign, a person of great character and full of compassion.

'You're rather young for a first officer, aren't you?' she said, beginning to take stock of this pleasant, rather plump young man with dark curly hair falling attractively across his forehead.

Culpepper blushed. 'Thirty-three, ma'am.'

'You look younger.' She closed her eyes and took a deep, appreciative breath. 'It must be a happy life out here.'

Culpepper couldn't think of anything to say. With enormous guilt he watched her small, firm breasts move beneath the thin cotton T-shirt. The nipples were disturbingly apparent, pointing at him with a devastating boldness. Perhaps she wasn't a Bathsheba at all, he thought. She certainly had the breasts of a Salome.

He dragged his eyes up to her face and found her looking at him with a surprisingly warm smile. He blushed and began to stammer an apology. She stepped up to him and placed a finger on his lips.

'My dear Mr Culpepper, I've taken up far too much of your time already.'

'Oh, no,' he said quickly. 'Not at all.'

There was a polite cough behind them and he turned to find Tommy staring at him with bulging eyes. 'My watch now, sir,' he said, his gaze flicking to Mrs Hartford-Jones and back as though he couldn't believe it was happening.

'Does that mean that you're off duty?' she asked. Culpepper blushed and nodded. 'That's splendid. Shall we?'

She slipped her arm through his and led him across the bridge to the companionway. Tommy watched them leave with stunned disbelief, then crossed to the helmsman.

'Did you see that?'

'I saw it, but I still don't believe it.'

'Jesus! Do you think I ought to tell the captain?'

'What can you say?'

'That's true,' said Tommy with a worried frown. 'If I told him Culpepper had gone randy he'd think I was having DTs or something.'

'She isn't even attractive.'

Tommy nodded, looking baffled. 'Maybe he's cracked. Let's face it, this has been a hell of a day. First the bodies, then the captain going on the wagon, then us attacking the wrong ship. Maybe it was all too much for him and he's gone bananas.'

'Then she's gone bananas as well,' declared the helmsman positively. 'You should have seen the looks they were giving each other.'

'After all this time,' said Tommy, a note of wonder coming into his voice. 'All those years, all those girls we laid on for him. My God, we even slipped one in bed with him that time in Tortola and he yelled like a scalded cat.'

They looked at each other, shaking their heads.

'It's been a hell of a day,' said the helmsman. 'One hell of a day.'

7

Lincoln Slade admitted defeat at five a.m. and hauled himself out of the bunk to sit with head in hands and acknowledge the fact that there was just no way he was going to get any sleep. The aching need for alcohol and the black depression that had been with him for most of the night made sure of that, and if he had succeeded in controlling those urges there was still the location of the German marauder to puzzle over.

He moved stiffly to his locker and rummaged through a heap of clothing until he found a reasonably clean, though wrinkled, pair of trousers. He put them on, then stood glaring at the barometer before deciding on an old grey sweater he hadn't worn for years. Slipping on a pair of canvas shoes he went out of the cabin and along the corridor that rolled gently to the swell of the sea. He paused at the radio cabin, surprised to find Torres dozing over a newspaper that was at least three weeks old. He jumped with shock when he saw the captain, glancing at the clock in bewilderment as though expecting to find that he had missed breakfast, perhaps even lunch. His relief at discovering it was five o'clock was almost as great as his astonishment at finding the captain up at this hour.

'How come you're on watch, Torres?' Slade asked irritably. 'You trying to impress somebody?'

'No, Captain. Oh no. It was just a little difficult to sleep. He paused, remembering Panacero's instructions the previous night. 'I needed a drink so bad it was impossible to sleep. You would not believe how much I wanted a drink.' He paused, watching the captain's mouth grow thin and a muscle begin to jump in his cheek. His spirits soared. 'It's terrible, Captain. How can I sleep when I keep thinking about a jug of rum, a bottle of gin, any kind of booze?'

'Alright, Torres,' snarled Slade, 'you made your point. We'd all like a drink.'

'Even you, Captain?'

'Even me.'

'Then why don't I get the keys and break out something for us now?'

'Good idea,' Slade replied. 'You can break out some coffee. Strong, black with plenty of sugar.'

Torres' face fell. 'It's a cold morning, Captain. Maybe a drop of rum in the coffee ...?'

Slade glared at him and moved on, climbing the stairs to the bridge. Tommy was collapsed over the chart table, Pasqual on the helm swaying sleepily with the rise and fall of the bow. Slade moved silently up to him and looked at the heading.

'You're ten degrees out, for Christ's sake!' he snapped.

Pasqual's head whipped round so fast he almost broke his neck. He gulped, the colour draining from his face, and quickly spun the wheel to bring them back on course. Tommy rose slowly from the chart table, looking as though he was fresh from the grave and began to scratch his head.

'I'll finish the watch,' Slade grunted.

The mate gave him an anxious look. 'You alright, Cap'n?'

Slade's menacing scowl was all the answer he needed. The captain was stone cold sober and looking mean enough to chew broken glass. Tommy groaned inwardly, already longing for the good old days when Slade would totter onto the bridge and squint at a hot noon sun with anguished eyes. He was even wearing clean pants, he noticed, and then wondered how long it would be before he was into white tunics and deck shoes.

'What's our position?' growled Slade.

'Position?'

Tommy looked at the helmsman who shrugged. He began to pull his ear nervously, bending over the chart and wondering if he dared make a guess. The plot lines from the previous day were still there, the last position timed at 1800 hours. He began to count on his fingers beneath the chart table, freezing as Slade crossed to him.

'Well, for Christ's sake?'

'Er . . . you mean our position now?'

'No, Tommy. Let's not be too ambitious. How about this time last week!'

'Sorry, Cap'n. Just give me a minute.'

He grabbed a compass and began to revolve it aimlessly over the chart. Slade glowered and took it from him. 'How many knots are we making?' he asked Pasqual.

'Ten, Cap'n. Steady ten all night.'

Slade grunted, measured off a hundred and ten with the compass, then drew a line from their last course change off Nevis. He handed the instruments to Tommy and stabbed a finger at the horizon, beginning to glow faintly in the east. 'Just in case you're wondering, that lump on the horizon is St Bartholomew . . . I'm talking about the island, Tommy, not the apostle!'

'Aw come on, Cap'n, we know these waters so well we never bother with plotting. In five minutes we'd have seen Bartholomew.'

'If you don't get the lead out, Thomas, it won't just be Bartholomew you'll be seeing. You'll be shaking hands with Peter, Paul and the rest of the gang!'

Tommy looked miserable and began to study his fingernails. Slade grunted and turned away, dismissing him with a gesture. He began to edge towards the companionway, glaring at Pasqual who gave him the sign of the cross as he went by.

Slade stepped out onto the wing of the bridge, suppressing a shiver as the chill air hit him. The horizon was now pink and gold, the edge of the sun just beginning to announce the day. He took deep breaths of the cold air, letting it sharpen his senses, watching the colours shift across the sky. Now they were deeper, blood red and melting gold, gilding the still dark waves so that, briefly, a glittering stairway stretched out across the sea. But in a moment it had gone, replaced by molten lead that rose and fell as the ocean breathed beneath it. The sky grew above, a dome streaked with light as the clouds burned in the east, as though an arsonist was at work.

Slade smiled at the thought. The grand arsonist was indeed at work, illuminating the world once again. It made him realize how long it had been since he stood the dog watch and witnessed the miracle of a new day. Far too long, he admitted. He was getting old and dissolute, thick-headed and thick-skinned. He turned from the east and searched for the peaks of St Martin, finding them low on the horizon to the north.

'Bring her round to three-three-zero,' he said without turning his head.

'Three-three-zero it is, Cap'n.'

For the next hour he stood on the wing, growing warmer as the sun rose, letting the silence seep into his soul. By the time the green slopes of St Martin were on their port he was relaxed and thinking clearly about the task he had set himself. The German could not afford to cruise around the Caribbean all day. Within the basin bounded by the Leeward and Windward islands there was a fair amount of shipping moving from the islands, or bound for Venezuela from Cuba and Puerto Rico. He would want to hunt at night, or certainly in the evening, which meant that he would probably head for the less populated islands within striking distance of the shipping lanes. He could shelter in any one of a hundred isolated bays or narrow straits, moving out at sunset with little chance of detection.

The first of these groups had to be the outer islands of St Martin, Anguilla and a few smaller islands to the north. Beyond them, no more than a day's sail, were the Virgin Islands. Once he got into those, Slade realized, it would take weeks to find him, but as they were further away from the main South American shipping routes he was hoping that the German captain would be content with either St Martin or Anguilla.

They held a course parallel to the rocky shoreline where sugar plantations rose up the hillsides, giving way finally to cotton on the higher slopes. It took thirty minutes to reach the northern tip of the island so that it was still only seven o'clock as they rounded the headland with the long flat island of Anguilla lying three miles ahead, like a thin green snake. He turned and looked back, remembering the wide bay beyond St Martin's Point. Even as he raised the binoculars his pulse was racing. A ship was anchored in the bay, well hidden from both sides of the island.

'Hard to port,' he told Pasqual quickly, 'I want us back behind that headland.'

Pasqual looked puzzled, but spun the wheel. Slade stepped into the bridge and blew down the engine room tube. He continued to blow for two minutes before the irritable voice of McVay came up the tube.

'If you blow that whistle once more I'll come up there and stuff the sodding tube in your ear!'

'Good morning, Mr McVay, this is Slade.'

'Is it, by God! Well let me tell you something, Cap'n Slade, my shift doesn't begin for another hour and it doesn't do any good at all blowing the pipes at seven a.m.'

'It's good of you to spare the time, Chief,' Slade said with a grin. 'I just thought I'd let you know that we might need maximum revs very shortly.'

'What the hell are you talkin' about? This floating scrap-yard has never even heard of maximum revs. Ten knots is all you get, and that's if you're lucky.'

'I want fifteen.'

'Man, you're dreaming. I couldn't get fifteen knots out of this cow if I fed her pure whisky.'

'You thought of it too?'

There was a long pause, then the chief engineer's voice

crackled from the mouthpiece. 'You blackmailing bastard, Slade. It can't be done.'

'It better be or you could be taking a bath before breakfast. I'll give you a whistle when I need it.'

'You can whistle as long as you bloody-well like but it won't do you any good.'

Slade waited until he had replaced the plug, then blew a long shrill whistle.

'What the hell do you want now?' screamed McVay.

'We might need smoke as well. Lots of black smoke.'

'What do you think I am? A bloody chimney!'

'Now I know you can do it, Chief.'

'What the hell are you running up there?'

'I thought you'd never ask,' Slade replied cheerfully. 'We're trying to impress the ladies.'

He listened to the stream of invective that crackled from the speaking tube, satisfied finally with the level of malevolence which ensured that the engineer was in no danger of going back to sleep. McVay was still in full flow when he replaced the plug and headed for the companionway.

'Will you be long, Cap'n?' Pasqual asked with a worried look at the approaching coastline.

'A couple of minutes. Take us in as close as you can. There's deep water up to a hundred yards from the shore.'

Slade entered the stateroom after the briefest of knocks, more concerned with getting Diana Curtis onto the bridge than with the niceties of the situation. He went to the closest bunk and pulled back the sheet. A tousled blonde head appeared followed by a face he hadn't seen before. A pair of large blue eyes opened, blinked, then widened with alarm.

'Diana?' said Susan Jamieson. 'Diana!' The figure in the bunk on the other side of the room began to move. 'Diana there's a man in our cabin. I think he's that captain you were telling me about. The revolting one without any manners.'

70

Slade gave her a frosty smile and moved to Diana, who was sitting up with a sheet clutched round her and the beginnings of a furious expression. 'I need you on the bridge right now,' he said.

'Do you have to make the request in person?'

'It's not a request, it's an order. There's a ship anchored ahead that might be the marauder.'

'Oh.' She frowned, then nodded. 'Alright.'

Slade waited. She made no move. 'Well come along.'

Diana glared at him. 'Captain, I am not wearing any clothes and I have no intention of getting dressed in front of you.'

Slade bowed mockingly. 'My apologies, Miss Curtis. I do seem to keep forgetting that you are a woman.'

There was a muffled giggle from the other bunk as he left the cabin. Along the passage he paused to hammer on Culpepper's door. 'On the bridge, Mr Culpepper, and make it fast.'

Most of the crew were beginning to appear on the foreward deck by the time the captain had returned to the bridge. They were less than a thousand yards from the looming cliffs that rose to three hundred feet on the headland, and the ship was beginning to feel the swell of the tide. Slade went out onto the wing and gestured to the men who were gathering along the port rails.

'I want everyone back on the aft deck,' he shouted. 'That includes the bos'un and the third mate.'

With mystified expressions they began to drift back towards the stern. Pasqual was sweating visibly at the wheel, giving the captain looks of growing horror as they began to round the headland. The freighter was at anchor in the centre of the bay, about a quarter of a mile from the headland and half that distance from the rocky shore. Slade studied it through his binoculars, noting that it was anchored bow and stern. If she was the German, he thought, it would take time to raise those anchors and get under way.

Culpepper arrived, looking harassed and quite baffled by the unaccustomed sight of Slade treading the bridge at such an early hour. 'What's the situation, Captain?' he gazed worriedly at the freighter in the bay. 'Surely you don't suspect that merchantman?'

'The name is *Tamerande*, registered in Panama. Look it up in the manual and be quick about it.'

Diana entered as he hurried from the bridge, Susan beside her. They crossed to Slade and gazed at the vessel ahead.

'Well?' he snapped impatiently. 'Is that the ship?'

They exchanged uncertain looks. 'We saw it from the side, not the back,' said Susan Jamieson. 'It could be, but . . .'

'But what?'

'Well, it's different from here,' said Diana. 'I suppose it's the right size, and the funnels are tall enough.'

'You're sure about the funnels?' Slade asked her.

'Yes.' Diana studied them carefully. 'I remember how tall they were.'

Slade trained his binoculars on the leading stack, studying the upper section. It could be false, he decided, and that would mean room for a gun. There would be vents beneath it to let out the smoke.

'I don't think it is,' Susan decided suddenly. 'It looks too ordinary.'

'Well that would be the whole point,' Slade said impatiently.

'What are you going to do if it is the ship?' Diana asked.

He glared at her, not at all sure of the answer himself. Culpepper returned with the Lloyds Register, looking pleased with himself.

'It's listed, sir. Definitely the same ship. Seven thousand eight hundred and sixty tonnes, four hundred and eighty-eight feet long. The *Tamerande*, registered to Janvor Line, Panama.'

'Where was it built?' Slade asked, unable to conceal his disappointment.

Culpepper searched for a moment, then looked up with alarm. 'Bremen, sir. In 1935.'

Slade's eyes gleamed and he moved quickly to the engine room voice tube. 'German yard, German ship. To hell with Panama.' He blew into the tube. 'Mr McVay, give me everything you've got.'

'I'll give it to you, you crazy bastard,' he screeched back. 'And if you wreck my engines I've got something else I'm going to give you as well.'

Slade grinned and replaced the plug, moving to the helm. 'I think you ladies better go below.'

Diana exchanged a look with Susan and shook her head. 'We'll stay. If we get closer we might be able to recognize it.'

'Oh we'll get closer all right,' said Slade, bringing the bow round until they were lined up on the *Tamerande*. He handed back to Pasqual as the deck started to shake beneath them and they began to eat up the distance. 'Hold that heading.'

'Aye aye, Cap'n,' croaked Pasqual, sounding like a frog with laryngitis.

Slade lifted the binoculars, sweeping the decks. There was no sign of movement, but when he swung the glasses up to the bridge he saw two officers in whites watching them. 'Right, you bastards,' he murmured. 'Let's play poker.'

'Captain, we don't have much room to manoeuvre,' Culpepper said, his voice pitched low so that the others could not hear. 'If it's the marauder he'll open fire.'

'The closer we get the less chance he's got to bring his guns to bear. Another five hundred yards and the only armament he can use will be on his aft deck and I can't see that he's got much there.'

Culpepper looked sceptical and reached for the binoculars. He studied the ship, biting his lip. 'That deckhouse looks odd. It's too wide for one thing.'

'Right, so let's make the bastard show his colours.'

'I don't really see what you're trying to accomplish,

Captain,' said Diana. 'From this angle all we can see is the back bit.'

'It's called the stern,' he said patiently. 'Or the blunt end if you prefer it. It's also the most difficult place for him to defend.'

'My God you're not going to attack him?'

'Good heavens no,' said Slade with mock horror. 'We're just popping over to pay our respects.'

The *Tinkerbelle* was making all of thirteen knots as it forged through the clear blue water of the bay, its rusty bow steady on the stern of the *Tamerande*. The German's siren began to blast out when they were a thousand yards away, the cliffs bouncing the sound back like thunder. Slade watched the distance dwindling between them, his eyes narrow slits.

'Another five hundred yards,' he murmured, 'and the bastard's lost the pot.'

'Activity on the aft deck,' said Culpepper quietly. 'And they're running up a flag.'

They watched the German War Ensign break on the after-mast at exactly the same moment as the front of the deck-house collapsed to reveal two massive six inch guns, the barrels already swinging to bear on them. Culpepper crossed himself and blew into the engine room tube.

'Mr McVay,' he said quietly. 'We are under attack.'

Slade turned to the white-faced women. 'Will you get yourselves flat on the deck and stay there.'

'But you've got no weapons,' Diana said helplessly.

There was an ear-splitting shriek that seemed to vibrate the very walls of the bridge. The women dived for the floor and Slade swung back to the window, grabbing the bino-culars from Culpepper.

'Too high,' he said. 'They've left it too late.'

The heavy guns fired again, both shells passing over their heads low enough to make them duck. Slade straightened with a gleeful chuckle. 'The bastard can't hit us without blowing off his stern.'

74

'Port and starboard lifeboats collapsing,' Culpepper reported calmly.

'Heavy machine guns,' Slade confirmed, watching a three man crew swing a twin set of 20mm towards them. 'Now if they can't hit us with those they're no bloody good at all.'

They were no more than five hundred yards from the *Tamerande* when the first heavy machine gun opened fire. The steel-jacketed bullets swept the foreward deck screaming off steel and blowing a line of ragged holes across the forecastle. The second machine gun opened up on the bridge, blasting out the windows and hammering at the steel superstructure.

'What do you intend to do when we get there?' Culpepper enquired in a tight voice. 'Which will be in approximately one minute.'

'We're going to ram him!'

Four pairs of eyes gazed at him incredulously. Pasqual was sweating so hard he looked like a melting doll. He let go of the wheel and pulled out a dirty neckerchief, frantically mopping his face. Slade crawled over to him, taking the helm and inching up until he could see over the steel coaming. Bullets were sweeping the deck and bridge, zipping and whining like hungry wasps.

'Tell the chief we need that smoke,' said Slade.

Culpepper blew down the tube. 'We're going to ram, Mr McVay. Can you give smoke?'

'It's not smoke you crazy bastards need,' he bellowed. 'It's strait-jackets!'

Slade held the bow steady on the high, bulging stern, already looming above their forecastle as they rushed across the last hundred yards. The machine guns were silent, no longer able to get a clear line of fire, the crews bracing themselves for the impact. It came with a grating shudder and a howl of tortured steel as plates buckled and rivets sheared. The *Tamerande*'s aft anchor chain took the full force of the collision and snapped like wet cotton, causing the big vessel to heel sharply over, swinging away from the *Tinkerbelle* as Slade put the helm hard to starboard.

Even as the Germans were picking themselves up the smaller vessel was pulling away from them, a thick oily smoke belching from its funnel to envelop the furious gun crews in a choking fog. In spite of the strident commands from the gunnery officer they had lost all sense of direction, unable to aim effectively whilst the ship swung sluggishly towards the shore.

Slade handed the helm back to Pasqual, who looked rather like a spectator at a particularly gruesome bullfight, fascinated by the spectacle but nauseated by the gore. The captain chuckled triumphantly, tapping his watch. 'They've got one minute, and then we're clear.'

They waited, the women brushing broken glass off their clothes with dazed expressions. Slade let a further minute pass before getting to his feet and surveying them happily. 'Now that's how to kick a kraut where it hurts,' he said. 'We caught him smack on the waterline and, with luck, made a mess of his steering.'

'I don't suppose our bow is looking very smart,' murmured Culpepper.

Slade dismissed it with a casual wave, ushering the women towards the companionway. 'We've got a watertight compartment up there. Even if we are shipping a bucket or two it's not going to do us any harm.'

'All the same, sir, I'd like to get a work party over the side as soon as possible.'

'Whenever you like, Mister Culpepper. Tell the chief he can have a drink on me and take his foot off the accelerator.'

The first officer grimaced. 'I hardly think he needs any encouragement, sir.'

Slade escorted Diana and Susan off the bridge and down to the staterooms where they found a harassed Mrs Hartford-Jones looking ready to abandon ship.

'Oh thank heaven,' she gasped, clutching at them. 'At first I thought I was having a nightmare, and then I woke up and it was still going on. What happened?'

'The captain decided to declare war,' Diana informed her. 'It was one of those spur-of-the-moment decisions.'

'Awfully exciting though,' said Susan. 'There were bullets all over the place.'

Mrs Hartford-Jones stared at them in horror. 'Bullets! My God, is Rodney all right?'

Slade looked puzzled. 'Rodney?'

'Yes, Rodney.' She was paling visibly. 'Your first officer.'

'Culpepper?' asked Slade in disbelief.

'Yes. Yes.'

'He's fine, Mrs Hartford-Jones,' Diana assured her. 'He's on the bridge.'

'Thank God,' she said fervently, closing her eyes and looking ready to faint.

'But you hardly know him,' Slade said in a bewildered voice.

Her eyes popped open and glared at him scornfully. 'I know a good man when I see one, Captain. I can recognize and respect integrity, honour, pride and . . . and courage. Excuse me, I must go to him.'

She hurried away towards the bridge, leaving them in varying degrees of astonishment.

'Whatever became of Dear Henry?' murmured Susan.

'Don't confuse me,' said Slade. 'I'm still trying to come to terms with Rodney. Are they really . . .?' He made a vague gesture towards the bridge, then just as quickly rejected the idea. 'No, not Culpepper. Not a chance. The last woman he kissed was his mother, and he probably felt guilty about that.'

'Well I'm sure you know your officers better than I do, Captain,' Diana said sweetly. 'But it does look as though Mrs Hartford-Jones is taking it all very seriously.'

She opened the door to her cabin and stepped inside, followed by Susan who was desperately trying not to giggle.

Slade stood in the passage frowning fiercely, then pushed his way in as Diana began to close the door.

'Have you any idea what the girls on these islands are like?' he demanded.

'It's not a subject I've devoted much time to,' she replied coolly.

'They're fantastic. Hair, eyes, face, figures . . . perfect. Any one of them loses the average American girl by a mile.'

'How about the average English girl?' Susan asked, fluttering her eyelashes.

'Not a chance,' said Slade.

'I'll say one thing for you, Captain,' said Diana in a voice that reminded him of breaking glass. 'You really know how to charm a lady.'

He grinned uncomfortably. 'I was just trying to make the point that Culpepper is hardly going to get excited over someone who's . . . well, who's . . .'

'Who reminds him of his mother?' suggested Susan helpfully.

'Right,' he said, then paused, frowning at the thought.

'If I were you, Captain Slade, I'd get us all off this boat as soon as possible.' Diana's smile went through him like a knife. 'Because Mrs Hartford-Jones strikes me as a very determined lady.'

8

The officers of the *Tamerande* were gathered in the wardroom, standing stiffly to attention as Captain Kroehner
paced before them. His square jaw was set hard, corded
with anger, his dark eyes condemning each man he passed.
Tellmann entered, a clipboard in his hands, moving to the
side of the room where he waited.

'Damage report, Mr Tellmann?' said the captain, continuing to patrol his area in front of the officers.

'We're taking water from two plates which are stoved
in, but the main leakage is about a metre above the waterline so the pumps can handle it without any trouble. The
rudder is jammed at an angle of forty-five degrees and the
upper bearing is warped out of line. The work party expect
to free the rudder before noon, but the bearing assembly
will have to be dismantled.'

'Can we navigate without repairs?'

'Once the rudder is free, Captain. But the bearing is likely
to shear in heavy weather or under full speed.'

'Thank you, Mister Tellmann. Kindly tell the duty officer
to prepare a course for Tortola in the Virgin Islands. We
will sail as soon as the rudder is free.'

The first officer came to attention and left. There was
silence as Kroehner surveyed the twenty-six officers before
him. Not a muscle moved in his face, yet the anger beat at
them until their mouths dried out and each man desperately
wanted to look away.

'In a few moments I will have to write in my log that at
0705 hours today we were attacked and disabled by the
Motor Vessel *Tinkerbelle*. The ship was built some twenty
years ago as a passenger-carrying coastal freighter. Accord-

79

ing to Lloyds Register she is leased to a Captain Lincoln Slade and due to lack of care and maintenance, is considered uninsurable.'

He took a crisp white handkerchief from his pocket, neatly folded and pressed, and patted his upper lip before continuing. The beads of perspiration ran down half the faces before him, but no man dared to take out his handkerchief.

'The *Tinkerbelle*, as some of you may have noticed, is now old and delapidated. She is sluggish in the gentlest of sea, makes no more than thirteen knots and at that speed it sounds as though the engine is coming through the hull.'

A junior officer grinned at the description, then froze as the captain's gaze lashed him with contempt. His cheeks began to burn as Kroehner continued, his voice now heavy with sarcasm.

'Some of you may even have noticed that this small coastal vessel was unarmed. She had no guns, no cannon, not so much as a pistol was used in the attack. Even the tactics were cumbersome, without skill or ingenuity. And yet we are at this moment disabled and at the mercy of the enemy.'

He glared at them, his lips white with anger. 'Do you have any idea of the shame, the humiliation, the stain on the reputation of this ship? We are supposed to be a ship of war, well armed and at constant readiness. But that was not the case this morning. We were an abomination! The officer of the watch and every station officer on call behaved like a party of prissy schoolgirls confronted by a rather unpleasant tramp. If it were possible I would replace every one of you. Unfortunately I must deny myself that luxury. But there will be no repetition of these events. Decisions will be taken quickly, efficiently, and carried out with the kind of discipline I expect, no demand, on one of the Fuhrer's fighting ships. It also means that in future either I or the executive officer will be informed immediately a situation occurs . . . *not one minute before impact!*'

He marched past them with stony features and left the

room, slamming the door behind him. Even after his footsteps had clattered up the companionway stairs no one spoke.

Tellmann was on the bridge supervising the delicate operation of lifting the *Tamerande*'s seaplane out of the hold. The covers of the foreward Number Two hold had been removed and a derrick swung out from the mast enabling the deckhands to winch up the Heinkel 114B and swing it over the side. The pilot, Flying Officer Hans Oberlechen, watched critically as the chief boatswain handled the winch bringing the seaplane gently over the armament crew waiting to fit a torpedo into the rack between the float stanchions. He stepped forward and checked the mountings, then armed it and signalled to the bos'un to swing it over the side.

'I want this whole operation speeded up in future,' Kroehner told Tellmann on the bridge. 'It's fifteen minutes since the order was given.'

'They do have problems, sir,' replied Tellmann. 'The hold is difficult to manoeuvre in, especially with a full torpedo load down there.'

'It's still too long.'

The Heinkel was floating free, a mechanic checking over the controls. A moment later the propeller began to turn slowly, the engine whining until it suddenly coughed into life, shattering the stillness of the bay with its steady roar.

Flying Officer Oberlechen entered the bridge and clicked his heels. 'Ready to leave, sir. Do you wish me to attach the trailing hook?' he asked Tellmann, referring to the hook and line used to destroy the radio aerials on ships under attack.

'Not much point now,' said Tellmann. 'Just make that torpedo count.'

'Yes, sir.'

Oberlechen turned and saluted the captain, then left the bridge. Kroehner moved out onto the wing with Tellmann, watching as the pilot swung out from the deck on the hoist and clambered into the cockpit.

'I wish I had more faith in the Heinkel, sir,' said Tellmann.

'I know,' sighed Kroehner, 'but we must make do with what we're given. At least the captain of the *Tinkerbelle* will have something to remember us by.'

'We're fairly sure he hasn't used his radio so if Oberlechen placed his torpedo well we might still have the element of surprise.'

The captain shook his head. 'Two kills were always the best we could hope for. The shipping companies will have guessed what is happening by now.'

'There's been no warning yet.' Tellmann pointed out.

'It will come. By tomorrow they will know there is a warship and will suspect a marauder. In a way I prefer that. We can attack in the open and do as much damage as possible during the next month.'

'You think the British will get a destroyer out here?'

'Not immediately, they have problems enough in the Atlantic. But there is nothing in the Caribbean to stop us, so eventually they must act.'

'We can do a great deal in a month.'

The captain nodded grimly. 'Indeed we can. That's why the damage must be repaired as quickly as possible.'

'It will be, sir,' replied Tellmann, then frowned thoughtfully. 'I wonder why that captain decided to attack us?'

Kroehner shrugged. He had been wondering the same thing for the past fifteen minutes. 'Whatever his reason, it was important enough to risk his ship and crew.'

Below them the Heinkel began to taxi across the water, turning into the light breeze. The engine roared and it began moving forward, the floats ploughing into the water at first, then as the seaplane picked up speed becoming steady, hissing through the gentle swell before lifting up into the sky. There was a ragged cheer from the crew lining the forward rails. The Heinkel waggled its wings, then vanished beyond the headland.

9

Lincoln Slade was stretched out in his hammock on the after deck, the tattered shade only just keeping the sun off his face, though he was hardly aware of it as he contentedly sipped a large pink gin under the envious eyes of the deckhands. All was once again well in the Caribbean, he told himself. He had effectively disabled the German with the minimum of effort and in a few hours time would present him on a plate to the British naval detachment at Barbuda. With a little luck he would even talk them into paying for repairs to the bow.

The alcohol was like a long lost friend, loosening the shackles of the mind so that he floated in a euphoric world. He would have a celebration party for the entire crew on Barbuda, he decided, as soon as the British gunboat based there had taken care of the *Tamerande*. He would also take great pleasure in handing the women over to the Royal Navy. He beamed with delight. Getting rid of the double-barrelled widow had become a maximum priority since he realized what life without Culpepper would really be like. Chaos was the most frequent word that came to mind. Sheer bloody chaos. The alternative would be a more sober life cluttered with the kind of decision-making he loathed. He took a long drink of his gin and contemplated the crisp white wake beyond the stern. Without Culpepper they were all lost. They'd probably go down one night on one of the reefs and every man on board would be too drunk to notice.

A shadow fell across the deck and he turned to find Diana Curtis gazing at him with veiled reproof. He raised his glass and winked. She wore the same faded trousers, but had now tied the shirt above her waist. The effect was definitely pleasing to the eye. He studied her navel, forced to admit that it was one hell of a navel. Small, delicate, like a fresh bud. He sighed. She turned her back and began to spread a blanket on the deck beside him so that she could utilise the meagre shade. Her buttocks were firm and sleek, suggesting both youth and maturity. He wondered about that. There was a certain arrogance in the thrust of the cheeks, a carnal invitation in the crease that separated them. He felt a stirring in his loins and groaned.

'Am I intruding, Captain?' she asked sharply. 'You do have the only shade.'

'Help yourself,' he replied. 'But if you wave that delightful ass in front of me much longer you're going to get goosed.'

She sat down, glaring at him: 'Captain Slade, has it ever occurred to you that your language is only fit for a brothel?'

'I wouldn't know, it's been so long since I was in one.'

'I hope you're not suggesting that I have.'

He beamed at her. 'That's a hell of a thought, Miss Curtis, but hard to believe. For one thing, if you had been in a brothel you certainly would never have got out.'

'I don't wish to continue the conversation, Captain.'

'Hell, you started talking about brothels. I was only talking about your ass . . . pretty as it is.'

She stood up, her face flushed. 'Do I have to find somewhere else to lie down? They're busy on the front deck as you know, and I don't particularly want to sit in my cabin.'

He started to wave a hand, then stopped, cocking his head.

'Well?' she asked furiously.

'Shut up!' he said.

The sound was beginning to assert itself above the thump of engines and the rush of water past the hull. It was sharp and urgent, like an angry wasp, and he felt the first cold premonition of disaster. Even as Diana was shaping an angry retort he was clambering to his feet, pushing past her without ceremony to run for the bridge.

The clatter of the work party who were making temporary repairs to the bow effectively drowned the sound of the approaching aircraft, but as Slade rounded the main deck superstructure he picked it out immediately about a quarter of a mile from the ship. He bellowed to Culpepper who was supervising the work party, stabbing a finger at the aircraft, then bounding up the stairs towards the bridge. The first officer glanced to starboard with a puzzled expression, then reacted with alarm as he saw the position of the aircraft. It was no more than a hundred feet above the sea, coming straight for them, its intentions unmistakable even before the torpedo fell in a shallow dive and splashed beneath the waves.

'Every man on deck,' he bellowed. 'Get the dolly up fast, Panacero.'

The bos'un was leaning over the side, watching Tommy and two of the deckhands working on a ruptured bow plate. He turned with a disgusted expression.

'Mister Culpepper, we ain't. . . .'

'Move you stupid bastard!'

Panacero blinked, unable to believe his ears, then quickly signalled the winch crew to start pulling up the work party.

Slade entered the bridge on the run. Demers was slouched at the wheel, half asleep in the heat. 'Hard to starboard,' roared Slade, bearing down on him with blazing eyes.

The helmsman froze with shock. The sight of the lanky figure of the captain at full speed was an awesome sight. He desperately tried to collect his thoughts, not sure whether he had said port or starboard. Slade hit him with his shoulder, knocking him on his back, then began to spin the wheel to its maximum position, simultaneously cranking the engine room control to full speed ahead. Demers picked himself up, wondering if the captain had finally snapped. It would come as a surprise to nobody. The engine room tube whistled and Slade reached out, grabbing him by the shoulder with fingers of steel.

'Tell McVay to give me full power and then get out of the engine room.'

Demers opened and closed his mouth, then as the fingers bit deeper nodded frantically and dashed towards the tube. Slade watched the bow coming round with agonising slowness, trying to count the seconds but each one seemed like an hour. Suddenly the aircraft was ahead, banking over the forward mast with a crackling roar of its large radial engine. He knew nothing about aircraft, but he knew Luftwaffe markings when he saw them. He gripped the wheel tightly, knowing the torpedo must be close. Culpepper was on the bow, looking out to sea, and then his arm whipped up sharply and stayed there. With a dry mouth Slade began to spin the wheel back to the midships position.

Culpepper watched the white foaming trail of the torpedo with a kind of stunned disbelief. He was only vaguely aware of the roar of the Heinkel overhead, or the clamour of voices from the bewildered deckhands. Panacero was still winching up the work party who were completely oblivious of the deadly white line that rushed towards them. The bow was almost lined up on it when he raised his right arm, praying that the captain understood. He felt the ship answer almost immediately and the bow began to steady. He was no longer breathing, his mouth leather dry as the torpedo closed the last hundred yards, hissing past the blade of the bow. He shut his eyes tightly and gripped the rail, certain that it must strike them somewhere along the hull. After the longest ten seconds of his life he opened his eyes and took a deep breath. It had missed. He shuddered then as he realized how close it must have been.

Panacero tapped him on the shoulder. 'Mister Culpepper, what in hell is going on?'

He turned, his face pale and beaded with perspiration. 'Get all the men under cover. Fast.'

The ship's siren suddenly blasted out, then as it died they heard the roar of the aircraft. Panacero looked towards it, his eyes widening with horror as he saw, for the first time, the German markings. 'Oh Jesus!' he said, and ran towards the work party who were beginning to climb over the side.

The Heinkel was coming in low, no more than fifty feet above the water, and even as the crew finally began to realize what was happening its twin machine guns opened fire from each side of the engine. A line of bullets ripped across the surface of the sea, then into the foredeck. Bullets exploded in the woodwork, screamed off metal and blasted ragged holes in the deckhouse which erupted into flames as cans of paint ignited. Panacero was shouting in terror, hauling the last of the work party over the side as the bullets hammered the deck around him. The man he was holding was Tommy and even as he pulled desperately at him the mate's chest spouted blood and he was torn away, turning in the air with blind, astounded eyes, before falling back towards the sea.

Culpepper ran for Panacero who was frozen with horror, looking at the space where Tommy had been. The aircraft was banking on the starboard side, turning tightly with the sound of its engine hammering at them.

'Get down,' Culpepper shouted frantically.

Panacero turned, shaking his head in disbelief. Culpepper began to push him towards the bridge superstructure, then the machine guns were chattering again and the air was filled with screaming metal. A bullet took him in his left arm and spun him round against the rail with enough force to shake every bone in his body. He looked at his shattered arm and wondered why he felt no pain. The aircraft roared over his head and he gazed up at it, no longer afraid. He wondered where it had come from, and then nodded slowly to himself as he saw the floats beneath the stubby fuselage and realized it must have been aboard the *Tamerande*. The deckhouse was a roaring inferno, but no one was doing anything about it. Everywhere he looked men were crouching behind any protection they could find. He pushed himself away from the rail and began walking towards the fire, wondering what he should do about it. He stumbled and almost fell, then stood gazing at his feet with puzzled eyes. His arm was now a shiny red, hanging at an odd angle. He considered it thoughtfully, noting the steady stream of blood that was already forming a puddle at his feet. There was still no pain, only a leaden feeling, as though he was carrying somebody else's arm.

'For Christ's sake, Culpepper!'

Slade grabbed him round the waist, pulling him round. Everything that had been going out of focus snapped back sharp and clear, and with it came the full cacophony of sound. Men shouting in terror, the roar of flames, the rising snarl of the aircraft coming in again.

'Captain, we'd better get down,' he said.

Slade cursed savagely and began to run with him towards the bridge, supporting him round the waist as he wobbled on legs that no longer functioned as they should. Behind them the Heinkel was coming straight at the bow, the machine guns opening up four hundred yards from the ship. Twin lines of bullets ripped over the bow, gouging holes in the deck and hammering past the lurching figures of Culpepper and Slade, blasting through the windows of the bridge where Demers was hanging onto the wheel in sheer terror. With horrified eyes he saw the wheel blow apart in his hands, his ears deafened by the scream and whine of bullets. The bridge revolved around him and then the deck smashed into his back and he lay there, resigned to death, thankful that there was no pain.

Slade came through the door with Culpepper, easing him down into a corner protected by the steel bulkhead, then crossed to Demers. Wooden splinters stuck out of his arms and face like darts, thin rivulets of blood coming from a dozen minor wounds. He checked the man, examined his eyes which were dilated and gazing fixedly at the ceiling. The sound of the aircraft was fading into the distance and he rose to his feet and watched it dwindle to a dot on the horizon before returning to Demers.

'On your feet, Demers.'

'Jesus, Cap'n, I'm dying,' he croaked.

'The only thing you'll die from down there is bloody boredom, so get below and find Santiano. Tell him Culpepper's hurt and get some antiseptic on those cuts.'

Demers staggered to his feet, feeling his limbs with growing disbelief. When he had finished the inspection he shuddered and crossed himself, murmuring a grateful prayer then tottered towards the companionway. Slade crouched beside Culpepper, tearing the sleeve of his shirt and examining the wound. The bullet had entered three inches above the elbow, breaking the bone, but making a clean exit. Blood welled slowly from the holes, but it was already beginning to clot.

'You'll be okay,' he said firmly. 'Can you manage until Santiano gets here?'

Culpepper nodded, his mouth pinched white as the pain finally began to surface. 'Tommy went over,' he whispered. 'He looked dead.'

Slade nodded grimly and went out of the bridge and down the outer stairs to the deck. Half a dozen of the crew, led by Panacero, were already tackling the fire. The bos'un had dropped a sea hose over the side and was connecting it to an auxiliary pump. Slade watched long enough to satisfy himself that they would soon have the blaze under control, then headed for the after deck, beginning to wonder apprehensively about Diana.

The only damage was a shattered lifeboat hanging drunkenly on its davits and a few bullet scars across the deck. His chair and shade were untouched, even the glass of gin safe beside it. He went over and picked up the glass, drinking the contents in one gulp, then looked around for Diana. There was no sign of her and with a feeling of relief he decided that she must have gone below when the shooting started. He was heading back towards the bridge when he heard a muffled exclamation. He stopped, glancing round. Nothing moved, then he heard another muffled cry and a clatter from the port ventilator stack. He went to it and gazed in astonishment at a pair of bare feet waving frantically just above the bend.

'I wouldn't try to get down there, Miss Curtis,' he said in a conversational tone. 'It's a long way down to the engine room.'

The voice was muffled, but savage. 'Then get me out you stupid man.'

He grinned and took hold of the feet, heaving on them until her knees appeared. He paused, considering her grimy bottom half. 'You alright?'

'Well of course I'm not all right!' she fumed, her voice echoing in the ventilation shaft. 'It's filthy in here.'

He reached into the stack and gripped the waistband of her trousers and heaved again. This time there was very little movement. He grunted and took a firmer hold, jerking hard. The only thing that gave was her trousers, which came down to her knees leaving him looking at a very pink bottom. The shriek of fury echoed all the way down to the bowels of the *Tinkerbelle*. He hastily pushed the trousers back over her hips.

'I think we've got a problem here,' he said.

The ventilator stack rattled as she beat at it with her fists, shouting something that sounded like 'sex fiend'.

'Okay, work your own way out,' he shouted. 'I just happen to be busy.'

The legs that had been kicking furiously went still. When her voice came again it sounded close to tears. 'You can't leave me in here.'

He sighed and moved back, reaching as far into the stack as he was able. With difficulty he managed to get a hand on either side of her waist. 'Alright, get your arms over your head and go limp.'

She squirmed for a moment, then relaxed. He braced himself and heaved, staggering back suddenly as she popped out of the ventilator like a cork. He tried desperately to keep his balance, his hands still round her waist, but the momentum was too much and they both sprawled on the deck. He sat up with a disgusted expression whilst she frantically pulled up her trousers which were once again around her knees. He grinned as she fumbled with the buttons glaring furiously at him.

'I'll say one thing for you, Miss Curtis,' he told her finally. 'You sure as hell know how to get attention.'

'You . . . You . . . You did it deliberately!'

He got to his feet, his mouth tightening. 'I've got better things to do than pull your Goddamn pants down. And if you had any sense you wouldn't have dived in there in the first place.'

'There was nowhere else!' she shouted.

'Well if you'd gone all the way down we'd never have got you out.' He gazed at the smears of oil and grime on her face and clothes, his nose wrinkling. 'If you don't mind my saying so, you could do with a bath!'

Her cheeks flamed and for a moment he thought she was going to take a swing at him. Instead she turned abruptly and marched away, her bare feet slapping the deck like gunshots. He followed after checking the starboard area for damage, finding nothing more serious than a punctured oil drum.

Panacero had the fire well under control on the foredeck so Slade went back to the bridge where Pasqual and Torres were rigging a makeshift wheel to the helm. McVay was there supervising the work, his features contorting with anger as he saw the captain.

'You're a mad bastard, Linc Slade,' he bellowed. 'If you're not chasing women you're chasing sodding warships. Women I can understand, warships I cannae raise any enthusiasm for. Will you look at this bridge.'

'How are the engines?'

'Shakin' their wee hearts out, that's what they're doing. The next time you ask me for full ahead they're going to blow themselves right out of the bloody funnel!'

'Well if you go out with them it will be worth it,' growled Slade, checking the compass heading and telling Pasqual to bring them twenty degrees to port.

McVay bristled, pulling out a half bottle of whisky and taking a long, gurgling swallow, before stepping close to Slade to breathe the fumes at him. 'Why in hell didn't you use them rifles?'

'There wasn't time. Anyway, they're not much use against a plane.'

'Oh, you've worked that out, then. Has it also penetrated that gin-sodden brain of yours that this ship isn't any use against anything more dangerous than an out-island canoe. Correction, a *leaking* out-island canoe!'

'Chief, shut your mouth or I'll fill it full of broken glass.'

McVay's eyes bulged, but he bit off the angry retort and took a drink instead. Pasqual and Torres looked longingly at the bottle as the whisky gurgled down the engineer's throat. Slade took it from him and passed it across.

'One drink each. You've earned it.'

They nodded gratefully. McVay snorted and moved to the broken windows, looking down at the smouldering ruin of the deckhouse. When he turned back he was bristling with indignation again.

'Where the hell is that lazy bastard, Tommy?' He demanded. 'If Culpepper's got a bullet in him he should be up here.'

'Tommy is dead,' Slade replied bleakly.

Torres and Pasqual stopped drinking, staring at him with shocked features. All the anger went out of McVay and his face was suddenly lined and old, as though a light had gone out somewhere. The effect made Slade realize that the engineer was well into his sixties, a fact he had never bothered to consider before. He felt a surge of guilt as he remembered how many times he had driven McVay through one day to the next, baiting him mercilessly when he complained.

'You're sure?' the engineer asked.

Slade nodded. 'Panacero was with him. He went over the side, but it wouldn't have mattered.'

McVay nodded, rubbed his nose and gazed intently at the

deck. 'A fair lad, Tommy. A fair wee lad.' He brushed a hand across his eyes and turned towards the companion-way. 'It won't seem the same without him.'

Slade watched him go, then told Pasqual to stand the watch and went below. He found Culpepper propped up in his bunk with his arm swathed in bandages and Mrs Hart-ford-Jones feeding him something that looked like yester-day's stew.

'How is it?' he asked.

'Not too bad thank you, Captain. Helen did a fine job with the dressing. She's had nursing training, you know.'

Slade groaned inwardly. The bloody woman would have to be a Florence Nightingale as well. He beamed at her, knowing what she was going to say before she said it and trying to come up with a logical alternative.

'He'll have to go into hospital, of course,' she said, her mouth small and stern. 'I trust there is one on Barbuda.'

He bent to examine the dressing, thinking furiously. She had used splints from the first aid cabinet and lashed them tightly with a lanyard. It was a very efficient job. He glanced up. 'How about the break? Was it clean?'

'A simple fracture. But I would like it checked. We don't want Rodney to have a short arm, do we?'

'Definitely not,' Slade replied. 'That'd play hell with his golf.'

Her eyes glittered. 'Is there a good man on Barbuda, Captain?'

He gazed gravely at Culpepper, relieved to see that he was embarrassed by the woman's concern. 'Well, now, the British naval people will have a sick berth orderly, and the locals have got a kind of voodoo man. Apart from that there's not much.'

'I'm sure Rodney will not be requiring voodoo medicine.'

'That's very true, ma'am. Maybe we should take him on to the Virgin Islands. The young women there are pretty good at nursing. They have a form of remedial massage that's . . .'

Culpepper glared at him. 'I don't think that's what Helen is meaning, Captain.'

'Ah.' Slade tried to look innocent. 'Well it was just a thought.'

'I can see I'll have to nurse Rodney myself,' she said, patting the first officer's hand.

Slade gritted his teeth. Her smile reminded him of a barracuda who had just scented lunch. 'I really don't see how that's going to be possible, Mrs Jones.'

'Hartford-Jones,' she said, teeth glinting.

He forced a tight smile, wondering whether the barracuda comparison was being a bit too kind. *Maybe a shark would be closer*, he thought. *One of the tigers, hard and mean as hell.* 'I'm so sorry,' he said. 'The point I was making is that we'll only be spending a day or so at Barbuda. I don't see how it's going to be possible for you to do much nursing.'

'Then obviously he'll have to remain behind. I shall find a place for us and stay with him until he is well.'

'For as long as ye both shall live' Slade added silently, then managed a vaguely puzzled expression which was not easy when he felt like snarling. 'But don't you have to return to Caracas? I thought, with your late husband going down with the *Cormorant*, you'd have to go back and take care of the legal affairs?'

Her eyes probed him like twin scalpels searching for the right nerve. *Give her half a chance*, he thought, *and she'd lay me open from stem to stern.* 'Henry had no family,' she said in a cold, clipped voice. 'I can tidy things up in Caracas at any time.'

That's after you've tidied things up here, thought Slade. 'It's very good of you to spare the time,' he told her. 'I'm sure that er, Rodney, does appreciate it.'

Her eyes misted over and her thin lips began to tremble. Slade turned away, knowing that if he remained another minute he would lose control and end up in a slanging match which he suspected she would win hands down.

The trouble with women like Mrs Hartford-Bloody-Jones,

he told himself on the way back to his cabin, was that they had you by the balls the minute you opened your mouth to disagree. A quiver of the lips, a tremulous sigh, a perfectly choreographed display of feminine frailty and everyone was looking at you as though you had just mugged Florence Nightingale.

10

HMS *Expedient* was located on the west side of Barbuda on a wide, sweeping bay flanked on both sides by the coral reef which surrounded the remainder of the island. The bay provided a natural harbour for visiting ships with deep water anchorage within five hundred yards of the beach, whilst the position of the island put the Royal Navy within striking distance of both the Leeward and Windward islands. There was a village of about two hundred people at Spanish Point, which marked the southern tip of the bay, and a larger fishing village on the far side of the island where Polmetto Point jutted out to the reef itself. From the palm-fringed beaches the land rose in gentle waves to dense forest which convinced most people that it was easier to paddle round the island rather than trudge the eight miles across.

Lieutenant Charles Purley was in command of the naval detachment, which consisted of two maintenance engineers, six shore-based personnel, and the ten strong crew of No 25 – a Fairmile 'A' class motor patrol boat which was their only reason for being in the Caribbean. The boat was one of the Fairmile company's early prefabricated craft built of hard chine and powered by a three'shaft Hall-Scott petrol motor which normally allowed them to cover the wide sweep of islands once a month and occasionally make the run to Cuba where 'showing the flag' was a convenient excuse for a long weekend in Havana. Unfortunately, for the past month, the seventy-foot launch had been wallowing in its moorings with a broken prop shaft and a burned out main bearing. The fact that World War Two had broken out the very day after it happened was the kind of co-incidence Lieutenant Purley could have done without. It confirmed, if confirmation were needed, that the fickle finger of fate was still pointing in his direction.

He was a tall, morose man with sandy hair and features that lacked both character and strength. His eyes were a watery blue and his mouth, neither small nor wide, seemed to be there only to underline a bulbous, unhappy nose that would have looked better on a prize fighter. What little chin he had seemed to disappear into a scrawny neck below ears that looked ridiculously small. It was a forgettable face with a memorable nose, which could well have explained his assignment to Barbuda and why his men referred to him as 'Pug'.

He stood on the rickety wooden jetty that jutted out from the beach watching the *Tinkerbelle* drop anchor in the bay. The vessel looked even more battered than usual and, shading his eyes against the setting sun, he studied the crumpled bow with a grimace of distaste. Of all the captains in the Caribbean he considered Lincoln Slade to be the worst by a mile, and it therefore came as no surprise to him that he'd managed to bend his bow on somebody or something. There were footsteps behind him and the jetty sagged even further towards the water as Petty Officer Hardcastle arrived.

'Beats me how they keep it afloat,' he said with a mixture of awe and reverence.

He was a gangling, freckle-faced man of twenty-five with untidy fair hair and an engaging smile that had so far survived the humid heat and aching boredom of life on Barbuda. Jimmy Hardcastle was the armourer and spent most of his time tinkering with the old fashioned Mark 8 torpedoes and the World War One two-pounder that occupied the launch's foredeck, collecting salt and rust with exasperating speed. The broken prop shaft was an added frustration for it prevented any useful exercises and limited his gunners to occasional dry runs, loading and unloading the Lewis guns to fire imaginary bursts at imaginary targets. The visit of the *Tinkerbelle* would at least break the boredom.

'I wonder if he's carrying any stores?' he said hopefully.

Purley glowered at the shore boat being lowered from the freighter. 'The only thing they'll be carrying is pink gin and local rum.'

'Well we could certainly do with some gin,' Hardcastle said cheerfully. 'The mess has been dry for two weeks now.'

'I'm fully aware of that,' Purley said waspishly. 'It will probably remain dry until Number 25 is operational again.'

Hardcastle grimaced behind his back and returned to the group of ratings who were gathering on the beach with hopeful expressions. Ginger Bates, the bos'un, was flexing huge hairy hands and already licking his lips.

'They'll have plenty,' he said to no one in particular. 'Maybe no beer, but rum, gin and whisky. I'll lay odds.'

'We might have a problem,' murmured Hardcastle.

Bates looked towards Purley and spat on the sand. 'You mean Pug?'

'I mean that our CO isn't too keen on doing business with the *Tinkerbelle*.'

'For Christ's sake!' exclaimed Leading Seaman Johnson, who was in charge of stores. 'We're down to bully beef and biscuits. If it wasn't for the local fishermen we'd be eating each other.'

'I quite fancy a piece of roasted Pug,' said Bates. 'Especially if it was done slowly over an open fire.'

'Stow it, Bates,' said Hardcastle, his pleasant smile taking the sting out of the words. 'We'll work something out.'

The shore boat was half-way to the jetty by now and they could pick out the half dozen occupants, the lanky figure of Captain Slade prominent in the bow.

'They're great lads for a party,' said Able Seaman Dower, looking hopeful. 'Time before last, when we had Chalmers as CO, it lasted three days and took a week for us to recover.'

'They can knock it back alright,' said Bates. 'Jesus can they knock it back.'

Johnson nodded agreement. 'And they've always got it. We could get a few crates at least, and probably meat as well.'

'Screw the meat,' said Bates. 'I haven't had a drink for a fortnight.'

'Who's that with them?' asked Hardcastle, shading his eyes. 'That blonde hair in the stern.'

They all concentrated on the approaching boat. After a moment Dower said in a shocked whisper: 'It's a woman.'

'Three of 'em,' said Bates confidently. 'It gets more like the Good Ship Venus every day.'

They grinned. Hardcastle continued to watch the blonde head that glowed like molten gold in the dying sun, beginning to drift back along the jetty towards Purley. When the boat bumped alongside one of the Puerto Ricans jumped out, tying up, whilst Slade stepped onto the jetty and solemnly shook the lieutenant's hand, nodding to Hardcastle. The petty officer barely noticed. His eyes were fixed on the slim beautiful girl with the golden hair who was smiling radiantly at *him*. He felt his cheeks burning and knew he was gaping like an imbecile, but managed to step forward without tripping over his feet to offer his hand. She took it and adrenalin fizzled in his heart like a type four detonator.

'I'm Susan Blain,' she said, stepping onto the jetty, 'and this is Diana Curtis.'

He croaked a hello, helping out the second girl who was dark haired and almost as attractive, then found himself facing a stern-faced woman in an off-white T-shirt and dungarees. Susan was introducing her as Mrs Hartford-Jones and he was beginning to notice that they all wore men's clothing.

'Thank you, Petty Officer Hardcastle,' said Purley in the slightly nasal voice which sounded more like a sulky wasp. 'I'm sure the ladies would like to get into the shade.'

He felt bewildered until he realized that he was blocking

99

the jetty and jumped aside so quickly he almost fell into the sea. Purley glowered at him and led the way with Slade and the women. A younger man, in crisp white trousers with his arm in a sling, was being assisted by Mrs Hartford-Jones. He began to understand that these people had been in some kind of trouble.

The remainder of the men from the shore boat began to climb onto the jetty. One of them, a tubby man with prominent ears he remembered as being called Panacero, came over to him.

'Jimmy Hardcastle, isn't it?' he said, holding out his hand.

He took it, nodding. 'What's been happening to the *Tinkerbelle?*'

'Happening!' Panacero rolled his eyes. 'You better ask Paul Jones about that. He's our new cap'n, by the way. I know he looks like Linc Slade, even talks like Linc Slade, but ever since we saw that German raider he thinks he's John Paul Jones.'

'Come on, you're kidding.'

'Listen, we got that busted bow by ramming the Kraut when he was blasting away at us with more big guns than I've ever seen in my life.' He paused, suddenly curious. 'You do know there's a war on?'

'Yes,' Hardcastle replied dryly. 'We did hear, but there's been nothing about any raider.'

'You have now, mate, and she's waiting for you to pay her a visit at St Martin.'

Hardcastle groaned. 'Oh no!'

'Now is that the attitude? Look, we've stopped it cold. All you need to do . . .' He stopped talking as the petty officer groaned again.

'We're laid up,' he told him. 'Busted prop shaft and a bearing that'll take a couple of days even when we get the part, which could be weeks.'

'Jesus!' said Panacero. 'I'd hate to be around when Cap'n Slade finds that out.'

*   *   *

Captain Slade was at that moment in the process of finding out, his face reddening with fury as Purley repeated it for the third time.

'There's just no way we can get operational. We can't even take it across to Antigua for supplies.'

'Tell me, Lieutenant, just what kind of a fucking navy are you running!'

Purley stiffened, his cheeks flushing, glancing across to the women who were being served iced lemonade by Dower. They were on the veranda of the long, thatched hut which served as mess hall, officers club and general recreation room for the entire complement of HMS *Expedient*.

'Kindly respect the ladies, Captain, and moderate your language.'

'I'm not here to hold hands with the Goddam ladies,' roared Slade, causing Mrs Hartford-Jones to glare furiously at him, 'I'm here to give you a bloody Kraut on a plate. All you can tell me is that you're not ready for a war out here.'

'Captain, you will lower your voice,' Purley snapped, his watery eyes looking into the wall a foot above Slade's head. 'It's not my fault that our launch is out of commission. We've been waiting for the spares for a month.'

'Are you seriously telling me that you represent the British Navy in the Caribbean and you can't even get a spare prop shaft.'

'Yes,' replied Purley, flushing. 'Furthermore, we can't even get assistance from the two frigates that covered us from Jamaica. The *Loch Syne* is on Atlantic convoy duty and the *Loch Cheran* is on her way to Montreal.'

'Oh that's great! That's bloody marvellous! You've got a bastard Kraut half a day's sail from here and you can't even show the bleeding flag. You realize what he'll do once he gets himself sorted out? He's already wiped out a passenger liner full of women and kids?'

'And a tanker,' said Purley. 'We didn't know it was a

marauder, but both ships have been missing for two days now.'

'There you are, then. He'll turn the Caribbean into his own private shooting gallery. For Christ's sake, Lieutenant, get on the bloody radio.'

'I shall do that of course,' Purley replied tightly, 'but every ship with any kind of firepower is in the Atlantic. Have you any idea what's happening out there, Captain? The German U-boats are sinking merchantmen every day. Already, after one month, two million tons have gone down. I can ask, I can beg, but we'll be lucky if we see any kind of vessel before next month.'

Slade glared at him as though it was his fault. Purley blinked, his eyes like muddy pools, and started to back away towards the women at the other end of the veranda. Inwardly he was seething at the effrontery of this uncouth and unprincipled rogue of a captain. To question the role of the Royal Navy was bad enough, but to stand there handing out tactical advice was intolerable. He wished he could boot him off his island, or at the very least cut him to pieces with a few well chosen words.

Instead he said: 'I'm afraid all we can offer you is lemonade.'

'Jesus!' said Slade and stalked off towards the beach.

Purley gazed after him with his mouth tightly compressed and an aching knot in his stomach. He felt totally ineffective and, unaccountably, filled with enormous guilt. He despised Slade and everything he stood for, yet he had to swallow the unpalatable fact that he had attacked the German with an unarmed ship when his own country wasn't even at war. He tried hard to understand that, but finally gave up and wandered towards his bungalow at the rear of the mess hall.

The radio transmitter was set up in the spare bedroom and he had already begun to compose the request for assistance when he reached it. The message would have to be firm, he decided, though not aggressive. A request, rather than a demand. A suggested course of action, rather than a statement of intent. He went into the bedroom and sat beside the transmitter, irritated because he had forgotten to call out the radio operator. He lifted the telephone and wound the handle, waiting a full minute before accepting that everyone was on the beach.

He reached for a pad and wrote the message out in block letters, underlining each word.

> CONFIRM PRESENCE GERMAN
> RAIDER SAINT MARTIN
> REQUEST EARLY ASSISTANCE
> AND/OR URGENT REPLACEMENT
> PARTS. PURLEY. BARBUDA.

He went into his bedroom and took the code book from the steel chest beneath his bed, then went back to the transmitter and read the message again. He picked up the pencil and deleted a few words, then scratched his chin nervously as he read it over again.

> CONFIRM PRESENCE
> GERMAN RAIDER
> REQUEST ASSISTANCE
> OR REPLACEMENT PARTS
> PURLEY.

He chewed on the pencil and went over it again, wondering if it wasn't perhaps a trifle strong to send to Command Headquarters. He tore off the sheet and began again.

11

The sea whispered along the shore like a band of cheerful ghosts that urged each other forward with quiet chuckles and gurgles of secret delight. Above the palms at the head of the bay the moon was edging through cloud, gilding the gentle ripples and turning the turbulence along the reef into pale blue fire. Slade watched contentedly, feeling the beginnings of a breeze along his cheek and a dampness in the air that heralded a change in weather. By dawn it would be starting to blow, coming out of the south with lowering clouds and scudding veils of mist that clung to the indigo waves like shrouds.

He watched the dark bulk of the clouds moving across the stars, gauging their speed. It was early yet, perhaps this time tomorrow would see the weather system covering the Caribbean basin, beginning to churn the sea, sucking it into the sky in ghostly towers. It was the hurricane season and although there had been no distant thunder for weeks he suspected they would hear it tomorrow. In the past that had always been the signal to head for a friendly island, to anchor deep and load up the tender with tobacco and booze.

'Not this time,' he thought. 'Not with Tommy dead for no good reason and the Tamerande getting ready to go out and kill again.'

He felt, rather than heard, the pad of feet on the fine white sand and turned his head, identifying the tubby silhouette of Panacero long before he spoke.

'The food's lousy,' he grunted, squatting down beside him. 'Bully beef and sweet potatoes. Jesus!'

'I suppose we could let them have some of Felipe's meatballs. That'll bring the tears to their eyes.'

'They could do with some booze, Cap'n. Dry as a dromedary's armpit round here.'

'Do them good. That Purley's a prick.'

'The rest of them are okay.'

Slade glared at him in the gloom. Panacero shifted uncomfortably, then pointed off into the darkness. 'Couple of the lads would like a word.'

'So what am I? The chaplain?'

Panacero beckoned and shapes materialised out of the shadows beneath the palm trees, padding across the sand to drop down in a circle around them. He recognised Johnson, the navy storeman, and the bos'un. There were two younger faces he didn't know and with them Santiano and Barbeza.

'What the hell is this?' he growled.

'Well, Captain Slade, sir,' replied the bos'un, 'we were kind of wondering if you felt in the party mood. Things are a bit quiet around here and, though I don't remember every little detail, the last time you came we had one hell of a party.'

'That was in peacetime, before we got shot at and lost a bloody good man.'

There was an uncomfortable silence and the ratings began building sand castles with their hands. Barbeza cleared his throat twice and then said nothing. Slade turned back to the sea, feeling depressed.

'Doesn't help Tommy none,' Panacero said gruffly. 'It's not the fault of these lads.'

'I don't give a shit,' said Slade. 'All I know is that we found and disabled the bastard just so they could have a go. We didn't just waste our time, we wasted Tommy's life.'

Johnson was still for a moment, then slapped his fist into the mound he had been building. 'You think any of us like that? We can't help, we can't fight, about the only sodding thing we can do is get drunk with you.'

'Listen,' snarled Slade. 'If I had that patrol boat I'd find some way of using those torpedoes. Even if I had to row the bastard over to St Martin.'

'Alright,' said the bos'un quietly. 'If you want the torpedoes you can have them.'

'Christ, Ginger, we can't do that,' Johnson said in a shocked voice. 'I'd be topped for sure.'

'Crap! We've got six on the boat and ten in store. If the cap'n here decides to steal one, even two, who the hell is going to know about it?'

'I'll know. Hardcastle will know. After that it's just a matter of time before the whole bleedin' navy knows.'

'Pug won't say a bloody thing if they're used,' replied the bos'un. 'The problem is how Captain Slade could go about using them.'

They turned to Slade who was staring out to sea, not a muscle moving in his face. He had the stillness of a guru about him and Panacero feared the worst. He tried a snort of disgust that faltered into a nervous clearing of the throat. 'You crazy?' he asked them. 'What the hell do you think we are?'

'He is crazy,' said Johnson. 'All this sun and sand has finally got to him.'

'He's a genius,' said Slade softly and turned towards them. Panacero felt a shiver of alarm as he saw the captain's eyes. They glowed like luminous smoke and the moonlight on his face showed it clear, unlined, as though his years had rolled out with the tide. Felipe was nudging him with his foot, his wizened features glistening with fear.

'I don't think we'd really go along . . .' Panacero's words trailed away into silence.

'What's in the torpedoes?' Slade asked the bos'un.

'Torpex. They're Mark 8s. The warhead carries eight hundred pounds of the stuff.'

'And will the warhead come off the torpedo?'

'Dead easy. You just unscrew the bolts.'

'Then we'd have a charge big enough to put a hole in him?'

'If you could place it,' said Johnson. 'But that's one hell of a trick.'

'We think about that later. Right now we want two of your torpedoes, the Lewis guns and that two-pounder on your foredeck.'

They looked at him as though he was quite mad. Even the bos'un, until then beginning to warm to the idea, was speechless.

'You've gone off your bloody trolley,' said a young rating named Levison. He was the most junior member of the crew of No 25, a deckhand and support gunner, and he had been listening with awe to the calm voice of this legendary captain casually discussing a major naval engagement.

'If you took our guns we'd all be up the creek,' said the bos'un in a reasonable tone. 'It's not on.'

'You're up the creek now,' Slade pointed out. 'No engine, no war. By the time you get the parts or assistance that Kraut could have sunk a dozen ships. All I'm suggesting is a little bit of trading. We borrow your guns for a couple of days, give them a bit of a work out. In return we'll leave a few cases of rum, gin, whatever you need 'till we get back.'

The bos'un looked up at the sky and licked his lips. Levison was whispering furiously to Johnson. He sighed, running the knuckles of a heavy hand across his mouth, then told them to 'stow it' before turning to Slade.

'How many cases?'

'Five rum, one scotch, one gin,' the captain said quickly.

'Jesus, Ginger!'

'Shut your yap.' He looked out across the bay to the dark silhouette of the *Tinkerbelle*, its mast lights glowing like tiger eyes. 'We'd need your derrick and winch gear. That's going to make a clatter.'

'We'll make a bigger one here,' replied Slade. 'Felipe will go out with you and come back with a crate of gin. We'll mix it up with lemons and limes, add a bit of soda and pass it round with the compliments of the *Tinkerbelle*. If you keep it good and strong, Felipe, we'll have everyone in a party mood before Ginger's even ready to lift.'

'Deckhands?'

'Panacero will organise that. A dozen of the strongest, the rest come ashore to liven up the party.'

'Cutting gear?'

Slade frowned, then nodded. 'McVay can handle it. He'll curse a blue streak, but he's good. Why do you need it?'

The bos'un shrugged. 'If we're going to do the job we might as well do it right. That two-pounder has a steel base that bolts into the deck. As long as we can cut the holes it shouldn't take more than eight hours to spud it in.'

'I'll need to sail before daylight.'

'So we're wasting time.'

The bos'un looked at his own men who were watching him with sickly expressions. 'They'll bleedin' hang you, Ginger,' whispered Johnson.

'Crap,' he said calmly. 'In the first place the Pug won't know who coughed, and in the second we'll all be bloody heroes if the captain gets to that marauder. So if any of you bastards are out, now's the time to get lost.'

He glared at them. Levison shivered and nodded. 'Alright. But Hardcastle's going to get it in the neck.'

The bos'un grinned. 'He's young enough to take it.'

*   *   *

The war and the armament on No 25 were a long way from Jimmy Hardcastle's thoughts at that moment. He was sitting in the shadows at the end of the veranda with his arm draped at an excruciating angle over the back of Susan Blain's chair. If he flexed his fingers he could just touch the coarse cotton shirt and feel the warmth of her body. He held his breath and scraped his fingertips across her shoulder. She stirred and looked at him, smiling.

'Why don't you put your arm around me. I'm sure it can't be comfortable like that?'

He gulped and croaked a reply, dragging his arm down

towards her. Pins and needles laced up to his shoulder but he barely noticed. Susan was leaning towards him, nestling into the crook of his arm with her golden hair smelling of honeysuckle and her eyes so dark he was lost inside them. With growing panic he realized that his other arm was going round her waist and that, incredibly, hers were circling his neck. He tried frantically to think of something witty to say, but then his brain froze as her lips pressed against his and something very like a sigh rose between them.

*　　*　　*

Culpepper was beginning to wish that he had stayed on board. Helen Hartford-Jones was telling Lieutenant Purley for the third time how he came to be wounded and the naval officer was agreeing, for the third time, that in His Majesty's Royal Navy this would put him in line for a medal. They were in the mess hall, which had long since been cleared of the frugal meal that had been eaten without enthusiasm. In spite of the lieutenant's apologies, the bully beef and watery sweet potatoes had come as a shock to them all.

Slade had appeared towards the end of the meal with half a dozen of the crew and had huddled with them in a corner of the room for a while. After the meal he drifted over, accompanied by Felipe and a large bowl of punch, cheerfully inviting them all to drink the health of the *Tinkerbelle*. This was rapidly followed by the Royal Navy, His Majesty, the United States Navy, the President of the United States, and finally the future success of Lieutenant Purley.

Purley, at first reluctant to sample the brew, was soon searching for a toast of his own whilst agreeing vigorously with Mrs Hartford-Jones that Culpepper should at least be mentioned in despatches. Only Culpepper's confirmed teetotal status had excused him from the rounds of punch and he had watched, with mounting alarm, the rapid deterioration in speech. Even Diana Curtis was losing her poise and occasionally tripping over words that had more than one s in them. The naval ratings were well into a large pan of a similar mixture, lounging around one of the long cane tables with exaggerated poses, as though each was determined not to be the first to fall down.

Culpepper intercepted the captain as he moved towards Diana with a fresh glass of punch. He wore that sleepy, laconic expression which usually meant he was three parts drunk and working hard on the final quarter.

'Captain, is this wise?'

'Is what wise?'

'This – ah, this concoction you're handing round. I mean, with the ladies present and a degree of intoxication clearly evident things are likely to get out of hand.'

Slade regarded him owlishly, then draped his arm around his good shoulder. 'Rodney, lad, you worry too much. You know that? Always a worrier. Good officer though. Bloody fine officer. Got to hand you that.'

'Thank you, Captain,' Culpepper said quickly, trying to edge from under the arm. 'I just wish you could reduce the amount of alcohol in the punch.'

There was a burst of raucous laughter from across the room and Culpepper winced as he saw that one of the ratings had fallen backwards off his chair and was now sprawled in a drunken stupor on the floor. He nodded towards the scene. Slade grinned and patted his arm, this time choosing the injured one. Culpepper paled visibly.

'Jesus, Rod, I'm sorry.' Slade pulled away from him, peering at the arm. 'I clean forgot that one was busted. How is it?'

'Painful,' replied Culpepper.

'You ought to have a drink. Best thing in the world to kill the pain. Couple of glasses of rum and you'll be doing hand stands.'

'I doubt it, Captain.'

'Listen, Culp, you could at least get something from the medic here.' He leaned forward, lowering his voice. 'We're pulling out at dawn and unless you want to spend a couple of months here waiting for that spare engine, you'd better come along.'

'Why so soon?' Culpepper gave him a worried look. 'And why is it a secret?'

Slade grinned and tapped his nose. 'You just trust old Linc. Weather's turning foul and we got places to go.'

Culpepper started to look around the room with growing suspicion. He turned back, opening his mouth to voice the question when Diana stepped between them, glaring aggressively at Slade.

'What's this about you leaving, Captain?'

Slade grimaced and stared at Culpepper as though it was his fault. Diana saw the glass in his hand and took it, her cheeks flushed and her eyes bright enough to light a Christmas tree.

'Well, Captain?'

'Well, ma'am, the movements of my ship are not something that should concern you any longer.'

'So you're leaving us here?' she snapped.

Slade blinked. 'Why the hell shouldn't I?'

'They haven't got a boat for one thing,' she told him in a voice that crackled with indignation. 'And they're at war for another thing.' She paused, frowning as she lost her train of thought.

'You said yourself that it could be a long time before the navy could move them,' Culpepper pointed out.

'Right,' said Diana, in control again. 'And the food is appalling.'

Slade gave Culpepper a murderous look.

'We could drop them off on one of the main islands,' Culpepper suggested, ignoring his gaze. 'I might take a few weeks sick leave with Helen.'

Slade muffled a curse and looked around for a drink. He was just in time to see Purley wandering out onto the veranda, managing to hit the door frame twice before lurching through. He started after him, but Diana caught his arm and pulled him back to face her.

'I want an answer, Captain?'

'Fair enough,' he replied. 'It's no.'

He started to move but was again jerked back so forcibly that she lost her balance and swayed against him. He looked at her eyes and estimated she was about ready to fall down. He grinned at the prospect.

'We're leaving with you,' she said. 'If you don't take us I will complain to Lieutenant Purley. If necessary he can commandeer your boat to take us to . . . to . . .' She glared at him. 'Where we want to go.'

Slade glanced towards the veranda again, aware that Culpepper was intrigued by his interest. If Purley saw the lights on the *Tinkerbelle*'s deck, or heard the winches, he had a better than even chance of spending the next few months on Barbuda himself. He turned back with a bitter expression. 'If you insist, ma'am. But only if you insist.'

Diana watched him move towards the veranda, his tall, angular frame leaning forward from the waist as though he was walking in water. He was by far the most aggressive and infuriating man she had ever met. She turned to Culpepper as Helen came towards them, her mouth trembling as a wave of despair engulfed her. 'He doesn't like me at all, does he?'

'Oh, it's just his way,' replied Culpepper, alarmed by the tears in her eyes.

'No. He really detests me. I can tell.'

Helen reached them, beaming at Culpepper. 'And what have you two been up to?'

Diana leaned forward and buried her face in his chest, sobbing. Culpepper felt his cheeks go bright red as he opened and closed his mouth in a soundless plea for understanding.

* * *

Petty Officer Hardcastle was convinced that if he kissed Susan Blain once more he was going to rupture something. It was not so much her technique, or even her soft, warm, pliable body that squirmed so delightfully in his arms. It was the sheer overwhelming enthusiasm with which she threw herself into the business.

They had slipped from the veranda to the beach beyond the jetty an hour ago, but the rising wind and occasional sheets of spray were adding up to one of the most frustrating evenings of Hardcastle's life. He lay on his back in the damp sand with Susan nestling on his chest trying to think of a way they could get into the room at the end of the long hut he shared with sixteen sex-starved ratings. He groaned at the thought.

'Darling,' said Susan, as though she had been calling him that for years. 'Why don't we go out to the *Tinkerbelle*? There's a dinghy by the jetty and I'm sure Captain Slade won't mind. I could always say I left something on board and didn't want to bother him.'

'What a marvellous idea,' said Hardcastle, wondering how it was that she always seemed able to read his mind. 'We could . . . well we might . . . I mean, at least we'd be alone.'

She kissed him, her small mouth opening wide on his and her silken tongue slipping between his teeth and threatening to blow his head off. She pulled back, her eyes dark, her breath warm and eager. 'If I don't make love to you, Jimmy Hardcastle, I'll just die before morning.'

Petty Officer Hardcastle rose like a drunken man, wondering what gods had cast their kindly eye on him that day and unlocked the gates of paradise. 'I think you're the most fabulous creature I have ever known,' he said.

She sighed and wrapped herself around him. 'And you're adorable. I've been thinking about you since I was fifteen years old, but I never imagined I'd meet you here on Barbuda. It must be fate.'

He could only nod and look gratefully at the stars.

'I don't mind telling you, Captain . . . Captain Shlade,' Purley was saying with a decided list to starboard. 'That you're not my kind of . . . of . . .'

'Sailor?' Slade offered hopefully.

'Sright. No. No, you're not. But by God you're a man of . . . of . . .'

'Action?'

'Couldn't have put it better miself. I like you, Slade. Salt of the . . . of the . . .'

'Earth?'

'Sea, old boy. Sea.'

They clung together like nostalgic lovers in the oil-lit depths of the veranda. Felipe hovered in the shadows, his wizened features taut with anxiety as he watched the macabre duet. Captain Slade's hand rose from the lieutenant's shoulder and beckoned. He stumbled forward with the large jug of punch which had gone through subtle changes in the past hour. It was now flavoured with lemon juice and sweetened with cane sugar and molasses to conceal the fact that it was almost one hundred per cent gin. He poured some into Slade's glass then turned, looking apologetic, to the lieutenant.

'I beg your pardon, sir. Can I fill your glass?'

Purley swayed at the thought. 'No. No, I'm . . . I'm jusht about . . . about . . .'

'Empty,' supplied Slade and topped him up. 'Now here's to one of the great fighting ships, HMS *Nelson*.'

'HMS *Nelson*,' gurgled Purley, then lifted his head from his glass. 'Do you know her sister ship, the *Rodney*? We ought to drink to her.'

'There never was a finer ship,' said Slade, wondering if Culpepper had any idea how famous he was.

Purley drained his glass, gazed at it with pride and flung it towards the beach. Felipe and Slade caught him before he hit the floor, easing him down until he was stretched comfortably against the wall.

'You going to leave him here?' Felipe asked, taking a drink from the jug.

'You want to take him home?'

Felipe shook his head and sat down abruptly, spilling sticky gin onto his trousers. Slade sat beside him and took long gulps of the cool air. 'Jesus,' he said, 'that bastard can drink.'

'He's navy,' said Felipe, as though that explained it all. 'In there they've drunk twelve bottles of rum and eight of gin and they still know who's talking.'

Slade peered at his watch, then shook it. 'What time is it?'

Felipe looked at the waning moon. 'About four o'clock.'

'Time to get moving. Pass the word.'

Felipe nodded, took another drink from the jug and levered himself to his feet.

*   *   *

The last two conscious ratings were stubbornly squeezing handfuls of lemon and lime pulp from the bottom of the pan with that dedication which only comes to the totally inebriated. Felipe appeared and began hauling *Tinkerbelle*'s crew unceremoniously to their feet, pummelling them back to life with a malicious satisfaction that was quite unwarranted considering it was he who had put them in that condition in the first place.

'Shore leave's over,' he whispered in each man's ear. 'On the jetty now or the captain says we go without you.'

The general opinion appeared to be that he could go much further than the jetty without them, but one by one they began to totter out, holding each other up as the night air hit them. The two ratings staggered along with them declaring eternal comradeship until they were turned around by Panacero at the jetty. One of them, a gunner who was in his

early twenties and convinced that this was the greatest
night he had ever had, paused and squinted across the water
at the *Tinkerbelle*.

'Hey, mate,' he said, waving his arm wildly, 'some daft
bugger's stuck a gun on your stern.'

Panacero exchanged a look with Felipe and went to stand
beside him, gazing out towards the ship which was brilliantly lit as Ginger Bates and his crew worked to fix the
heavy two-pounder to the afterdeck.

'That's not a gun,' Panacero told him after a moment.
'That's a harpoon we use for hunting whales.'

The gunner started to nod then stopped, grinning. 'You
must think I'm pissed, mate. That's a two-pounder.'

Panacero sighed and tapped him gently behind the ear.
The gunner folded up, taking his companion down with
him. They arranged them neatly on the beach, then herded
the rest of the men into the shore boat.

*   *   *

Diana Curtis was awakened from a fitful sleep by a hand
shaking her none too gently. She felt strangely light-headed
and her eyes refused to focus, but the tall, angular figure
before her could only be Slade.

'If you're coming, it's now,' he said shortly.

'Why? What time is it?'

'It'll be dawn in half an hour and I want to be ready to
sail by then.'

She pushed herself to her feet and stood swaying, wincing
at the throbbing in her head. 'What did you put in the
punch,' she said weakly. 'I feel terrible.'

Slade grinned and took her by the arm, leading her towards the door. 'Nothing special. It was probably something
you ate.'

She gave him a disgusted look and gestured towards the
snoring figures around the table. 'Those too?'

He shrugged. 'Weak stomachs.'

They went out into the night air and she felt a wave of nausea, hanging onto his arm until it passed. He waited, looking strangely perturbed as he watched her.

'Are you sure you wouldn't rather stay?'

'No thank you. I'll be alright in a moment.'

They went down to the jetty where the shoreboat was moored. It had taken the crew out to the ship and returned with Bates and Johnson who stood waiting for the captain, a number of crates beside them. Culpepper was already in the boat with Mrs Hartford-Jones who looked like Diana felt and seemed to be blaming it all on Slade.

'I find your behaviour appalling, Captain,' she snapped as he helped Diana into the boat. 'First you get everyone drunk, then you drag us out at a most uncivilised hour.'

Slade gave her an irritable glance. 'Nobody's forcing you to go, ma'am. I've already told you that I'd rather you waited for a boat on Barbuda.'

'You mean without Rodney,' she said sharply. 'Well I don't intend to let him be bullied into serving on your ship with a broken arm.'

Culpepper seemed bemused by it all. He patted her hand whilst giving Slade a puzzled glance. 'You could come back for us, Captain? A few days. Even a week or two.'

'Not possible,' Slade replied shortly and turned to shake hands with Bates and Johnson.

'Take care, Cap'n,' said Bates. 'Wish I was going with you.'

'Maybe next time,' grinned Slade.

He stepped into the boat and nodded to Barbeza at the helm. He cast off and slipped the engine into gear, pulling rapidly away from the two figures on the jetty. Diana watched them with growing bewilderment. They didn't smile or wave. They looked as though they would never see any of them again.

'What *is* going on?' she asked with exasperation.

Slade was hunched in the bow. He turned, his eyes bleak. 'You'll find out soon enough.'

The tattered bow of the *Tinkerbelle* came out of the darkness and a moment later they were bumping against the ladder. Culpepper went first, helped by Mrs Hartford-Jones, then Diana followed. On the deck Felipe was serving mugs of coffee to the shore party, most of whom looked as though they would be better off with embalming fluid. It was not until she turned to speak to Culpepper that she realized something was wrong. He was gazing up at the bridge in horror and when she followed his glance she understood why. Mounted on each wing was a machine gun.

Culpepper's face was grey when he turned back to Slade. He shook his head slowly, almost with despair. 'You can't get away with it, Captain. You just can't go around pinching the Royal Navy's weapons.'

'I signed for them,' Slade replied calmly. 'We've got the two-pounder on the stern and two torpedoes in the hold.'

Culpepper groaned. 'They'll hang us. It's an act of war.' He swayed, his face glistening with perspiration. Helen put her arm around his waist and gazed accusingly at the captain.

'Can't you see he's ill. He shouldn't even be out here.'

'If I left him behind they'd make him responsible,' Slade explained heavily. 'I didn't have much choice.'

'Well he's going to bed now,' she said firmly. 'And he's going to stay there.'

She turned Culpepper towards the companionway and led him away without waiting for an answer. Slade swung back to Diana, glaring at her.

'Now don't you give me a hard time.'

She shook her head, only to regret it immediately. She reached for the rail to steady herself. The deck had begun to throb beneath her feet and she was far from sure whether it was the ship's engines or her condition that was responsible. 'I haven't seen Miss Blain,' she said. 'We can't leave her behind.'

Slade's face went grim and he seemed lost for a reply.

After a moment he said: 'She came aboard a few hours ago.'

Diana frowned. 'That's not like her.'

Slade suddenly seemed anxious to find something else to do. He began to look around the deck, beckoning to Felipe who was skulking in the shadows. 'Where's Panacero?' he asked.

Felipe shrugged and gestured towards the bridge. 'You told him to get under way, Captain. You want some coffee?'

'No, I don't want any damned coffee,' snarled Slade and headed for the bridge, avoiding Diana's glance.

She went slowly towards the companionway, trying to arrange her muddled thoughts into some kind of coherent pattern. Even the simplest things didn't seem to make sense any more. She went down the companionway and along the passage to her cabin. A deckhand she vaguely remembered as Torres was standing outside, trying to look as though he wasn't there. She tried the door. It was locked.

'Why is the door locked?' she asked, wishing everything would stop going out of focus.

'Captain's orders, ma'am,' he mumbled.

'I've just left the captain. He knew I was coming here.'

Torres gave her a tortured grin and said nothing. There was movement in the cabin, then the voice of Susan. 'Diana? Is that you?'

'Yes. What's happening?'

'Everybody's gone bonkers. I came on board with Jimmy and now we're prisoners.'

'Don't be silly,' Diana said and turned to Torres. 'Open the door please.'

He grinned again and shook his head. 'Not without the captain.'

She sighed, wishing she could understand what was going on. 'Are you alright, Susan?' she asked.

'I'm fine, but Jimmy's furious.'

Diana nodded and started to turn away, then paused and turned back. 'Susan? Who's Jimmy?'

'Petty Officer Hardcastle. We've just got engaged.'

It was all too much for Diana. She turned and made her way back along the passage to the captain's cabin. Switching on the light she crossed to the bunk and sat down, wondering how long he would be. From the clanking sounds above they were raising the anchor and the steady thump of the engines had increased. She yawned and lay down, thinking about Susan Blain. She could have sworn she said they were engaged.

12

'Ahead one third. Come to two-four-zero.'

The helmsman rang up the instruction on the engine room telegraph and began to bring them onto the new heading. Slade stood at the window, watching the line of surf break across the reef as they moved slowly out of the bay. The sky was smoke-grey, smouldering in the east, and the sea was molten lead rolling sluggishly beneath them. The wind had dropped, but he could smell the weather that was building the cloud above. He turned to Panacero, aware of his nervousness.

'Set a course for St Martin, Panacero. Ask Mr McVay for the best he can muster.'

Panacero nodded, reaching for the voice tube only to pause, gazing at him miserably. 'Captain? We are not men of war.'

Slade opened his mouth to snarl a reply then closed it, biting back his anger. He turned away from him, staring at the leaden sea with brooding eyes. How could he begin to expect them to understand the emotions that drove him? He barely understood them himself. The Germans had brought this war to the Caribbean in the shape of a disguised marauder that killed by stealth and deception. Fate had decided that they should be witness to the victims of that deception and suddenly the past that he had sought so long to bury had risen up and confronted him. Even now, twenty-seven years later, he could still hear the screams of the fear-crazed passengers as they fought for the few boats that meant their only chance of survival. If he closed his eyes he could see the faces, grotesque beyond belief as terror brutalized the features, distended eyes and contorted mouths that spewed obscenities of hate as he pushed them away. And all around the sea was wrought with flailing limbs as the ice cold water drove them to hysteria. He felt again that awesome guilt as his lifeboat had pulled away from the scene whilst beyond it, hanging in the sky like a black mountain, the huge bulk of the *Titanic* began to tip slowly towards the waves.

'No, we are not men of war, Panacero.' He gazed at the barrel-shaped man with tousled hair who wanted to understand his motives. 'But we are men and we have a ship under us. If we do nothing how many more will it sink? How many more bodies will float in the Caribbean? Is that the price you want to pay, Panacero?'

He swallowed and shook his head. 'No, Captain.'

Slade put his hand on his shoulder, gripping it hard. 'The first time we tried it was crazy and we were lucky. This time we're going to think it out, do it right.'

Panacero sighed, his eyes filled with despair. 'It is a warship, Captain. One shell from those guns . . .'

'Then we must find a way to do it without giving them the chance. If I can't find that way, Panacero, then it's no deal. Okay?'

Panacero managed a shaky smile and nodded, picking up the voice tube and blowing into it with some relief. The grating response made him wince.

'Chief, it's Panacero. The captain would like the best possible speed.'

'Would he now. Well you tell that maniac that we've still got a leaking bow and I've been up all night playing Ali Baba to his forty-frigging-thieves. I've got a torpedo on the other side of my bunkhole and a boiler that sounds like my Aunt Lizzie's kettle so any time he wants to live dangerously all he's got to do is come down here and I'll weld his balls together faster than he can cough. Have you got that, Panacero?'

'Yes, Chief,' Panacero said patiently. 'You'll be on half speed while you're making running repairs.'

He quickly plugged the tube as McVay's scream of fury erupted from it.

*   *   *

Slade entered his cabin and crossed to the chart table, collecting a bottle and glass on the way. He sat down and uncorked it with his teeth, pouring gin up to his fingers. After the first drink he allowed himself a shudder, then leaned over the chart and tried to think of a plan. His brain felt stuffed with cotton wool and his eyes had begun to burn, but the friendly warmth of the gin was building a pleasant enough fire in his belly. He took another drink and topped up the glass, wondering if he would be able to persuade the British petty officer to take the warhead off the torpedo. He had been pretty mad last night. He grinned as he remembered Hardcastle's fury.

There was a sigh from his bunk and he spun round to stare with astonishment at the girl lying there. She was curled on one side, fast asleep, her hands cupped beneath her chin. He remembered then that he had locked the petty officer in with Susan Blain. He rose and went over to the bunk, looking down at her. The black hair framed flawless features, more delicate in repose. He swallowed another mouthful of gin and sat on the bunk beside her, wondering what had brought her here.

After a while he went to the chart table and brought the bottle back to the bunk. It was a difficult journey for his legs had begun to develop that elastic looseness which was a sure sign that the gin had penetrated below the kneecaps. By the time he reached the bunk he was glad to sit down, placing the bottle carefully on the shelf above it. She stirred briefly when he stroked her hair back from her forehead, but that was all.

He wasn't sure precisely when he had the idea, only that it amused him enormously. The picture of prim Miss Curtis waking at noon all tucked up with the captain had the kind of madness that appealed to him. The only problem was

123

how to accomplish it without waking her. He began by removing his clothes and folding them neatly, a feat which had him tottering from one side of the cabin to the other. During the course of that operation he finished the bottle of gin, then turned his attention to her. Taking her plimsolls off was no problem at all, but the trousers represented a major obstacle. He solved it finally by kneeling on the floor at the foot of the bunk and tugging them gently towards him. They were loose enough to descend as far as the hips, but there they stuck. He glared at them, determined not to be beaten. With great care he managed to unfasten the top two buttons, but gave up the rest when she almost awoke, muttering in her sleep and rubbing a hand across her face. In the process she turned onto her stomach and with a surge of triumph he pulled the trousers off in one swift movement.

Diana mumbled to herself and reached blindly for the blanket. He chuckled and covered her with it, easing himself onto the bunk beside her. He lay for a few minutes congratulating himself on the entire operation, only to become uncomfortably aware of the warmth and softness of the girl. His erection seemed to come out of nowhere and with it a whole set of new ideas. She had begun to move restlessly in the narrow bunk, turning so that her flat, silky stomach was sliding over the very part of his anatomy he was suddenly anxious to forget.

'*Christ!*' he thought. '*How the hell did I get into this?*'

He steeled himself to think only about how to get out of the situation, knowing that if she awoke whilst he was half out of the bunk, or half into his clothes, no one was ever going to believe that it was all a joke. She was moving again. He lay perfectly still, his head clearing rapidly as the full implications of his action began to penetrate. Her head was now on his shoulder and her arm draped across him, but the most disturbing feature was the slim leg that was sliding over his own.

With growing desperation Slade tried to think about his marauder, and when that didn't work, about the course corrections needed to bring them to St Martin after sunset. That didn't work either. He was acutely conscious of the girl, aware of each breath she took, the smell of her hair and the silky texture of her skin. With clumsy hands he stroked her back down to the flaring buttocks, groaning inwardly as she nestled closer to him. His hand went down to her slender thigh intending to move it away but, in a moment of weakness, pulled it around him instead. Perspiration rose out of his skin like a fine dew and his heart was pumping faster than the engines below as he positioned himself and then slowly, tentatively, pressed forward. He slipped into her without any difficulty, a fact which filled him with both astonishment and despair.

The aching need that had been with him since he climbed into the bunk beside her took over and he began to move, slowly at first, rocking her gently in his arms, but as she began to sigh and moan against him he forgot all caution and began to plunge deeper and deeper into the girl until they both cried out in strangled voices and he found her staring at him with enormous eyes. They were filled with incredulous surprise and something else he could not even begin to understand.

She fell asleep almost immediately and he eventually drifted off without any clear idea of how he was going to cope with the situation the following morning. He wasn't even sure he felt guilty about it any more.

*   *   *

When he awoke she was sitting fully dressed by the chart table, watching him without emotion, as though he was a long way away. He raised his head and winced as small hammers began to beat unevenly behind the temples.

'Bad?' she asked in a flat, uncompromising voice.

He sat up and closed his eyes, taking deep breaths. When he opened them she was holding out a mug of coffee. He took it gratefully, wondering how much she remembered.

'Do you do this sort of thing often?' she asked coldly.

'Do what?' he asked back, feeling his stomach turn over.

'I think it's called rape.'

'Oh,' he said, his face beginning to burn. 'You er . . . you remember?'

'Not all of it, of course, but enough to be able to fill in the rest of the details.'

He tried to stand up and realized he had no clothes on. He gestured towards his trousers. She passed them over, her eyes cold, watching impassively as he manoeuvred them on beneath the blanket.

'Why be modest, Captain? After all, I don't suppose I had much chance to be modest last night.'

He winced and sat down, wishing he could think of something urgent to do elsewhere. She went on remorselessly, as though she had been rehearsing it for most of the night. 'I suppose on this ship it's your word that counts and nobody else's.'

'No. You'd be wrong about that.'

'Then you admit rape?'

He flushed and gave her an angry look. 'That's an ugly word.'

'It's an ugly act.'

'It wasn't like that.'

'What's that supposed to mean?'

He made a weak, evasive gesture. 'Can't we talk about this later.'

'You mean when you've got me drunk again?'

'I didn't get you drunk,' he snapped. 'If you can't tell when you've had enough that isn't my bloody fault!'

'Well at least I thought I would be safe,' she said contemptuously. 'In spite of your revolting language and enormous arrogance I still assumed you were a gentleman.'

Slade glared bitterly at the floor, unable to meet her eyes. 'You're entitled to that opinion,' he said heavily. 'God knows I would be too.'

'Then what do you suggest we do about it?' she asked furiously. 'Just forget it ever happened?'

He shrugged uncomfortably. 'You're doing the talking.'

'If I was a man I'd know exactly what I'd do.'

'If you were a man you wouldn't have anything to complain about in the first place!'

'Captain Slade, you're a bastard!'

He stood up, his face pale and gaunt, nodding slowly. 'Yes, Miss Curtis, I am. And if it makes you feel any better, I am unlikely ever to forget that fact.'

'Oh.' She looked at her hands, biting her lip. When she lifted her head he was surprised to see that her cheeks were flushed. 'You mean that don't you?'

'Every word.'

Her eyes were large and unreadable again. He remembered the way they had been when she awoke, so incredulous and . . . and . . . something he couldn't define.

'It wasn't entirely your fault.'

Slade was still trying to identify the emotion and almost missed the words. He looked at her, frowning. 'What was that?'

'I said it wasn't entirely your fault.' Her cheeks were very red and she was almost glaring at him. 'It wouldn't be fair for you to blame yourself completely.'

It took a minute for him to fully comprehend the words. 'What the hell are you saying? You mean you weren't asleep?'

She bit her lip and turned towards the door. He grabbed her wrist and pulled her round. 'You weren't were you? It was just too bloody easy anyway.'

'Oh that's charming! That's absolutely charming!'

'You know what I mean. I was drunk to start with.'

'Well I wasn't exactly sober myself.'

'But you *were* awake?'

She glared at him. 'Some of the time.'

'You bitch!'

Her eyes flashed and she swung a small fist at his jaw. He ducked, then caught it, pulling her against him.

'What the hell was going on?'

'I didn't think it would go that far.'

'One word from you would have stopped it.'

She blinked, her eyes filling with tears. He realized he was holding her wrist too tightly and let go, shaking his head in bewilderment. 'You're one hell of a confusing woman, Miss Curtis.'

A tear ran down her cheek and she wiped it away with the back of her hand. He took it in his, genuinely puzzled. 'Why did you?'

She stifled a sob and shook her head. 'I don't know. I thought I'd make a fool of you and . . . and then it just happened.' She glared at him through the tears. 'Don't ask me why I should want a man like you. I haven't the faintest idea.'

He shrugged. 'I don't suppose you would when you're sober.'

Her eyes flashed and she opened her mouth to disagree only to change her mind, gazing at him with an exasperated expression before turning towards the door. 'If you say so, Captain,' she murmured.

After she had left he went and gazed into the battered mirror above the bulkhead washbasin. The face that stared back had not changed miraculously overnight, a possibility which might have explained Diana's surprising behaviour. It was still deeply lined by the years with a square, stubborn chin and eyebrows that rose like moss-covered mounds from the wide forehead. The eyes beneath were smoke grey, as cynical as the mouth that curled contemptuously at the question he dared to ask himself.

His hair was fairer than it used to be, bleached by sun and time, but the whiskers showing against the deep tan of his face were as grey as winter. He grunted and turned away, irritated by his own stupidity. There was only one explanation: the silly cow had been too drunk to notice.

13

They had St Bartholomew Island on the starboard bow as the light began to fade in a sky that had been lowering all day. The wind was gusting at forty knots and capping the waves, which were steadily deepening as the storm centre approached. Slade studied the weather with Panacero and Felipe, gauging the tide that was running against them before he offered his view that the storm would be weak and blow itself out by tomorrow.

'Maybe,' Felipe grunted, 'but something bigger is coming. The air's too warm.'

Everyone respected the wizened cook's knowledge of the weather. He possessed that sixth sense that only comes from a lifetime at sea, coupled with the hazards of cooking in a galley that could become a rollercoaster if things really turned nasty. Yet Felipe had never been caught with his pans out when the bad ones came.

Slade sniffed the air, feeling the edge of coldness in it. He grunted cautiously, not eager to disagree with Felipe. 'Feels cold enough.'

'Not for December in a depression.' Felipe spat over the side as though to emphasise the point. 'Too hot. We could meet a hurricane soon.'

They gave him disgusted looks. 'That's a pretty lousy thought, Felipe,' said Panacero.

'So don't believe me. Get out the barbecues and we'll have a meal on deck tomorrow.'

'How sure are you?' Slade asked him.

He spat over the side again. 'Something's coming. This is just a fart from the big one.'

Slade made his way back to the cabin and glared at the chart. They would make St Martin by midnight, but if the marauder had moved from the bay it would be no easy job to find her with the weather worsening. They would have had two whole days to work on the damage and if her captain was anything like efficient he would have moved to a safer anchorage the moment he freed the rudder. His only option was the Virgin Islands, no more than ten hours from St Martin and with many uninhabited islands to choose from. He glowered at the chart, wondering which group he would aim at. There was a sharp, determined knock on the door and he leaned back, grimacing.

'Come in, Hardcastle.'

The petty officer entered and stood stiffly before him. 'Can we have our discussion now, Captain?'

'I suppose so.'

'How long do you intend to keep me on board?'

'Until we reach a suitable port where you can be put ashore.'

'I take it that I can then report your actions, sir?'

'You may. Of course, it might be a bit difficult from inside a cell.'

Hardcastle looked puzzled. 'I beg your pardon, sir?'

Slade put on his most condescending look. 'Stowaways, Hardcastle. They put them in jail round here.'

'A stowaway? Damnit, Captain, your men grabbed me and locked me in a cabin.'

'Your story.'

'It's damned well true. You stole No 25's guns and me along with them.'

'Well, Hardcastle, you'll be able to make a clean breast of it all in court. The way we'll tell it is that you sneaked on board with Miss Susan Blain for the kind of activity nice young ladies aren't supposed to know about!'

Hardcastle's face went so pale that Slade thought he was going to faint. The freckles stood out around his nose like buckshot and he began to stammer a denial so laden with guilt that he finally gave up and stood in miserable silence.

'I don't suppose it will read too well in the papers,' Slade said, turning the knife still further. 'You know how these court reporters love to build up a scandal.'

'Captain, you wouldn't involve Miss Blain,' he said beseechingly. 'I mean, it just isn't the thing. Her parents don't even know we're engaged.'

Slade gave him a disgusted look. 'That isn't surprising .. you only met the girl yesterday!'

'We know what we're doing, sir,' he replied stiffly. 'But if you made it public people are bound to get the wrong impression.'

'You mean they would wonder why you were sneaking into a cabin only two hours after you were introduced?'

'I . . . I must take exception to that remark, sir,' said the petty officer, his complexion going from white to red.

'Your privilege,' Slade replied, then frowned as though he had just come up with a completely new idea. 'Of course, there is a way you could turn the whole thing to your advantage.'

Hardcastle grabbed the straw with both hands. 'How? I mean, naturally I would welcome any suggestions you care to make.'

'Well, if you stayed with the ship for a couple of days you could take the guns back. The navy won't ask any questions if you've helped us sink the Kraut.'

The young man gaped at him for a full minute before whispering: 'Help you what, Captain?'

'The marauder. We're going to sink the bastard tonight.'

This time Slade was sure he was going to faint. A tap at the door saved him. It inched open, revealing a mass of blonde hair and wide inquisitive blue eyes.

'Can I come in, Captain?' asked Susan Blain.

'You're half in already.'

She entered with a crisply purposeful smile, glancing enquiringly at Hardcastle. 'Is he bullying you, James? He does, you know.'

James winced. 'The captain's being very helpful.'

'Oh,' she frowned at Slade. 'You must want something.'

'That's a pretty cynical remark.'

She nodded brightly, undeterred. 'All the same . . .?'

He glared at her. 'I want the warhead taking off a torpedo.'

'That's all?'

'What are you? His agent?'

'Fiancée.' She lit up at the word, looking at Hardcastle with a dreamy expression. He was busy making frantic semaphore in the vicinity of his right ear. 'I'm sure he's the best possible man with torpedoes.'

Slade almost choked at the analogy. 'I'm glad to hear it,' he managed. 'How about it, Hardcastle?'

'May I ask how you intend to use it, sir?'

'Put it next to her during the night and set it off.'

'Ah, not quite that simple.' He looked apologetic. 'It's really designed to go off when it bashes into something.'

'Well can't we get round that?' Slade demanded.

'I suppose it's possible.'

Susan tapped his arm, giving him a warning look, then beamed at Slade. 'If he did manage to do it, Captain, would that be worth a great deal to you?'

'I was right,' growled Slade. 'You do think you're his agent.'

'I'm just exploring the situation,' she answered sweetly. 'If James did this for you, perhaps you could do something for us?'

'Such as?'

'Marry us.'

Slade's mouth dropped open. 'Marriage!'

She nodded, suddenly nervous. 'It would solve all sorts of problems if you did. I mean, we wouldn't need a licence and as Jimmy is technically under your command he wouldn't need to get permission. Then there's the war and everything. It could be ages before we see each other if he goes back to Barbuda. Everyone would try to stop us, including mummy and daddy, not to mention Hitler and the Admiralty. And we're absolutely one hundred per cent sure, so if you could . . .' She stopped, breathless.

'Jesus!' said Slade. 'What kind of finishing school did you go to?'

'It is what we both want, sir,' Hardcastle said, his voice quiet but firm. 'We talked about it last night.'

'I'm surprised you found the time,' the captain said sourly. 'What the hell's the rush?'

Susan's incredibly blue eyes misted over and she reached blindly for Hardcastle's hand. 'I love him terribly, Captain. And it would be good for him.'

'Ah,' said Slade, not at all sure he followed her logic. 'So I perform the ceremony and Jimmy here comes up with a bomb?'

'Yes,' they both said, nodding vigorously.

Slade gazed at them in exasperation, wondering if the young petty officer really knew what he was getting into. But when he looked at the girl he had to admit that she had guts, even though she clung to Hardcastle's hand with tears sparkling in her eyes and her lips pale with dread. She would take on the world if she had to.

He sighed: 'Are the pair of you doing anything at seven o'clock?'

14

The council of war took place immediately after the wedding which was held in the saloon where mahogany and deep red leather glowed warmly in the lamp light. Culpepper stood beside Hardcastle as his best man whilst McVay, to everyone's astonishment, appeared reasonably sober in kilt and dress tunic to give the bride away. Diana and Mrs Hartford-Jones served as bridesmaids, looking somewhat incongruous in faded shirts and trousers although two of the slimmer members of the crew had parted with their best shore pants for the occasion. Diana's were white and tight enough to distract every man present, especially Slade who worked hard to conceal his interest.

The bride arrived in bare feet and a sarong that Torres swore he had bought as a souvenir. No one believed him and the general opinion was that the last girl who wore it was the one who left in a hurry the previous summer during a slight fraças when her husband unexpectedly came on board. But it suited Susan, who floated dreamily across the saloon like some exotic bird of paradise. Her radiance was such that when Hardcastle dared to look his knees gave way and only Culpepper's firm hand at his elbow kept him upright.

Slade had put on a tunic that was yellowed with age and stained with something that looked suspiciously like mildew around the armpits. But the mellow light was subdued enough to flatter and when he stood before the leather-topped writing table with Culpepper's bible clasped in his hands, his angular features etched with reverence, even the most cynical member of the crew could not help but be impressed. It was a chilling reminder to them all that beneath the brash, dissolute exterior lurked the soul of a master. As Torres put it, summing up the feelings of them all in a doom-laden whisper: 'The cap'n's only been sober for the best part of three days and he's already holding Culpepper's bible like it's the *Bartender's Guide*. Another week and he'll start baptizing us!'

It was a moment of pride for all the chief participants. Mrs Hartford-Jones was proud of Culpepper because he looked so smart and dependable, a worthy groom in any woman's eyes. It was a comforting thought for she knew, with that quiet confidence that comes to the experienced woman, that this wedding was even now strengthening the bond between them. 'Here, in the sight of God,' droned the captain, and there in the sight of Mrs Hartford-Jones was Culpepper nodding reverently, blissfully acknowledging the Holy state of wedlock. She smiled contentedly. The ground was being prepared and soon, very soon, she would plant some seed and watch it flourish. All men were little boys at heart and with the right encouragement would usually do the things expected of them. The ones who wouldn't were the male chauvinists, a breed she avoided like the plague for they were surely destined for hell.

It was a proud moment too for Diana Curtis because she had come to love this romantic girl who was such a strange blend of innocence and wisdom. She knew that Susan was as sure as any woman could be that this was the man for her, and as such her adoration of Jimmy Hardcastle would surmount every obstacle, reject every doubt. Her brand of loyalty transcended human weaknesses, imbuing others with the strength and fibre of her own dreams. Turning the thought over in her mind Diana compared it with her own feelings towards Lincoln Slade. They appeared to be founded on antagonism, a healthy dislike of a man who nevertheless fascinated her. And yet, when she recalled last night, there was no doubt that she felt a glow of something. But what? She sighed, looking at him now as he conducted the ceremony, wishing she knew what it was that drew her to him. Even the difference in their ages presented an unbridgeable gulf . . . or did it? She tried to remember the rule that someone had once told her. The right age for a husband was the woman's age plus one third . . . but was it a third of the woman's or a third of the man's? She grimaced. It probably didn't matter anyway.

McVay was also proud of the occasion, largely because Susan reminded him of his own daughter. Her hair was blonde of course, whereas Janie's had been red, but there was the same freedom of spirit he remembered most when he recalled the last time he saw his daughter, standing on the pier of the Queen Mary Dock in Dundee nigh on twenty years ago. She had been six then, jumping up and down with the streamer he bought so that she could be sure he would see her all the way to the horizon. He was off to Hong Kong, nine months at least, and there was no way he could know that less than a month later his loving wife would sell their terraced house in Tayport and head for Canada with the man who used to sell insurance.

During the next five years he took every ship he could to Montreal, spending his shore leave searching the little towns that stretched along the east coast through Quebec and Ontario. No one seemed prepared to help, or even care, but eventually he found her, lying in a cemetery in a quiet little town called Richeleau. The parish register told him how she had died, less than a year after her arrival in Canada, not yet strong enough to withstand the ravages of diptheria. His wife still lived in the town with her illegal husband, but he didn't bother to call.

Culpepper's pride was a quite unselfish emotion directed at the man before him. Slade handled the ceremony as though he had been performing marriages all his life, gentle yet firm, reverent yet joyous. To Culpepper it was the total vindication of all those nights he had knelt beside his bunk to pray for the soul of Lincoln Slade, whilst above and below decks roared the drunken brawls and lascivious orgies that would have brought shame to a Singapore brothel.

During those long nights he had prayed in spite of his conviction that the captain was in league with the devil, damned for ever to a life of sin. And yet here he was, an agent of the Lord, clasping the hands of two Christian souls and pronouncing them man and wife for as long as they both should live.

It was an unforgettably beautiful moment.

*   *   *

Afterwards, when the crew had returned to their own quarters to drink the health of the bride and groom with the captain's blessing, they gathered around the chart Slade spread out on the saloon table. Mrs Hartford-Jones took up a commanding position at the foot of the chart, fixing the captain with a steely gaze.

'I trust you are about to tell us when you will be putting us ashore. We have already passed two habitable islands.'

Slade gave her his bleakest smile. 'Only if you like bananas, ma'am, and are prepared to wait a month or two for an island ferry.'

She sniffed and looked at Culpepper, as though challenging him to dispute the statement. Culpepper shrugged and said nothing.

'This is the problem,' he began quietly. 'The weather is building to a storm, maybe tomorrow, and it could become bad enough to pin us down for days. We're on a westerly course for St Martin, whereas the only islands I could set you down are to the south.' He waited until Mrs Hartford-Jones had expelled an indignant breath before continuing.

'With Petty Officer Hardcastle's help I intend to place an explosive charge against the marauder's hull tonight. If the weather holds true it could be the only chance we'll have for days, perhaps ever. It's too important to jeopardise by making a detour for you ladies, as much as I'd like to.'

'And when you've had your moment of glory, Captain?' Mrs Hartford-Jones asked with heavy sarcasm.

He beamed at her. 'Then it will give me great pleasure to

make full speed for the nearest island on the main shipping route.'

'I think we all appreciate your dilemma, Captain,' Diana said quietly, her tone sympathetic enough to make the older woman bristle. 'I just hope we're not going to have to endure another attack.'

Slade shook his head emphatically. 'No question of that. We go in with the launch, place the charge and get out. The *Tinkerbelle* will be well clear, and it'll be late tonight so even if we failed there's little chance of being followed.'

'Oh I hope so,' said Susan, squeezing Hardcastle's hand. 'It's not at all the sort of thing I had planned for our honeymoon.'

Hardcastle had the grace to blush whilst McVay and Slade tried to keep their faces straight.

'There is a chance that the German has managed to repair the damage and get out of that bay, sir?' Culpepper pointed out.

'I've been thinking about that,' replied Slade. 'He had two alternatives. Either carry out all his repairs at St Martin, or free his rudder which must have taken a battering and make for a safe anchorage somewhere else. If he chose the second course, which is what I'd do, then his range is limited and he wouldn't be starting his main repairs until sometime today.' He placed the palm of his hand over the cluster of islands to the west of St Martin. 'That's the only place he could go. The Virgin Islands.'

Culpepper and McVay nodded together, then the engineer took a pencil from his pocket and drew a small circle around the two outermost islands, Virgin Gorda and Anegada. 'I'd agree with you, Captain, and I'd go so far as to say it will be one of these two. Probably Virgin Gorda.'

'Remember that bay on the east coast? Deep water anchorage with hills rising on either side. It's a natural spot,' Culpepper added, eyes gleaming. 'And easy to get at.'

Slade grinned. 'We're all in agreement, gentlemen. If she's not at St Martin, she'll be sitting in Berchers Bay at Virgin

Gorda. We'll be there in nine hours, unless Mr McVay has other ideas?'

McVay snorted. 'I'll have you there, Cap'n, providing I can promise the old girl a wee rest when it's over.'

'How does two weeks in Santo Domingo sound?'

'Och, now you're talkin',' chuckled the engineer and headed for the companionway.

After he had left Hardcastle spoke quietly to Susan before moving to Slade. 'I think I'd better get to work on the Mark 8, sir?'

'I'd be obliged, Mister Hardcastle.' Slade glanced across at Culpepper who was moving calipers across the chart, working awkwardly with one hand. 'Can you check the bridge, Mister Culpepper? Panacero could do with standing down for an hour?'

Culpepper nodded, transferring the calipers to the edge of the chart and noting the distance. 'Right away, sir.'

He began to turn towards the door, smiling at Mrs Hartford-Jones. Her response was cool, but she said nothing until he had left the saloon. Once the door had closed, however, she made no effort to conceal her fury.

'That man is in no condition to be on duty, Captain.'

'Mister Culpepper is quite able to speak for himself,' Slade replied coolly. 'An hour on the bridge won't hurt him.'

'And tonight? I suppose you'll expect him to take command whilst you're gadding about in the launch!'

Slade's eyes were like chips of flint that seemed to smoulder with a heat of their own. When he spoke his voice crackled with authority. 'This is the last time I will remind you that I am the captain of this vessel and you, madam, are a passenger without a ticket. What my first officer chooses to do is no concern of yours unless there's some special relationship which nobody has bothered to tell me about.'

Mrs Hartford-Jones went white around the corners of her mouth and for a brief moment her eyes blazed with anger, but it died long before she opened her mouth to speak as she realized that the captain had a point. There was no special relationship with Rodney, at least not outside her own imagination. She forced a sickly smile. 'How thoughtful of you to remind me, captain. My concern for Rodney is natural and I'm sure anyone who knows me would expect no less. Here is a man, gravely wounded with his arm bound in a splint, continuing under your command out of loyalty. I would be a strange person indeed if I did not protest, nay demand that you spare a moment from your blood-soaked vendetta to think of the consequences of an infection in that wound. Your medicine cabinet would hardly qualify as a first aid kit and your so-called sick-bay orderly is more at home swabbing decks. An infected wound in this climate is very serious. It spreads, turns to gangrene, has to be amputated quickly before the patient dies. That's my concern, Captain. I don't want to see a brave young man going through life with only one arm!'

Slade gazed at the woman with hooded eyes, wishing they were alone so that they could have a real conversation. He knew all about the Mrs Hartford-Jones's of this world, filled with piss and vinegar and enough righteous anger to launch a dozen crusades. But strip away the façade of Christian fellowship and tearful compassion and you were right back in the jungle. She could rip you from gut to gizzard with a smile on her face.

He spent a moment enjoying the thought: *'Tell me, Mrs Hartford-bloody-Jones, what's so special about Culpepper's arm? Do you have any plans for that particular limb, or is it just that you want to keep him tidy?'*

'My dear Captain Slade, what a ridiculous question. Of course I want to keep him tidy. He's all I've got.'

'Well if you don't mind my saying so, and I imagine you do, he's a damned sight better off without an arm if you're going to be holding the end of it for the rest of his life.'

'I can think of quite a few pieces of your anatomy we can do without, Captain.'

'I can guess where you'd start, you sadistic old cow.'

'*Well it wouldn't be your arm!*'

Slade ground his teeth and found that everyone was looking at him with puzzled expressions. He glared at them and started towards the door, having to be content with. 'I'm sure that, between us, we can keep Culpepper's arm where it belongs, Mrs Hartford-Jones.'

After the men had left Diana looked at the older woman with a puzzled expression. 'He's only doing what he believes he must. And after all, he is trying to destroy the ship that killed your husband.'

'An eye for an eye has never been my philosophy, or Henry's for that matter,' she replied acidly.

'Well I think they're being terribly brave,' said Susan.

'Or stupid,' said Mrs Hartford-Jones with a thin mouth. They gazed at her silently, without understanding. She shuddered and sat down, pushing a knuckle against her teeth. After a moment she said in a choking voice: 'I'm just afraid. I'm just terribly afraid.'

*   *   *

They had set up one of the torpedoes in the engineer's workshop, a long, narrow room that ran the width of the ship with the forward hold on one side and the engine room on the other. McVay had a pipe berth beside the steel workbench and all the available space beneath it seemed to be taken up with cases of whisky. The room was lit by old fashioned spot lamps which tended to explode like grenades when the temperature got too high, but Hardcastle was reasonably happy with the tackle and used the overhead pulleys to attach cables to the torpedo.

'Do you need any special tools?' Slade asked, considerably subdued now that he stood beside the gleaming torpedo. It was much larger than he had expected, twenty-four feet in all, and the bulbous warhead with its detonator nipple a warning red, emanated danger.

Hardcastle was foraging in a tool chest and came up with a handful of flat-headed spanners. 'These will be fine.

We've got to unscrew the twenty-eight bolts around the warhead, then we'll ease it away from the drive section.'

He passed a spanner to Slade and they set to work. Each bolt was recessed into the casing, but once the spanner was locked on they began to unscrew smoothly. McVay came in from the engine room, wiping his hands on a filthy rag and sucking air through his teeth as he watched them.

'I'll thank you to be careful with that,' he said, as Slade's spanner slipped and clattered over the casing. 'If you set the bastard off it's likely to wipe out my entire stock of whisky.'

Hardcastle chuckled. 'It might indeed, Mr McVay. There's exactly eight hundred pounds of torpex in here. Enough to give us all a headache.'

'How about the Kraut?' asked Slade.

'It depends on where you intend to place it.'

'Up his arse would suit the cap'n,' said McVay, cackling at the thought.

'On the waterline, probably just above the stern. Right beside the engine room so that the chief is the first to go.'

'Och you're a sadistic bastard,' McVay said, sitting on his berth and sliding a bottle from under the pillow. 'The poor laddie is only there to drive the engines.'

Slade grinned. 'I hope he does a better job of it than some I know.'

McVay choked in mid gulp, spluttered a fine spray of whisky towards them as he gasped for air. When he had recovered he stabbed an angry finger towards the engines which filled the air with the steady thump-thump of the giant pistons that turned their single propeller. 'That old girl in there was ready for the scrapyard ten years ago, and you know it. She only keeps going because she's too bloody stubborn to stop.'

Slade heaved on the last bolt and spun it out of the casing. Hardcastle checked the pulley and tightened the cables around it.

'Now we have the tricky bit. I'll ease it away from the

drive section and once it's clear you swing that lot off the bench and let it down to the floor.'

McVay came over and watched as Hardcastle gently separated the bulky warhead until it was free from the fourteen foot length of torpedo which contained the impulse motor. Slade began to move it off the bench when something triggered the induction chamber and the propeller began to whine. They all froze, watching with alarm as the propeller became a silver blur, then began to smoke as the bearings heated up. Hardcastle picked up a hammer and hit the prop shaft a tremendous blow which produced a scream of tortured steel, then a clatter as the propeller came in contact with the steering vane and reduced the entire assembly to a mangled ruin in seconds.

'Now then,' said Hardcastle, as though he did it every day, 'we have to get the pistol out.'

'Jesus,' said Slade, 'are you telling me this lot is set off by a pistol?'

'Well, not exactly,' he replied, gently sliding off the outer casing of the warhead. 'It doesn't really look like a pistol, but all the same it fires a charge that explodes the detonators.'

He began to ease a steel cylinder with copper ends out of the front of the warhead. Various dials, knobs and small pins protruded from the cylinder and he was careful to keep these clear of the tube. Once it was free he placed it in a vice on the bench and began to unscrew the upper section. It came apart easily, revealing two stubby detonators that were set into holes through which a dark grey substance could be seen.

'This is the first primer,' said Hardcastle, indicating the explosive. 'Inside the tube which goes into the centre of the warhead are two more primers, each of them composed of a more sensitive explosive.'

'How sensitive?' asked McVay nervously.

'Enough to be triggered by the detonators, which are the percussion type. Each primer sets off the next. After that the torpex goes up.'

Looking at the massive steel warhead Slade began to realize for the first time the full magnitude of the forces involved. This was a gigantic bomb capable of blowing a ship in half. He grimaced. 'If I'd known all this a couple of days ago I don't think I'd have been so casual about swinging us towards that torpedo the Kraut plane dropped.'

'You're damned right you wouldn't,' said McVay in a shrill voice, 'because I for one would have been over the bloody side while you were still whistling for full speed.'

Slade moved closer and gently touched one of the detonators. 'So we've got to trigger this, somehow.'

Hardcastle nodded. 'If we had electric detonators it would be easier, but from the sea we'd have a new set of problems. We'd need waterproof wiring and a sealed generator box. About the best I can come up with is a Very pistol.'

They looked at him in astonishment. He held up the pistol assembly to explain. 'Look, we don't need this top section which weighs almost fifty pounds. That leaves a long tube going into the warhead with the detonator and first primer at the bottom. By fixing a Very pistol inside the tube, all we have to do is work out a way of firing it.'

'And then?'

'Wham. The heat and explosion of the cartridge will set off the detonators. They're already fixed into the primer, so everything happens in sequence after that . . . in about a hundredth of a second.'

Hardcastle put the heavy assembly on the floor and picked up the Very pistol. He placed this into the tube, keeping the handle and trigger outside. 'What have you got that we can pack around it, Chief?'

McVay scratched his head, then crossed to a pile of junk in a corner. He rooted around for a few minutes and came back with various lengths of piping. Using a vice on the bench he flattened the end of a pipe and placed it between the pistol and the side of the tube. Hardcastle got the idea and nodded, telling Slade to hold the pistol in position whilst he began to flatten more sections of pipe.

144

It took half an hour to gently tap in a dozen pieces of pipe, but by the time they had finished the pistol was held firmly in place by the metal wedges. Hardcastle used a hacksaw to cut off the protruding pieces and stepped back to survey his work.

'That will hold well enough,' he said. 'What we need now is about a hundred yards of wire.'

'There's plenty in the chandler's store,' said McVay. 'I use miles of the stuff to lag my moth-eaten steam pipes.'

'So all I do is yank the wire and up she goes?' Slade asked, astounded by its simplicity.

Hardcastle gave him a slightly nervous look, took a deep breath and said: 'No, Captain. I pull the trigger.'

'Forget it, Hardcastle,' Slade said harshly. 'You're not even there.'

'Sir, I will have to be there to insert this assembly into the warhead. It's far too dangerous to carry around live.'

Slade gazed at him unhappily. 'I can't ask you to take that kind of risk.'

Hardcastle shrugged. 'With respect, sir, I'm the only armourer you've got. And setting off eight hundred pounds of torpex is a dangerous business. We'll all have to go under water when I trigger it.'

Slade grimaced, realizing that such a precaution would never have occurred to him. 'Alright, you made your point. But for God's sake don't tell Mrs Hartford-bloody-Jones. That's all she needs.'

McVay toasted the warhead with the bottle that was already beginning to look empty. 'Here's to destruction.' He turned to Hardcastle, his eyes twinkling. 'You're sure it'll go off, now? We don't want to be helping the Jerry war effort.'

'It'll go off,' the petty officer said in a positive voice. 'And as long as we've got it snug against the hull it'll blow the ship in half.'

15

The ship in question, the *Tamerande*, was a hive of activity at that moment. Shielded lamps bathed the lower section of the stern as a dozen men worked to free a buckled plate less than a foot above the waterline. The repair crew had concentrated on the rudder during the few hours of daylight left to them after they dropped anchor in the bay midway along the east coast of Virgin Gorda, but as darkness fell they moved to the leaking hull section and began hammering out the buckled plates. One of the steel sections had to be replaced and this was causing the biggest delay.

Lieutenant Commander Wolf Tellmann, who had been driving the men hard for eight hours, stood at the stern rail with the chief engineer, a grey-haired man who had spent the past twenty-five years in the Kriegsmarine. His name was Hans Leinster and he had no intention of allowing Tellmann or Captain Kroehner to move the ship out of the bay until the hull was sound.

'It looks as though we're in for heavy weather,' Tellmann was saying, gazing off into the darkness as the wind freshened, stinging their faces. 'I'd like to get out before dawn.'

'I can see no chance of that,' replied Leinster, his mouth setting firmly. 'We'll need daylight to weld this plate.'

'The men have got enough light to work.'

'And they've been working for eight hours without a break. I want the hull sound again, especially if we're going out into a rough sea.'

Tellmann gave him an irritated look. 'There's a war on, Hans. We can't have everything we want.'

'I can,' said the engineer. 'I agreed to the ship being moved from St Martin, but on the understanding that the work would be carried out in the first safe anchorage. This is safe. I doubt if anyone even knows we're here.'

'That freighter must have told the British by now.'

'So? We know their frigates are deployed in the Atlantic. The only thing they have is a patrol boat and that won't be going anywhere tonight.'

'Alright,' snapped Tellmann. 'But I still think the men could work through the night.'

'Midnight is as far as I will go. With luck we'll be able to start at dawn and be ready to sail three, perhaps even two hours later.'

Tellmann turned abruptly and left him, crossing the aft deck and dropping down the companionway to the crew's quarters. Most of the ship's complement of three hundred and forty-seven were enjoying the unexpected chance to relax, stretched in their bunks reading magazines already dog-eared with the weeks at sea. A gramophone played somewhere, producing a scratched and tinny version of a Strauss waltz, and in the ratings' mess someone was competing with a mouth organ. The atmosphere was relaxed and, apart from the occasional hammering from the stern, there was little evidence of any urgency.

The lieutenant commander went past the galley and up the short companionway steps into officer country. Here the lights were dimmed and the long corridors silent, even the wardroom was almost deserted. He paused there, looking in. Four junior officers were playing cards, straightening quickly as they saw him. He gestured for them to relax and beckoned to the steward who was polishing glasses.

'The captain?'

'In his cabin, sir.'

Tellmann moved on, turning left and then right, past his own quarters to the last cabin which was directly below the bridge. He tapped gently, waiting until the captain told him to enter.

Captain Kroehner was sitting at his desk, a sheaf of radio flimsies in his hand. He waved a hand at a chair and continued to read. Tellmann waited patiently until he put them aside and turned to face him.

'Yes, Wolf?'

'It doesn't look as though we'll be ready for dawn, sir.'

Kroehner frowned. 'That's a pity.'

'Leinster wants that plate replacing in daylight.'

'He's a good man.'

'Yes, sir. A trifle over cautious, perhaps.'

Kroehner considered him, mouth pursed, then nodded slowly, as if reluctant to agree. 'Just a trifle. You think we should work through the night?'

'I don't like being vulnerable, sir. The chief doesn't have that worry.'

'Very well, Wolf, I'll talk to him. I don't think we need to worry too much, though, I've just had an intelligence report from our people in Cuba. Apparently the British patrol boat at Barbuda is out of commission. A broken prop shaft.'

Tellmann flushed, irritated that he had not checked this out himself. 'Then they have nothing at all in the Caribbean?'

'It would seem not, and the only aircraft they have are on Bermuda covering the convoys out of New York.'

Tellmann stirred uncomfortably in his chair, his clean cut features displaying the minimum of emotion, although the captain knew him well enough to sense his annoyance. 'In that case, sir, perhaps we should leave the chief engineer to do things his own way?'

'No, I think you're right. Things will be changing soon enough, so he should learn now how it's going to be. Ask the duty officer to send him along.'

Tellmann rose to his feet. 'Thank you, sir.'

Kroehner nodded, turning back to his intelligence reports. The two closely typed sheets that had been occupying his attention for the past half hour contained a complete report

148

on a Captain Lincoln Slade. It had been compiled by agents in Cuba, Washington and Caracas and represented a very thorough profile of the man. It included extracts from the board of enquiry into the sinking of the *Titanic* and the comments of the Press following the exoneration of Slade by the board.

He had been in charge of the boats on the aft promenade deck and, according to his testimony, had been supervising the lowering of one of the first lifeboats when hysterical passengers had knocked him over the side. He had managed to grab the davit cable and slide down into the boat as it reached the water where, faced with an impossible climb back to the deck, he had cast off and remained with the boat. At that time there had still been some six hundred passengers on board the liner, many of whom did not survive, and the question that remained in many people's minds long after the inquiry was to what extent Slade was pushed. Some newspapers openly accused him of jumping to safety when his duty was to have remained on board.

Whatever the truth of it was, Slade had found it impossible to join any of the major shipping lines and for ten years had served in the Far East on leaking old freighters with crews shanghied out of some of the roughest ports in the world. He had earned his master's certificate on a ship carrying rubber from Malaya and when it sank under him during a gale in the Pacific he had been accused of overloading. Six months later he had arrived in Caracas and talked his way into leasing the *Tinkerbelle*.

Captain Kroehner leaned back in his chair and closed his eyes, trying to visualise the man. On the surface he appeared to be a dissolute, irresponsible rogue who only survived in the Caribbean because no one had taken the trouble to haul him into court. He was in debt at half the ports and if he showed his face in Caracas or Cuba he would be arrested on sight. Yet he clearly had many friends for on two occasions when his vessel had been impounded he had managed to slip out of harbour during the night.

Why should such a man risk his life, and his ship, to find and then ram the Tamerande? Kroehner sighed and shook his head, baffled. There was absolutely nothing in Lincoln Slade's past to suggest a reason. And yet he knew the answer must be somewhere in the captain's background. He was not British but American and as such had no quarrel with Germany, nor owed allegiance to any of these islands.

He turned again to the report of the *Titanic* inquiry, wondering if that could be the link. Slade ran away once and perhaps this time, faced with an opportunity to redress the balance, he refused to run again. He grimaced. It was a tenuous lead at best, but Captain Kroehner was a methodical man who believed that all acts were motivated by past events. If this was true of Slade then he would not be satisfied with the inability of the naval detachment at Barbuda to take advantage of the *Tamerande*. It followed, therefore, that he would try something else.

The captain went to his chart table and gazed at the islands of the Caribbean basin. Finding a marauder would not be impossible for a man who had spent the past four years in these waters, but having found it what could he possibly do? He went back to his desk and put the report in a drawer, beginning to relax. There was, of course, nothing that Slade could do. Only luck had saved him the first time.

There was a knock on his door and he turned towards it. 'Enter.'

The chief engineer stepped in and stood stiffly in the centre of the cabin. 'You wished to see me, Captain?'

'Yes, Chief. How is the work progressing?'

'Well enough, sir. The rudder is functioning perfectly now and we are hammering out the last of the plates. In the morning we'll weld in a new section and be ready to sail.'

'What time do you estimate that would be?'

The chief engineer hesitated, his eyes wary. 'I would think ten o'clock at the latest, Captain.'

'Ten o'clock?' Kroehner leaned back in his chair and

gazed up at the ceiling, his brow furrowed. 'That would mean sitting here in the bay with a hole in our hull for four hours of daylight?'

Leinster nodded slowly. 'That is necessary, sir.'

Kroehner shook his head, smiling to take the sting from his words. 'Not necessary, Chief. Convenient, perhaps, but I would not say it was necessary. Suppose the work party continued through the night? What then?'

The chief engineer's mouth tightened, realizing that Tellmann had made his point. 'It could be carried out, of course, but it would mean that my men would be working for sixteen hours. The risk does not seem to warrant it.'

'Only I calculate the risks, Herr Leinster.' Kroehner's eyes were suddenly ice cold. 'The repairs have taken too long already. Instruct your men to work throughout the night and impress on them that we can no longer enjoy the luxury of peacetime standards. From now on all repairs will be running repairs.'

'Yes, sir,' the engineer said stiffly. 'As long as it is noted that these are not my recommendations.'

'I shall note it personally,' Kroehner said quietly. 'Kindly have your engine room ready with full steam at dawn.'

Leinster came to attention and left, his features pale and disapproving. Kroehner smiled bleakly and went to his bunk, considering the chief engineer's attitude as he un-dressed and donned the clean linen pyjamas his steward had laid out. Leinster had a great deal to learn, as did so many of his crew. They did not seem to understand that the *Tamerande* would never see Germany again. It's only value was its anonymity, its ability to move unnoticed and kill by surprise. Once its presence and identity were known its usefulness was at an end.

Kroehner grimaced at the thought, stretching out in his bunk, irritated by the knowledge that somewhere in the Caribbean was a man who had the ability to destroy the *Tamerande*'s usefulness almost before it had begun.

16

The wind had continued to strengthen during the night, coming out of the west with that deceptive warmth so characteristic of the Caribbean 'westerlies'. The warm, humid front that had been born in the Amazon basin had built steadily over the sea and as it met the incoming trades had begun to turn, creating towering cumulus that blacked out the stars. The mixture of warm and cold winds began to increase the momentum of upper and lower layers of air, but the process was still only in its infancy. During the day, in the heat of the sun, the system would continue to grow until it covered the entire Caribbean, turning on an axis that was already being established south of Cuba.

In Florida, Jamaica and Caracas weathermen were watching its growth, charting its potential, launching balloons to measure wind speed, humidity and barometric pressure. They were waiting for the system to become complete, to revolve at speeds of over a hundred miles an hour when the axis itself would begin to move. Where it would go was still unknown, but its characteristics were unmistakable. A hurricane was being born and at the weather centre in Florida it already had a name: Annabelle.

Slade and Hardcastle knew none of this. Whilst the sea off Virgin Gorda was beginning to run, pulling spray off the crests of the waves in ghostly spirals, the troughs had not yet deepened into ugly canyons and the wind was only a moan rather than the rising howl that would herald the approach of the monster from the south.

They had picked out the lights of the marauder when they were five miles east of Virgin Gorda, the brilliant lamps being used by the work party as bright as the beacon that flashed red and white at the tip of the island. They made their approach without lights, dropping anchor half a mile below the bay so that they were screened by hills.

Slade and Hardcastle were lowered in the launch whilst Panacero, who would take them to the mouth of the bay, was winched down on the life raft which held the eight hundred pound warhead. Once he had transferred the towline to Slade he climbed into the launch and took the helm, choosing a course that hugged the coast just clear of the breakers but close enough for the noise of the diesel to be drowned by the surf.

It took far longer than Slade had expected, largely because of the heavy sea which had them wallowing like a water-logged barge for most of the way. The drag of the raft and the difficult currents so close to the shore slowed their progress to the point where they could almost believe that the launch was going backwards. Hardcastle sat hunched in the bow, the heavy pistol assembly wrapped in an oilskin with the coil of wire around his neck. The sea was giving off an eerie phosphorescent glow where the waves broke, but the sky above was starless and black as a raven's wing.

When Panacero finally brought them pitching and rolling round the headland into the bay there was less than an hour to dawn and Slade was cursing savagely in the dark.

'If you'd gone any slower we could have brought bloody sandwiches!' he snarled.

'It's not a good sea,' Panacero replied defensively. 'Any faster and the bomb would pull us down.'

Slade growled and dropped over the side, treading water until Panacero had cast off the towline. Hardcastle waited whilst Slade manoeuvred the raft alongside, then put the pistol assembly beside the warhead and lashed it with lengths of rope already fastened to the raft. Once he was satisfied that it was secure he slipped into the water beside Slade, relieved to find that it was really quite warm.

Panacero watched them vanish into the darkness, feeling a deep sense of despair when he looked across the bay towards the bulk of the marauder. The work lamps at the stern were no longer lit, but lights showed on the decks and the occasional porthole glowed, indicating that many of the crew were still awake. He crossed himself and dropped the kedge anchor over the side, checking the shielded torch in his pocket that he would need to guide them back. The thought brought a shiver of fear.

Once they were clear of the mouth of the bay the water became less choppy and although the waves still rolled past towards the shore they were able to swim more strongly. They soon found that pushing the raft from behind achieved the best results, but it rolled alarmingly when any sizeable wave went past. There was no talking. Keeping the sluggish raft on course took all their strength and by the time they had covered half the distance they were both close to exhaustion. Slade signalled for a rest and they pulled themselves half out of the water, hanging onto the warhead lashings.

'Jesus,' gasped Slade, 'I must be getting old.'

'If you don't mind my saying so, sir, I'd hate to have tried to keep up with you twenty years ago.'

'You mean in your pram?' said Slade and started to laugh, spluttering as a wave slapped the raft and caught him in the face.

'I suppose they'll have some sort of look-out.'

'Why the hell should they? It's black as a witch's tit and as far as the islanders are concerned they're just a passing freighter.'

Hardcastle looked doubtful, but was reluctant to pursue the argument. They were close enough to the *Tamerande* to study the bridge and aft superstructure, alert for any sign of movement. After a few minutes the petty officer was forced to admit that there appeared to be no duty watch on deck, although there would almost certainly be somebody on the bridge. The ship was bigger than he had expected, close to eight thousand tonnes, and if it carried anything like the armament that Slade had suggested there must be well over three hundred men below decks at that moment. The thought depressed Hardcastle and he slid back into the water, looking at Slade who grimaced and joined him.

'Let this be a lesson to you, Hardcastle,' he said as they began to swim once more. 'Never volunteer.'

'I wouldn't have missed this for anything,' the petty officer replied. 'It's a privilege to be with you, sir.'

Slade gave him a disgusted look and shook his head. Kids, he thought. Bloody kids in uniform. He still had no clear idea of his own motives for being there. Half the time he felt that he was on a course of self-destruction with somebody else at the helm. If only the bloody navy had taken better care of their patrol boat he might already be stretched out on some friendly beach, a glass of gin in one hand and a warm little bundle in the other.

The thought reminded him of Diana Curtis and the way she had looked as he climbed into the launch. He just couldn't make her out at all. She reminded him of the dolphins that played with them in the summer, forever darting across and under the bow, emerging on the far side to arch gracefully in the sun before slipping back beneath the waves. It was as though they wanted to attract attention, but were afraid to become too friendly. She had that same kind of manner, drawn and yet repelled.

They had not referred to the previous night, as though it had been part of a shared dream, and her eyes had told him nothing of the thoughts that hid behind them. But her hand had been tense, clinging briefly to his, and he only just caught her whispered 'take care' as they swung the launch over the side.

The raft bumped gently against the side of the marauder and they began to manoeuvre it along the length of the hull until they reached the bow anchor chain. Slade fastened the towline securely to the chain whilst Hardcastle let a fifty-pound kedge sink to the bottom close in to the hull. Once it had grounded in the sand it held the raft alongside the vessel, concealing it from the deck above by the overhang of the bow.

Slade steadied the raft as the petty officer eased himself up onto it and began to unfasten the pistol assembly. The horizon was beginning to pale in the east and with a sense of alarm Slade realized that they were about thirty minutes from daylight.

'You're going to have to stick that in fast,' he said tersely.

Hardcastle shook his head, taking the covering off the heavy cylinder. 'There's no quick way of doing this, Captain. One slip and they won't even find our fingernails.'

Slade could only watch, his tension growing as the minutes slid by and the dull silver light stretched across the horizon, etching the lowering cloud base in gloomy shades of purple. It was a doom-laden sky and the wind was on the increase, whipping the crests of the waves and swinging the raft wildly from side to side. Hardcastle ignored it all, crouching over the warhead and slowly easing the pistol assembly into the tube. When he finally had it in place only the butt of the pistol projected from the end of the cylinder. The sea around them was turning from black to gun-metal grey and sounds were beginning to drift down from the deck above.

'Jesus, get a move on,' said Slade. 'I can smell cooking.'

Hardcastle glanced at him, his features chalk white. 'That means they're sailing at daylight.'

'Not if you get a bloody move on they're not!'

The raft was swinging regularly into the side of the hull, giving off dull thuds that would be heard by anyone in the forward hold. Any moment Slade expected to hear a sharp command from above, rapidly followed by the chatter of a sub-machine gun.

'Almost there,' said Hardcastle, tying the wire to the trigger of the Very pistol. 'You start swimming.'

'When I want you to start giving me orders,' snarled Slade, 'I'll join your bloody navy!'

Hardcastle grinned and cocked the pistol, then eased himself off the raft into the water, holding the coil of wire in both hands and starting to kick away from the vessel on his back. Slade struck out beside him, keeping clear of the wire, but ready to take it the moment he got into trouble. The tide seemed to be moving against them and in the rising wind their progress was painfully slow. The shout from the deck was almost lost in the wind, but there was no mistaking the alarm gongs that echoed through the ship ten seconds later.

Hardcastle, lying on his back as he paid out the wire, saw the figures appear at the rail high above them. He turned quickly, holding the coil in his hand, gesturing to Slade.

'You head for the launch.'

'Will you stop giving me fucking orders,' yelled Slade, grabbing for the wire.

Hardcastle hung on to it, taking a deep breath and going beneath the surface as small spouts of water suddenly appeared all around them. Underwater he could barely see, but began to swim hoping that it was away from the ship and that the wire would pay out freely. The vague outline of Slade appeared beside him, keeping close as he started towards the surface again. They emerged to find two search-lights sweeping the sea, gulped air and submerged before they found them. This time Slade swam ahead, pulling away to surface seconds before Hardcastle.

'How much have you paid out?' he asked as the petty officer sucked in air.

'Fifty feet, no more.'

'So pull it now.'

'We're too close. The blast will wipe us out.'

A brilliant light swept towards them and they dived, the surface erupting seconds later as a machine gun opened fire.

The clamour of the battle gongs was still sounding as the duty officer leaned out from the bow rail with a spotlight, shining it down into the gloom. Within seconds he had picked out the raft and realized what it must contain. The nearest man to him was one of the forward gun crew, running towards his station in the deckhouse.

'You! Over the side with me,' he shouted, climbing up onto the rail.

The startled man gaped as the officer tore off his jacket, screamed the order again and jumped out into the sea. He moved to the rail, wondering if the duty officer had realized he was gun crew, not maintenance. Other crewmen were rushing towards the bow, but no one seemed to know why the duty officer had jumped overboard. The man who had reached the rail gazed down, hoping to find the answer, but in the dim light he could only make out a lot of splashing in the water. He shrugged, wondering if the officer would remember his face.

In the sea beside the raft the German officer tried frantically to untie the towline attaching it to the anchor chain. He was close to panic, knowing he might only have seconds. The rope was tightly knotted and too wet to free. In desperation he swam back to the raft, only then seeing the anchor cable on the other side. He began to haul on the cable, pulling the anchor free from the bottom so that the raft started to swing away from the hull and clear of the bow.

Hardcastle surfaced, looking back towards the ship which was flooded with light. Slade swam towards him, gesturing at the wire. He glanced at it, estimating that at least seventy feet had been paid out.

'For Christ's sake, Hardcastle, we're not selling bloody tickets!'

'This time,' said Hardcastle, and dived.

The duty officer pulled himself onto the edge of the raft so that he could get a better hold on the anchor cable. He started to heave again, his breath coming in frenzied gasps, his eyes fixed on the huge cylinder beside him. Only then did he see the butt of the Very pistol and the wire running away from it into the sea. With a choking gasp of relief he let go of the anchor and leaned towards it, but even as he reached for the wire it suddenly went taut. His brain froze with terror as he watched the trigger jerk, the Very pistol recoil with a blinding light, heard the crack of the first detonator which he knew would be no more than a split second ahead of the first primer. He was only just beginning to comprehend his own death as the warhead exploded with a shattered roar.

Slade and Hardcastle were ten feet below the surface when the shock waves hit them, turning them like leaves in a storm, compressing their ear drums until it seemed that they must rupture. Blood vessels burst in their noses but they were unaware of the pain, concerned only with fighting their way to the surface. When they finally emerged the sky was lit by a crimson glow and all the pain was forgotten as they gazed towards the *Tamerande*, watching the flames leaping from its bow. With whoops of triumph they hugged each other, floundering in the water until they saw the frantic flashes from Panacero's torch and began to swim towards him.

17

Captain Kroehner stood on the bridge and watched the flames roar through ruptured plates with an ice cold detachment. Two junior officers waited for orders with pale, shocked faces. He ignored them, his hooded eyes fixed on the blaze as though hypnotised by its ferocity. The phone buzzed beside him and he picked it up without moving his head.

'Yes?'

'Forward damage control, sir. Watertight doors now locked, the fire is contained in the bow compartments.'

'I believe that was the paint store, was it not?'

'That's correct, Captain.'

'You're sure it's contained?'

'Yes, sir. The fire teams are starting to use chemical foam.'

'And the bow section?'

'No information yet, Captain.'

'Tell the chief engineer to see me as soon as he can.'

Two other phones were buzzing angrily. Kroehner picked up one and beckoned to the nearest officer to answer the other.

'Captain Kroehner.'

'Tellmann, sir. I'm pumping water on the starboard bow, but the pressure is low and I don't think it breached us below the waterline.'

'Very well, leave it to damage control and get the Heinkel ready for take-off. Use bombs, not a torpedo.'

There was a moment's silence and the captain's voice cracked like a whip. 'Did you hear that, Tellmann!'

'Yes, Captain,' he answered hurriedly. 'But the weather conditions are not good for flying.'

'I am fully aware of the weather. I'm looking at it. But it is my belief that the American vessel is very close. Tell the pilot I want it disabled at all costs.'

'Yes, Captain.'

Kroehner replaced the phone, his face devoid of emotion, but his eyes held the cold sheen of polished steel as he turned to the young officer who was holding the engine room phone. He swallowed and handed it to him quickly.

'Yes, Chief?'

'I'm about to vent steam pressure, Captain. I just wanted you to know.'

A muscle jumped along the captain's jaw and he paused, fighting to control the emotion that caused it. 'You will not vent anything, Chief. Not until I have a full damage report on the bow.'

'Captain, the blast has ripped it to pieces.'

Kroehner closed his eyes and took long, deep breaths. When he opened them again he said: 'I want a full report on the damage in five minutes. In person, Chief.'

He handed the phone back to the officer and went out onto the wing of the bridge. The wind was blowing fiercely across the bay, holding the smoke low over the water. There were no more flames and from the position of the fire crews he could see that they were on the edge of the damage area, pouring chemical foam through the ruptured plates. The winch began to clatter and he turned in time to see the Heinkel rising out of its special hold, three bombs clipped beneath each wing. The pilot was already in the cockpit, saluting the bridge as the winch crew swung him over the side.

Kroehner felt a moment's sympathy for the man. Taking off in the choppy waters of the bay would be extremely dangerous, possibly disastrous. It made no difference. The captain knew without a shadow of a doubt that the man behind the attack had been Lincoln Slade. He also knew that he had to sink the *Tinkerbelle*.

The Heinkel's engine started with a roar, the aircraft

drifting for a moment in the wind before starting to plough in ungainly lunges from wave to wave. Each time its nose dipped, cascading sheets of spray over the wings and fuselage, every man on the *Tamerande* was convinced it would flip over onto its back. But somehow the pilot kept the nose up and began to get lift under the wings. It was almost at the mouth of the bay when the floats began to plane and suddenly it was free, soaring up into the early morning light.

Kroehner went back onto the bridge, his features giving no hint of the relief he felt. The chief engineer entered, looking harassed.

'I've inspected the damage, Captain. We have a six foot gash about two feet above the waterline. Fortunately most of the blast seems to have gone outwards so that we only caught minimum effects low down. At deck level it took off a ten foot strip of the bow, buckled deck plates and of course ignited the paint store. It's a mess, Captain.'

'According to my first officer we are not taking water, and a six foot section does not appear to be beyond your resources.'

The chief engineer flushed. 'I didn't say it was, Captain.'

'Five minutes ago you told me that the bow was ripped to pieces. Even from where I stand, Chief Engineer Leinster, it is clear that such a statement is untrue. It is also obvious from this position that the fire is already under control, which would suggest that the damage to the bow plane and deck plates in no way impairs our seaworthiness.'

Leinster gazed at a spot a foot above the captain's head and said in a flat, emotionless voice. 'As your chief engineer, Captain, it is my duty to assess all damage and make recommendations regarding it.'

'Real damage, Herr Leinster. Not figments of your imagination.' Kroehner no longer made any attempt to conceal his contempt. 'As soon as this emergency is over I shall be relieving you of your responsibilities and passing them over to your number two. In the meantime, Herr Leinster, you will break out a sea mattress large enough to cover the hole in our hull and winch it into position. You will then make your engines ready and inform me here the moment we are ready to sail. Do you understand my orders, Chief Engineer?'

Leinster's face was ashen. He nodded, unable to speak. The captain dismissed him with a gesture and turned to the young officer whose eyes were bulging with astonishment.

'Tell the radio officer I want to know the moment the Heinkel has found the American.'

18

They had switched off the launch's motor and were coming alongside the *Tinkerbelle* when they first heard the roar of the Heinkel's engine. Slade glanced back towards the bay and shook his head in disbelief.

'He'll never make it in this wind. Not a hope.'

But still they listened as the crew lowered the davit cables and prepared to lift them aboard. The sound rose and fell, echoing off the hills so that at times it seemed as if an entire squadron of aircraft was taking off.

'It wasn't too bad in the bay, you know,' Hardcastle said nervously. 'He might just get off.'

'No chance,' said Slade, and signalled to the bosun above. But his mouth was pinched with tension as the winches began to clatter and lift them slowly up the side of the ship.

They knew before they saw the seaplane that it was in the air. There was a sudden change in the jarring roar, a smooth howl of power that was at first muted by the hills and then reverberating across the sea as the aircraft shot out of the bay, banking and turning in a wide sweep that would bring it towards them.

'Shit!' said Slade, waiting impatiently until they cleared the deck rail.

Culpepper was standing on the wing of the bridge, looking down on them with grim features. Slade made a winding up signal with his hands and he nodded, disappearing into the bridge. The crew stood around the launch, gazing nervously towards the plane as it banked a mile out to sea and started climbing into the grey sky.

'Get the lead out, Panacero,' snapped Slade. 'Raise the

anchor and let's get the hell out of here.' He turned to Hardcastle who was watching the aircraft. 'I don't think that bastard knows we've got any armament. You want to take the two-pounder?'

'Right, but I'll have to wait until he's made his run. It looks as though it's bombs. He's going too high for a torpedo.'

'Then you better keep your head down,' Slade growled and ran for the bridge.

Smoke was beginning to belch from the funnel as McVay, who was having one of his more difficult mornings, tapped his dials and yelled abuse at two sleepy boiler hands who had just woken up to find all hell breaking loose. 'Get number two lit you idle bastards,' he screamed. 'I want full pressure now!'

They ran to the old fashioned oil furnace, fumbling the jet choke so that it back-fired and blew clouds of sooty smoke across the engine room. McVay, almost dancing with rage, hurled a spanner at one of the men who only just ducked in time. The bridge tube whistled and McVay snatched at it, his face going purple.

'I'll tell you when I'm ready you flat-arsed baboon!'

'Good morning, Mr McVay,' said Slade in a perfectly calm voice. 'I just thought you'd like to know that we're about to be attacked. I suggest you open your forward hatches and think saintly thoughts.'

'You know what I'm thinking, Lincoln Slade?' he screeched. 'I'm thinking that you can go and take a flying fuck at the whole German Navy.'

He stabbed the whistle back into the tube and threw it at the wall. There was another thump from the number two furnace and more black smoke belched out. He gazed at the two men, speechless with rage. There was a shrill rising whistle ending with an explosion in the sea on the other side of the hull. He shook his fist at them.

'You see! You see what you've done! You've even got the fucking Germans trying to light your bloody boiler!'

The engine room telegraph rang for full ahead and he cursed it savagely as he pulled the throttle levers and engaged the turbine. The heavy pistons began to move, turning the prop shaft at minimum revs. He picked up an oil can and flung it into the smoke, feeling better when he heard a howl of pain.

Slade was manning the port Lewis gun, Barbeza the starboard, but so far neither of them had opened fire. The Heinkel stayed high for its first pass, the pilot having difficulty with the wind which suited Slade for the two bombs fell on either side of the ship and did no more than douse the deckhands with water.

He turned and shouted to Culpepper who was standing calmly in the open window, watching the bow come round with agonising slowness. 'Take us straight at him on the next run. We want to give Jimmy Hardcastle a chance from the stern.'

Culpepper nodded, debating whether to call McVay again and ask why they were only on one third. The Heinkel came into view, low over the water, lining up for its run. He turned to the helmsman, managing a sympathetic smile. 'Wheel amidships, Demers. Keep your head down.'

Slade pulled back the heavy bolt and cocked the Lewis gun, checking the ammunition drum for the tenth time. He glanced across at Barbeza who was crouched behind his gun, perspiration running off his face like tropical rain. He turned back, holding the sight steady on the aircraft. He could hear the engine now, a deep-throated roar, and began to tighten his finger on the trigger. The bombs were clearly visible beneath the wings, two on each side. He tried not to think of the damage they could do, of the women in their cabins whose lives he had placed at risk. His ship, his crew, his friends who had obeyed him without question.

He pushed the thoughts from his mind and pressed the trigger, trying to hold the gun steady as it jerked and pulled against him. The noise was deafening, the acrid smell of cordite sharp in his nose, and a stream of empty cartridge cases were flying out over the wing of the bridge like pennies from heaven. There was no way he could tell if he was hitting the aircraft, but before it reached the ship the pilot must have become aware of the guns because he pulled up steeply, mistiming his bomb release so that they fell harmlessly a good hundred yards ahead of them. Slade laughed triumphantly, stopping firing as the Heinkel roared overhead. With luck the machine guns would convince him that he should make his next run towards their stern.

Flying Officer Oberlechen pulled the Heinkel into a sharp turn, feeling the vibration from the wings as the wind buffeted them. Grey tendrils of cloud whipped past and the lush green hills of Virgin Gorda soared lazily towards him, turning on their side to fall away past his wing. He held the turn, sick with anger at his cowardly response to the gunfire. The first indication that the ship below was armed had been the ripple of bullet holes that suddenly ran across his wing. Instinctively he had pulled back on the control column, but the movement had made him also pull on the bomb toggle he had been holding in his left hand. Now he had only two bombs left and nothing at all to show for it.

With grim features he straightened out and dropped down towards the sea. The ship was four thousand yards ahead, stern on and a sitting target. He forced himself to relax, taking hold of the last bomb release cable, reducing throttle so that he would have more time. The *Tinkerbelle* begin to drift towards him, moving slowly out to sea. It wasn't even taking evasive action, just moving ahead in a straight line. He licked dry lips, his eyes fixed on the target, beginning to count the seconds as the distance narrowed between them. He was a thousand yards from the ship, some three hundred feet above the sea, when he saw a steady flash of light from the stern. Only then, with stunned disbelief, did he understand why the captain was holding a straight course.

Hardcastle couldn't believe his luck. With his shoulders cradled in the firing rests he had been holding the Heinkel in the middle of his sights for a full two thousand yards. The pilot was even coming in slow, as though this was all a bit of friendly target practice with blank ammunition instead of the lethal two-pound shells. He waited until it was a thousand yards away, then pressed the button beneath his thumb and held it down. The gun began to buck against him, the pom-pom action sliding the barrel back into the breech and out to flash blue-white and recoil again. In his sights he could see the first shells exploding, correcting ever so gently, watching the dark puffs of smoke beneath and above the wings. It was flying straight into him and he stopped breathing, knowing he couldn't miss.

The exploding shells were buffeting the Heinkel wildly, but Oberlechen held the control column steady in his hand. Only five hundred yards, less than ten seconds, and he could pull the bomb release. There was a dull concussion beside him and a stinging in his eyes. He blinked, trying to clear them, feeling the aircraft falter and begin to yaw to starboard. His vision returned and he saw that half his wing had gone, the stick already loose in his hand. With a bitter sense of defeat he watched the sea begin to revolve. Another explosion shook the aircraft and there was smoke everywhere. His hand moved automatically towards his harness, but he knew it was far too late for a parachute. The aircraft began to spin, the engine howling in protest as the sea and sky became a kaleidoscope with him at its centre. He felt very cold, but unafraid, surprised that he could still think clearly. He thought of his mother, wondering how they would tell her, and then his world disintegrated.

When Susan rushed out onto the deck following the sound of the exploding aircraft she was just in time to witness the unlikely sight of her young husband cavorting in some kind of barn dance with the ungainly figure of the captain. She rushed towards them, fearing the worst, but as she drew closer felt some relief when she saw that at least he was laughing. The confusing part of it was that they kept punching each other, admittedly not terribly hard, and then they would hang onto each other and cackle with laughter.

'Jesus, did he walk into it,' gasped Slade, tears in his eyes.

'Walk? He almost strolled. I tell you, Captain, I couldn't believe it when he sat there in my sights.'

They began to laugh again. Susan was getting pink around the cheek bones because her husband hadn't even noticed her yet.

'James,' she said coolly.

'You know what?' chuckled Slade. 'I think he thought those balls of smoke were indian signals.'

'Peace talk!' howled Hardcastle and they collapsed again.

'James, I'm so glad you're safe!'

Hardcastle glanced around at the icy tone, then grinned. 'Hey, did you see that, Sue? Did you see that?'

'No,' she said crisply. 'I was only concerned about seeing you!'

Slade sobered and turned the petty officer firmly around and pushed him towards her. 'I've got a feeling the war isn't over yet, Jimmy.'

'Oh come on, Sue. That was the first enemy aircraft I ever shot down.'

'Splendid,' she said. 'It'll be something to remember every year – instead of our anniversary.'

Slade choked and had to turn away, his shoulders shaking. She glared at Hardcastle, daring him to grin. He grinned.

'We blew the marauder up too.'

'Marvellous. I'd no idea you were so good at destroying things.'

The laughter left him instantly. 'I'm not. They're the ones who are good at that, or have you forgotten all those nice dead people you took a swim with?'

Her eyes flashed and she stepped close to him, polishing her most crushing retort. But suddenly the words seemed to stick in her throat and her knees went weak. He really was the handsomest man she had ever met. 'Jimmy,' she said, leaning towards him.

'Darling Sue,' he said, putting his arms around her.

Slade shook his head, grinning, and started towards the bridge. Diana was by the rail, looking at the plume of smoke that hung over the sea where the Heinkel had vanished. She glanced at him, her mouth lifting at one corner as though she was about to make a sarcastic comment. He glowered at her.

'I suppose you think we should have fired a warning shot?'

'Why should I, Captain? Only a gentleman would do that, and if I remember rightly you strike first and apologise later.'

He smiled tightly, covering his embarrassment. 'You really know how to twist that knife, Miss Curtis.'

'Diana,' she snapped.

'Oh that's right, I forgot,' he said sarcastically. 'Now that we're on *intimate* terms we get to first names. Well mine's still captain!'

She clenched her fists, fighting to hold back tears. 'You are the most . . .' She stopped as Culpepper appeared in the companionway, looking nervous.

'Excuse me. Er, Captain, we have a problem.'

'Well now that makes a change. Tell me about it?'

'We're operating on half pressure and, according to Mr McVay, there doesn't seem to be much chance of full power until he's done a fairly big repair job on number two boiler. That means we're getting no more than a third out of the prop and with this wind against us we're not making much progress.'

'Alright, so hold it at a third. We'll make five knots and still be there by dark.'

Culpepper shook his head, his face expressionless. 'We don't have that long, Captain. There's a hurricane warning for this whole area. Annabelle, heading right for *Tinkerbelle.*'

Slade absorbed the information, then patted him on the shoulder. 'Rodney, there are times when you can be quite poetic. Tell you what, we'll go around the point and head west for Tortola. How does that suit you?'

'That would have been my recommendation, sir.'

He smiled happily and left. Slade turned back to Diana who seemed to be having difficulty maintaining her anger. He decided to help her out, 'You're in luck, sweetheart. You get to spend another night on board.'

'Then I want a padlock on my cabin door!'

''Fraid I just had the last one fitted on mine.'

He grinned and stepped quickly through the companionway hatch. She turned to the rail, hitting it with her fist and muttering through her teeth something that sounded very like 'drop dead' to the Hardcastles who were passing unnoticed on the way to their cabin.

'Did you hear that?' whispered Susan as they went through the companionway hatch. 'Imagine!'

Hardcastle nodded uncomfortably, wishing he had not overheard. 'Not a very nice thing to say.'

Susan rolled her eyes in despair. 'Darling, it's marvellous. Absolutely marvellous.'

'Oh,' said Hardcastle, feeling disloyal. 'He's not such a bad chap.'

Susan gave him a patient smile. 'Not that, silly. I mean it's marvellous that Diana has fallen in love.'

She moved on, filled with delight at the thought. Hardcastle followed more slowly, struggling with her logic, deciding finally that he must have missed something quite important.

Slade, still in his euphoric mood, was telling himself there was no cause for concern if Annabelle did come their way. The Caribbean was the world centre for hurricanes and each year they had to cope with at least a couple. He went into his cabin and broke open a fresh bottle of gin, blowing into the engine room tube just for the hell of it.

'What now you Goddamn Yankee bastard!' bellowed McVay. 'Do you want me to get the oars out and start rowing?'

'I just wanted to congratulate you and your men, Chief. Against all odds we sorted out the Kraut.'

'So what do you expect me to do? Pin a medal on your arse!'

Slade grinned. McVay always felt insecure in the presence of a compliment. 'No need for that, Mr McVay, but if you can see your way to getting your finger out and starting number two boiler we just might survive the hurricane that's moving our way.'

There was a five second pause, then the engineer's howl of rage filled the narrow confines of the cabin. Slade estimated that it was about strength eight, almost a record. He stretched out on his bunk, sipping gin and listening to the tirade that began with a painstaking description of his anatomy and its genetic origin and ending with undiminished fervour on a recommendation that was both unsanitary and impracticable.

Although the wind continued to rise during the next hour it was not until they rounded the tip of the island and started across Sir Francis Drake Channel that things really began to look bad. Waves were rolling through the six mile channel that separated Tortola from Virgin Gorda, and the wind being funnelled by the hills was banking the sea into mountainous crests that could capsize bigger ships than the *Tinkerbelle*.

Culpepper was taking the bridge watch, accompanied by Mrs Hartford-Jones who had given up insisting on rest and was now fully committed to a more subtle form of persuasion which was half medical and half maternal. She wasn't quite sure which of the two was succeeding, only that Culpepper was responding to treatment and seemed content just to have her beside him. The ugly seas ahead filled her with dread, but he was quick to assure her that he had no intention of risking either her or the ship. He told the helmsman to bring them round and blew into the captain's voice tube.

'Captain, this is Culpepper. We're not going to make it

across the Sir Francis Drake Channel. I'm going about and will drop anchor behind Copper Mine Point.'

'Okay, Culpie,' replied Slade, 'but don't forget there are a lot of angry krauts at the other end of the island.'

Culpepper smiled and replaced the whistle, watching as they began to plough back around the point which was some two thousand yards to port.

'He's right about the Germans isn't he?' said Mrs Hartford-Jones. 'If they're on the same island they could find us.'

'Not really. Berchers Bay is five miles along the coast and the vegetation is too dense to travel overland. As they no longer have a ship that floats, we're quite safe.'

She nodded, beginning to relax. Outside the wind was beginning to buffet them as the rocky headland fell away. Culpepper crossed to the chart, checking depths around the point where they would anchor. He was studying the best position for shelter when Mrs Hartford-Jones tapped him on the shoulder. He glanced up, smiling. Her face was very pale, making her look much older.

'Rodney,' she said quietly, 'is it possible that Captain Slade didn't sink the marauder?'

He frowned and started to shake his head, then went very still. Beyond her, through the broken window, the rolling sea stretched far along the coast of Virgin Gorda. And plunging through that sea, less than a mile away, was the unmistakeable lines of the *Tamerande*.

'Bring her round!' he told the helmsman quickly, lunging towards the voice tubes. He was about to blow down the captain's tube when an ear-splitting scream passed over their heads. Mrs Hartford-Jones threw herself to the deck, covering her ears, whilst Demers on the helm spun the wheel faster than he had ever done in his life.

'Jesus!' said the voice in the tube. 'What the fuck was that!'

Culpepper winced. 'The marauder, Captain. You know ... the one you sank this morning!'

173

19

The stretch of water named after the visit of Sir Francis Drake in 1571 extended from the western tip of Virgin Gorda to Beef Island, which was separated from Tortola by a narrow channel no more than two hundred yards wide at its narrowest point. Atlantic currents entering the Caribbean through Gorda Sound to the north of the islands created one of the most difficult stretches of water at the best of times, but with the wind gusting at forty miles an hour and beginning to rise up the Beaufort Scale as Annabelle moved in from the south west, the sea was a churning maelstrom that began to roll the ship as soon as she cleared the shelter of the island.

Slade gazed at the channel with grim features, estimating the speed they would make and coming up with all the wrong answers. He turned to Culpepper beside him. 'How long to reach Beef Island?'

The first officer grimaced, looking at his watch. 'With luck I'd say half an hour.'

'And the *Tamerande* should clear Virgin Gorda in ten minutes.'

'He must have some damage,' Culpepper pointed out. 'He could be on reduced speed the same as us.'

'Alright, say he's down to seven knots. He'll have to go wide round the point to clear the shallows, but he'll still be in the channel in fifteen minutes. That would put him two miles behind us and gaining half a mile every five minutes.'

Culpepper nodded slowly, his face very pale. 'And his big guns can open up a mile away.'

Slade cursed softly and turned towards Hardcastle who stood with Panacero. 'Jimmy, I might have to ask you to man the two-pounder again.'

'I understand, Captain. It won't be much use if he stands off and uses his big guns.'

'I don't think he will. If we can reach Beef Island there's a narrow channel that we can just about get into. He'll know that, guess what we're planning, so try to make the best speed he can. If you can get any shots near his bow he won't like it.'

'I'll do my best, sir.' Hardcastle tried a smile that jerked nervously. He knew better than anyone what the marauder's heavy guns could do. 'I still don't understand how he could put to sea so quickly. He was on fire and holed.'

'We keep forgetting the bastard's at war,' Slade replied wearily. 'He was probably carrying sea mattresses and all the clamps he'd need to do a temporary job. But he'll take plenty of water once he gets into the channel. Let's hope his pumps can't handle it.'

Hardcastle nodded, but without conviction. He thought of Susan and felt his stomach lurch. 'Sir, what about the ladies?'

Slade stared at the ugly sea. 'We can't put them off in that, not if there's a chance of making the island. Mister Culpepper, you're badly handicapped with that arm and it may get rough up here. I want you to get the ladies into life jackets and stay with them. Keep close to the number three lifeboat. It's the best one.'

Culpepper hesitated, biting his lip. 'Captain, I'm sure I could . . .'

'That's an order, Mister Culpepper.'

After they had gone Slade went to Demers at the helm. He had been on duty since dawn and the exhaustion showed around his eyes and mouth. The captain patted him on the back and beckoned to Panacero. 'Take the helm, Mister Panacero. It'll be you and me on the bridge.'

The mate swallowed and nodded jerkily, taking over

from Demers who looked both relieved and sad. He started towards the companionway only to turn back, reluctant to leave them. 'I'm not too bad, Cap'n,' he said awkwardly. 'If there's anything I can do ...?'

Slade gave no sign that he had heard. He stood in front of one of the broken windows, the wind tearing at his long pale hair, his hands gripping the metal coaming as though he was trying to push the ship faster over the surging sea. After a moment he reached for the engine room tube and blew into it.

'What the hell is it now?' squawked McVay.

'The captain, Mister McVay. What chance is there of repairing number two boiler?'

'No chance if you keep asking me bloody stupid questions.'

'Answer me, McVay!' said Slade in a brittle voice. 'I have no time for your tantrums now.'

Demers and Panacero winced, waiting for the explosion. There was a brief silence and then, to their astonishment, a briskly efficient voice from the engine room.

'We've got a damaged jet that's difficult to reach, captain. We might have to cut our way in, but that's going to need repairing later.'

'Go ahead with it, Chief, and leave your hatches open. If we're hit get out fast.'

'Aye, Cap'n. But I expect I'll be giving you a call before then.'

Slade replaced the tube and turned to Demers, hovering by the companionway. 'Pass the word to the crew. Everyone in life jackets and clear on boat stations. I want four fire parties, two on the foredeck, two on the aft. If we're badly hit I'll sound two blasts for prepare to abandon ship, continuous blasts for take to the boats.'

Demers swallowed and nodded. 'Aye aye, Cap'n.'

When he had gone Slade went out onto the wing, looking back towards Virgin Gorda. It seemed a good distance away now, but when he looked forward to the rolling grey channel and the low hills of Tortola he felt a cold hand of fear. It seemed an impossible task.

*   *   *

The *Tamerande* turned its slab-sided hull as it cleared the headland beyond Copper Mine Bay, feeling the full force of wind and sea. The junior navigation officer out on the wing measured its force and gritted his teeth, looking instinctively towards the south where the sky was now black and touching the sea. Flashes of lightning were beginning to glow along the horizon, flickering like St Elmo's Fire. He went back into the bridge where Lieutenant Commander Tellmann was studying the chart with the navigation officer.

'We have gusts of seventy miles an hour, sir.'

Tellmann nodded, tapping a pencil on the chart and gazing at the navigation officer with grim features. 'You better plot a course north out of Gorda Sound, just in case we have to run with the wind.'

The navigation officer nodded, glancing towards the captain who sat motionless in his seat in the centre of the bridge. He had been like that for the past hour, saying nothing, just watching the bow lifting and falling.

'My recommendation is that we shelter in the lee of Virgin Gorda,' he told Tellmann quietly.

The executive officer nodded, his mouth thin. 'Naturally.'

'You will convey that to the captain?'

Tellmann's eyes were ice cold, but he nodded and moved across the bridge. Captain Kroehner glanced at him briefly, his face stony. They both knew that the conversation was going to be meaningless.

'Navigation officer reports gale force winds with hurricane forces in two to three hours, sir.'

'Thank you, Mister Tellmann.'

'He recommends standing off the lee shore of Virgin Gorda.'

'Of course he does.'

Tellmann spoke quietly, so that his voice would not carry to the helmsman. 'That is also my recommendation, Captain.'

Kroehner glanced up at him, a shadow of disappointment on his face. 'Are the forward guns ready, Mr Tellmann?'

'Yes, sir.'

'And the torpedoes?'

'Armed and ready, sir.'

'Are we taking more water than the pumps can handle?'

'Not yet, sir,' replied Tellmann, gazing stiffly ahead.

'Then we will continue to follow the *Tinkerbelle* and you will instruct the gunnery officer to commence firing the moment we are in range.'

'Yes, sir.'

Tellmann turned away and went back to the chart table where the navigation officer studiously avoided his furious glance. Captain Kroehner rose from his seat and went out of the bridge onto the wing, taking his binoculars from their case and searching the channel ahead. The wind whipped at his immaculate white jacket, but it was a warm wind that was more of an inconvenience than a discomfort. The sea was gun metal grey, reflecting the lowering clouds which had begun to darken. He raised the glasses, finding the ship almost immediately. It was half-way across the channel, pitching and rolling in a violent fashion. He lifted the binoculars, looking beyond the *Tinkerbelle* to the small island that seemed to be part of the coastline of Tortola. It would be close, he thought. Very close.

There was movement beside him and he turned to find Tellmann there. The executive officer lifted his own glasses, studying the channel. He spoke without turning his head. his words almost lost in the wind.

'Is this very important to you, Captain?'

Kroehner frowned, considering his answer carefully. He had only known Wolf Tellmann for three months and in that time he had learned little about the man. There was no doubt about his ability as an officer, but there were times when he detected a cool reserve in him. It was probably due to the fact that Tellmann had been a regular officer whereas Kroehner had spent most of his career in the Merchant Navy. If this had been any other ship instead of a marauder the chances were that it would be Tellmann who was the captain and Kroehner his first officer.

'This man Lincoln Slade has almost crippled us twice and succeeded in destroying our Heinkel. He has accomplished the impossible, Wolf. In spite of our superiority in every way he still succeeds.'

'He was lucky, sir. No more than that.'

Kroehner turned to him, shaking his head slowly. 'No, Wolf, not lucky. Unorthodox, courageous, determined, even irrational, but not lucky. I feel that if we let him escape today then next time, somehow, he will destroy us. That is why we must sink him now, whatever the cost.'

Tellmann stared at him for a long moment, his expression one of puzzlement. 'With respect, Captain, he is no match for us. We have no need to fear an unarmed freighter.'

Kroehner sighed. 'It is not the freighter, Wolf. It is the man. Why he hunts us I do not know. How he finds us is a mystery. All I can be certain of is that if we lose him now that will not be the end of it. And we have more important things to do.'

The executive officer returned his binoculars to their case and nodded, his gaze steady and direct. 'Very well, Captain. I will attend to it.'

20

The massive 5.9 inch guns of the *Tamerande* fired their first salvo when the *Tinkerbelle* was still half a mile from the rocky coastline of Beef Island. The shells exploded harmlessly four hundred yards behind, but the members of the crew who were on deck gazed back towards the German with worried features. It didn't take an expert to work out that before they reached the island the shells would not be falling short.

Jimmy Hardcastle checked the magazine on the two-pounder, lifting the pan lid and easing the stubby shells up and down. There were two rows of ten inside, ready to feed into the sliding breech below. He felt curiously detached, as though this wasn't really happening at all. There was another shrill scream in the sky and he tried to ignore it, moving round to the steel shoulder supports and leaning into them, only glancing up when the shells exploded with dull concussions. Fountains of foam hung briefly in the air, wide to port but only a hundred yards behind.

There was a calmness in him that was surprising, as though it had all happened before. A dream long forgotten. He tried not to think of Susan, knowing instinctively that he would not have the strength to hold back the fear. Instead he busied himself with the gun, dragging ammunition boxes across, checking and rechecking the breech mechanism. Every minute or so he would lean into the metal braces, looking through the sight at the tall, dark bulk of the *Tamerande*. It was still small in the distance, but full of menace as it rose and fell in the sea. As he watched the guns flashed from the foredeck, the gun crew firing as they crested a wave to give them maximum range. He heard the scream almost immediately, gripping cold steel, not breathing until they detonated in the sea. Again they were closer, no more than fifty feet away.

On the wing of the bridge Slade was a solitary figure hunched around his binoculars as he watched the twin spouts of water move inexorably closer. Most of the crew crouching below the weather decks now, wedging themselves into corners, many of them praying for the first time since childhood. He wondered if, between the prayers, they were also cursing him and the mad arrogance which had brought them here.

There was a thin whistle from the engine room tube and he hurried back onto the bridge, every nerve stretched tight as he pulled the plug. 'Yes, Chief?'

'We're firing it now, Captain. Give us one minute.'

He closed his eyes, letting his breath ease out like a sigh. McVay started to repeat the words, thinking he hadn't heard. He interrupted him. 'That's alright, Mister McVay. We'll go to full power the moment you have steam.'

He replaced the tube and looked at Panacero whose eyes were like glass marbles. He held up two crossed fingers. 'We just might do it yet, Panacero.'

The gunnery officer on the *Tamerande* felt confident enough to stop ranging for three minutes before tilting his guns to maximum elevation again. His range finder on the top of the bridge was reading out the bearings. He checked them, frowning. The ship had increased its speed. He spoke sharply into his mouthpiece, feeling the jolt that ran through the hull every time the heavy guns fired. Three seconds later the white spouts of water reared up in the distance. He smiled with relief. The shells had straddled the *Tinkerbelle*.

Culpepper had put the women in a recess beneath the companionway at the front of the bridge. The steel superstructure was heaviest there and they were within ten feet of the midships lifeboat that was already hanging out in its davits. Culpepper felt useless and futile, sitting closest to the rail, only barely conscious of Mrs Hartford-Jones's hand clutching his arm.

Diana sat with her arm around Susan talking to her constantly in a low cheerful voice. Susan was hardly listening. Every shell that landed brought her to her knees, but each time Diana spoke reassuringly, pulling her back. The girl was shaking, her face blanched with fear. What made it so much worse was that they knew the fear was not for her own safety. She wanted to be with Hardcastle and only the combined efforts of them all had kept her there so far.

They waited, counting the seconds. At thirty the harsh shriek came once more and less than ten feet from the ship a tower of water suddenly erupted, hanging there as they ploughed on past it. Susan lunged to her feet, freeing herself from Diana's grasp with a sudden violence.

'No!' she said, shaking her head as she backed away from them. 'You can't make me stay here. You just can't.'

'Please, Miss Blain,' said Culpepper, and could have bitten his tongue.

'I'm not Miss Blain,' she said, tears in her eyes. 'I'm Mrs Hardcastle. I'm his wife!'

She turned and ran and no one had the heart to follow and bring her back.

Culpepper stared at the approaching island with blurred eyes, a voice in the back of his mind repeating the Lord's Prayer endlessly. He could see the trees on a rocky knoll now, make out the waves breaking over the coral reef that marked the entrance to the narrow inlet between Beef Island and Tortola. *Just three more minutes,* he thought. *'Just three.'*

Susan ran across the heaving deck with her hair flying like a bright yellow scarf. Hardcastle was hunched against the gun which was tilted so that the barrel pointed at an extreme angle into the sky for maximum range. She reached him, sobbing, clutching his arm. 'I'm sorry, Jimmy,' she sobbed. 'I'm so sorry.'

His young face seemed so old when he turned to her, but the way he smiled sent such a wave of emotion through her that she felt sure she would faint.

'It's all right,' he said quietly. 'I understand.'

'Do you?' she wanted to explain. She wanted him to know the terrible pain, to tell him that now she was there it didn't matter. Nothing mattered at all.

Neither of them noticed the scream in the sky. The first shell took off the rear corner of the bridge in a roar of flames, the second hit the after deck within six feet of the gun. An entire section of deck disappeared in a shower of jagged metal and searing flames. The blast killed them instantly, before they even knew that this time the shells were on target.

On the bridge Slade ignored the lurch of the ship, the concussion that was unmistakable. They were less than a hundred yards from the rocky promontory that leaned out over the sea. Beyond it the island curved back in a crescent at the end of which was the channel that narrowed until you could throw a stone from one island to the other. There was a scream and a shell burst on the island, showering rock and sand towards them. There was a massive explosion on the starboard side and smoke began to billow across the deck.

'Take her round it now,' said Slade.

Panacero gritted his teeth, spinning the helm so that the rocks lurched towards them. Slade ran out onto the wing, looking back along the starboard side. A section of the saloon was blown away and the interior was a mass of flames. Even as he took in the scene Demers appeared running towards it with a fire crew. He looked beyond them to the aft deck and felt the clutch of fear as he saw more smoke. He tried to see Hardcastle's gun but it was impossible.

They plunged and rolled as Panacero brought them round the promontory in a hard turn, but the motion of the vessel changed almost immediately as they moved into calmer water. Another salvo of shells exploded on the island, but

they were shielded by it now. Slade went back to the bridge
and rang for slow speed, then took the helm from Panacero
who immediately sat down and looked at his hands.

They were making no more than eight knots across the
bay that stretched for almost a mile, running back at an
angle so that the further they went the more they were
shielded by the island itself. Slade was beginning to relax,
knowing that they would be into the narrow channel before
the marauder cleared the promontory. Even if he sent salvos
of shells over the island he would be firing blind and unlikely to hit them.

'Give me two blasts on the siren,' said Slade.

Panacero rose and pulled the siren choke twice. The long
blasts boomed out, bringing the crew up on deck to their
boat stations. Smoke was still billowing from below the
bridge, but it was whiter and Slade guessed that they had
the hoses on it by now. He rang up dead slow, easing the
Tinkerbelle over the shallow entrance to the channel. He
could make out the choppy water beyond the inlet, surging
restlessly between the islands, but that was the least of his
worries.

He felt the ship shudder as it passed over the spit of white
sand, then surge forward again between the steep slope of
Tortola and the jagged cliffs of Beef Island. Panacero was
at the side window, his face grey as they lurched towards
jagged rock, then as quickly rolling away towards the slop-
ing white sands of the main island. But Slade's hands were
sure on the helm. He had been through the channel twice
before, admittedly in calm weather, but he knew that by
hugging the cliffs of Beef Island they would have enough
water beneath them. In little more than five minutes he
rang for 'All Stop' and stepped away from the helm.

'Alright, Panacero, they can't see us or get to us now. Just
let her drift towards the sand.'

He went out onto the wing and climbed down the steel
ladder to the deck. A dozen of the crew were putting out
the last of the fire in the saloon. It was a charred and gutted

184

ruin, half the length of the living quarters ripped away by the explosion. He moved on, his heart pumping, trying to see the damage on the rear deck. A small group of people were gathered near the stern. He quickened his pace, every nerve taut as he approached. Mrs Hartford-Jones was there, supported by Culpepper, and he could see she was sobbing hysterically.

Faces blurred in front of him and he pushed them aside, the sounds around him distorting as though he was in a giant echo chamber, then his vision shimmered and he felt a terrible spasm of pain. Lying before him, like a broken doll, was the body of Susan Blain. There was so much blood it was hard to believe it was all hers, and then he realized that it wasn't. Jimmy Hardcastle, mangled beyond belief, lay partly beneath the wreckage of his gun.

There were tears in his eyes that stung like fire and he desperately wanted to cry out, to give some substance to his anguish. But he could only look and feel the pain. Her face was quite untouched, still beautiful against the golden mane of her hair, and her eyes were still the clearest blue as if dying was no effort at all.

When he turned away he found Diana before him, her face streaked with tears. She tried to speak but the words would not come. He pushed past her, almost running, knowing he didn't need to hear it from her or Mrs Hartford-Bloody-Jones or Panacero or Culpepper or even McVay. On the way to the bridge he grabbed Barbeza and Panacero, telling the rest of the crew to take what they could in the boats and get to the shore.

'I want that torpedo we've got stuck on the bow,' he told the mate. 'Can it be wedged in that damaged section?'

Panacero's mouth opened and closed. Barbeza grabbed his arm, shaking his head. 'No, Cap'n. The German can't reach us here.'

'That's not the problem,' snarled Slade. 'The problem is how do I reach him!'

They fell silent, watching him nervously. His grey eyes

185

burned with rage and grief, striking into them each time their glances met like steel knives.

'If you bastards won't help I'll do it myself.'

'We'll help, Captain,' said Panacero quietly. 'We just don't want you to do it.'

Slade left him, heading for the bow. There was a sizeable tear in the crumpled section, high up near the rails, and it was this area that he intended to use. Panacero and Barbeza went reluctantly to the derrick and swung it over the forward hold, shaking their heads with baffled expressions to those who asked what they were doing.

Slade was hanging over the bow in a sling when McVay came to peer down at him with haunted eyes. He said nothing for a while, watching Slade hammer jagged edges back into the hole.

'You saw the lassie?' he said.

'I saw her.'

'You cannae blame yourself, Linc.'

'I can blame who the hell I like!'

McVay blew his nose loudly on a dirty rag. 'Do you need any help down there?'

'No. I just want everyone off this fucking ship!'

'Most of them have gone,' replied the engineer. 'There's just a couple of hands and Mr Culpepper waiting for you on the bridge.'

'Tell Mr Culpepper to get his arse over the side. That goes for you too.'

McVay's face went red and he glared over the rail. 'You keep your bloody nose out of my engine room. Do you hear?'

Slade caught his hand on a piece of metal and cursed viciously. He stuck the hammer in his belt and began to haul on the tackle, pulling himself up to the rails. Panacero and Barbeza were swinging the torpedo towards them on the derrick. He looked up at the bridge and waved to Demers on the helm who began to bring the bow round slowly in the narrow channel. The wind was starting to howl over the cliffs above them and the clouds hung dark and heavy overhead. Now that he was on the deck Slade became aware of the rumble of thunder in the south.

'You can plug it in through the hole and let it rest against the inner bulkhead,' he told them.

'You really think a crazy scheme like this is going to work?' snapped McVay. 'Man, it'll likely as not fall out the minute you hit a heavy sea.'

'I'm not going into heavy sea,' growled Slade. 'If I can get back out of this channel in time that bastard will be sitting out there in the bay wondering how to get at us.'

'If he's got any sense he'll have gone along Tortola to drop anchor.'

'Then I'll still have him.'

'You'll have nothing you crazy Yankee bastard! You'll never get close enough to ram him and even if you do there's no guarantee the warhead will explode.'

Slade was supervising the lowering of the torpedo. He paused, turning on the Scotsman with furious anger. 'What the hell has it got to do with you, McVay? You've spent the last four years complaining about the bloody engines and now I'm going to put them where you've always said they ought to be. On the fucking bottom!'

'And yourself too,' screeched the engineer, 'because if ever a captain deserved to go down with his ship it's you, you long-armed pissy-eyed American git!'

Slade grabbed for the Scotsman's scrawny throat but he kicked him in the ankle and bounced away, his face almost purple with rage.

'Get off my ship,' snarled Slade, hopping on one foot with clenched fists. 'If you're here in five minutes I'll stuff you so far up the bilges they'll need a block and tackle to get you out!'

Panacero and Barbeza had stopped work, gaping at the two men who looked ready to tear each other to pieces at any moment. Slade swung round on them, his gaze malevolent. 'I can find room for you two as well!'

Culpepper had viewed the scene from the bridge and was now hurrying across the deck towards them. He arrived as Slade took the hammer from his belt and waved it at the chief engineer who was looking for something to throw.

'Captain Slade,' the first officer said quietly, hoping his nervousness would not show. 'I estimate that the hurricane will be with us within the hour. I suggest we drop anchor and get everyone off the ship.'

Slade glowered at him. 'Nobody's dropping any anchors. As soon as that torpedo is in place I want the rest of you away.'

'You can't handle the *Tinkerbelle* yourself, sir.'

'Don't get any smart ideas, Culpepper. Just get yourself ashore and watch me do it.'

'We need you with us, sir. We have to get everyone up in the hills before the hurricane reaches us. I can't manage that on my own.'

'So get help. Felipe, Demers, Torres, even Mrs Hartford-Bloody-Jones.'

Culpepper stubbornly shook his head. 'We want you with us, Captain.'

There was a screech of metal that put their teeth on edge. Slade went to the rail and watched as Panacero unfastened the sling from the torpedo which now jutted some ten feet from the hole in the bow. He climbed up onto the deck and signalled to Barbeza who swung the derrick away.

'That's wedged in tight, Cap'n.'

'Thanks, Panacero. Now get going.'

The mate looked at Culpepper, then at Barbeza. 'I think we'd rather stay, sir. You'll need help.'

Slade opened his mouth to make an angry retort then snapped it shut, glaring at them all.

'If you're determined to go, Captain, then we'll all go with you,' Culpepper said quietly.

'You stupid bastards! That Kraut will probably blow me out of the water.'

Barbeza winced and rolled his eyes. McVay, still seething with anger, stabbed a finger at the darkening sky.

'If you've got a second to spare,' he said sarcastically, 'the thing that's going to blow you out of the water is coming from the south.'

Slade looked up at the sky, then at the four men who faced him. His eyes were deep in their sockets and his features slack with fatigue. When he rubbed his jaw with the knuckles of his right hand they could see the shake in it, feel the exhaustion that was weighing him down. He looked like an old bull getting ready for the last charge.

'It won't bring anyone back, Linc,' Culpepper said softly. 'And losing the ship hurts us all.'

'The ship is already lost,' he replied bitterly. 'You've seen the damage. We'd never find the money to put it right, and who the hell would help us? No, she's just as dead as . . . as that boy and girl I killed just now.' He gazed at them, his eyes very bright. 'But at least it would all mean something if I could get to the marauder.'

'Linc, he's too good, too powerful,' Culpepper said helplessly.

'You're wrong. He knows where we are and it'll stick in his throat. Maybe he'll send a shore party, maybe just drop anchor and wait. But he won't leave. Not without settling it.' He raised his fist, the knuckles standing out white against the tanned skin. 'I'll be doing the last thing he expects, and that might just give me enough time to reach him.'

There was a long silence broken finally by McVay who shuffled his feet and blew his nose loudly, then began to search his pockets as he spoke, as though hoping to find a bottle there. 'I'll run the engines. You'll need all the speed you can get.'

Slade hesitated, then as the engineer began to bristle, grinned crookedly. 'Alright, you old bastard. But I want you in a life jacket and ready to get out fast.'

'I'll take the helm,' said Culpepper.

'Not this time, Mister. You've got to get everyone into the hills. The only man on that bridge will be me.'

'You're wrong about that, Cap'n,' Panacero said stubbornly. 'You've got two machine guns up there that can give covering fire. You'll need that or they'll be sweeping the bridge with their own machine guns the minute you try to get close.'

Slade chewed his lower lip, knowing it made sense. They waited nervously, afraid he would say no, as though neither of them understood the odds against their survival. But Slade knew they did, even though their motives were as great a mystery as their eagerness to go out with a captain who had got them into this mess in the first place. He remembered the way he found them in Caracas four years ago, a couple of drunken bums looking for an easy berth.

He shook his head. 'Jesus, you guys. How the hell did I manage to find you!'

21

Far above the black storm clouds that marked the front of the hurricane Annabelle the immense dome of the system had begun to develop along classic lines. A glittering mane of ice particles hung above it in the troposphere, the powerful winds in the upper levels stretching the frozen moisture into streamers a hundred miles long, curving them into an enormous spiral around the revolving storm fifty thousand feet below. In that past twenty-four hours the hurricane had become a sleek white blister over the turquoise basin of the Caribbean and lying before it, like an emerald necklace, lay the Virgin Islands.

The hurricane had been expanding all day as the enormous forces within tore up the surface of the sea and shot it to the roof of the dome at speeds approaching a hundred and fifty miles an hour. And the entire system was spinning, using the interaction of barometric pressures and the rapidly changing temperatures, so that it was now a gigantic gyroscope composed of dense cloud revolving at increasing speed around its 'eye' at the centre. The dome was already two hundred miles across, and still growing, and the winds inside had the destructive energy of a dozen atomic bombs.

So far Annabelle's course had been across open sea, but soon its nature would change as it felt land beneath it. The heavy mass of Puerto Rico was sufficient to guide it into the shield of the Lesser Antilles where the smaller masses of the Virgin Islands would be no match for its fury. Already the islands of St John and St Thomas were being battered by winds that were ripping trees out of the ground. Ahead of it, less than an hour away, lay Tortola.

Wolf Tellmann stood on the bridge of the *Tamerande* and watched the approaching hurricane with mixed feelings. The wind had begun to howl across the calmer waters of the bay, lifting the waves and pulling white streamers of foam from every crest so that the air was already filled with droplets of moisture giving it a thick, unreal quality, as though they were looking at the world through wet glass. They were two thousand yards from a coral reef that prevented them from entering the narrow channel, a feat of seamanship that would have been foolhardy in his opinion even if they did have clearance.

He glanced casually towards the captain, hunched in his chair, gazing with brooding eyes towards the small island. He could not wait much longer. Soon they would have to move up the coast of Tortola to Trellis Bay where the hills in the centre of the island would protect them from the full fury of the storm. Even in the bay, with every anchor rigged, it would be difficult enough. The alternative favoured by most of the officers on board was to turn and run for the shelter of Puerto Rico, although Tellmann suspected it was already too late for that. A radio man entered with a flimsy, moving towards him. He took the sheet, scanning it quickly, then told the man to take it to the navigation officer.

Captain Kroehner glanced up when he approached, the corners of his thin mouth lifting in a wisp of a smile. 'Yes, Wolf?'

'The weather bureau in Miami reports that the hurricane now has winds of one hundred and twenty miles an hour at sea level. We are in its path.'

'We cannot outrun it. Not with a sea mattress on the hull.'

'I agree, sir. We can make Trellis Bay and anchor.'

'True. Unfortunately Captain Slade knows that too and I suspect he is used to hurricanes.'

Tellmann's mouth tightened. 'With respect, sir, we scored three hits on his ship. I doubt if he is feeling like going anywhere.'

'Perhaps.' Kroehner leaned forward, staring through the heavy air towards the island, almost lost in the misty gloom. 'But suppose he did catch us at anchor. What then?'

'I can think of less complicated situations,' Tellmann said dryly. 'The hurricane is bad enough. Add Slade and I'd rather give it a miss altogether.'

'Exactly,' replied Kroehner, nodding vigorously. 'I think he will come. Soon.'

Tellmann glanced through the heavy armoured glass streaked with rain. He was quite convinced that Slade would sit tight in his natural harbour until tomorrow at least and then, only then, would he venture out. As though aware of the thought Kroehner looked up at him and smiled bleakly. 'I cannot ignore my instincts, Wolf.'

'No, sir. But we cannot stay here much longer.'

The captain sighed and nodded. 'I suppose not. Tell the navigator to plot us along the coast to Trellis Bay, then have the gun crews stand down.'

Tellmann's cheeks went pink. 'I'm afraid I stood them down some time ago, Captain.'

Kroehner's mouth tightened angrily, but before he could speak the duty watch out on the wing stuck his head inside and announced that something was moving in the channel. Kroehner went quickly to the window, raising his binoculars. When he turned to Tellmann his lips were thin and pale, twisted into a bitter smile.

'Battle stations, Mister Tellmann, and if the gun crews are not ready to fire in one minute I shall be forced to prefer charges against you and the senior gun commander.'

Tellmann stiffened, nodded his head and stabbed the battle alarm. The gongs began to sound throughout the ship, bringing two hundred men to their feet. Tellmann lifted a microphone and switched it on, speaking without emotion.

'All hands to battle stations. This is Tellmann. I want

torpedoes ready to fire and all guns ranging for salvo in one minute. I repeat. One minute.'

*   *   *

When the *Tinkerbelle* cleared the narrow mouth of the channel and crossed the sandbar into the open bay, Slade howled with triumph on the bridge.

'I'm coming you bastard,' he bellowed, bringing nervous glances from Barbeza and Panacero on the Lewis guns. 'And nothing this side of hell is going to stop me!'

He gripped the helm with knotted hands, as though urging the ship through the water with his own driving hatred for the marauder. The vessel sat in the middle of the bay like a tall grey ghost, the wind tearing its smoke away and throwing veils of spray between them. He could reach it. He knew he could reach it if only those big guns would give him the time.

'Mr McVay,' he shouted into the tube, 'leave your throttles open and get the hell out of there.'

'Suppose you get torpedoes you ignorant Yankee bastard? I'll just have to come all the way back down again.'

'To hell with torpedoes. I'll have the bastard in two minutes.'

'Then I'll come up in one.'

Slade glared at the tube, but there was nothing else he could say. The big ship was beginning to churn water up along its hull and he realized that the captain was going astern, keeping bow on. He cursed him savagely for his wisdom. A lesser man would have started to bear away to get more sea room. But they were nearly half-way there, surging through the sea with the storm howling behind them like a thousand demons driving them on.

Barbeza and Panacero opened up with the Lewis gun and almost immediately there was the rattle of bullets across the bridge. The last unbroken window dissolved in a shower of glass, then Barbeza turned towards him, as though to ask a question, leaning through the broken window with his mouth wide in a soundless cry. Slade watched him, unable to understand why he did not speak, and then the blood came in a rush from his throat and he coughed and fell out of sight.

Slade crouched down, grabbing the engine room tube again. 'Get up here, Chief. Port side, straight over the rail as soon as you hit the deck.'

'Alright, alright, you don't need to shout you disagreeable bastard.'

He threw the tube away and bellowed to the mate who was changing magazines. Panacero glanced back, nodded, then cocked the breech and opened fire on the ship that was now less than a thousand yards away.

Slade gritted his teeth, watching the two sets of guns on the foredeck. They were moving, slowly, stopping when they pointed directly at him. He swung the helm, heeling to starboard, his nerves ice cold as he watched the barrels flash. The shells screamed over the bridge, then as the second pair fired there was an explosion in the bow and he felt the entire hull shake. Almost simultaneously there was a tremendous blast above and behind him followed by a rush of wind. He turned, looking out at a grey sky, astonished to see that the entire rear section had been torn away. Jagged steel and tattered wood was all that remained.

He felt the copper taste of fear in his mouth and swung round spinning the helm to bring them back on a collision course. Panacero came through the door, crouching low, his eyes wide and terrified. Slade gestured to the rear companionway.

'Out. Straight over the side.'

'You too,' he pleaded.

'Move, damnit!'

Bullets were cracking through the air over his head, shrieking off the steel walls like demented wasps. Panacero shuddered, then gave a despairing curse and ran for the companionway. Slade lifted his head slightly, just enough to gauge the distance. Less than five hundred yards, the marauder dead ahead, churning the sea as it went full astern. He could feel the *Tinkerbelle*'s speed slackening, the helm beginning to get sluggish. Whatever had hit the bow had obviously holed them. He watched the guns, a hammer going in his chest; knowing that the next salvo would probably be their last.

He never saw the flash of light from the barrels. An enormous hand picked him up and smashed him across the bridge into the cubby hole beneath the chart table. The front bulkhead was torn away in the blink of an eye, shrapnel screaming in the smoke-filled air. Other shells exploded in the forward hold, the engine room and the bow, blasting a massive hole where the torpedo had been.

The *Tinkerbelle* reared up out of the water as though hit by a giant hand, then slammed back into the sea and rolled, almost capsizing. When it righted itself the forward hold and engine room were taking water by the tonne. The boilers exploded, blasting a fountain of steel and steam out through the funnel which was still miraculously intact. Then the bow, as though weary of it all, dipped slowly towards the waves and the stern lifted high until its propeller hung clear of the water.

Slade felt the unmistakable movement beneath him and tried to get up. Pain lanced through his side like hot knives going all the way into his spine. He groaned and fell back, hearing the grating and screeching from the hull as it began to break up under the strain. The hand he lifted from his side was red with blood and the sight brought a chill of fear which just as quickly gave way to a bitter sense of defeat. It had all been for nothing. The thought was almost too much to bear.

He could hear the sea rushing through the hull beneath him and he knew it would not be long. He wondered if Culpepper was watching from the hillside, and then he thought of Diana and the way she had looked such a short time ago. Everyone else had started up the hillside from the beach as he moved slowly back up the channel, but she had stood there alone on the sand, her very stillness an accusation.

He sighed. What the hell could he have said? *Goodbye, honey, see you later.*

'What the bleeding hell are you lying there for you ridiculous Yankee bastard!'

He opened his eyes and looked into the angry face of McVay. His hair was all wrong, only on one side of his head, and his face looked as though he had come up through the funnel. *Maybe he had*, thought Slade, *I always knew the bastard was too awkward to die!*

'What happened to your hair?' he asked.

'Oh you'd have to ask about that, wouldn't you?' snarled the engineer. 'You couldn't just pretend it was all there.'

'I was curious for Christ's sake!'

'Well it caught fire. Does that satisfy your bleeding curiosity? I was getting out of the engine room when that clever bastard blew the lot up underneath me. It's called a half back and sides!'

Slade started to laugh, then wished he hadn't, doubling up. McVay cursed and got him under the arms, dragging him out from beneath the chart table. Water was surging across the floor which was now tilted at an impossible angle.

'Jesus,' groaned Slade. 'I think we're sinking.'

'Well of course we're bloody sinking. Now will you stop passing the time of day and get off this bridge.'

Slade began to crawl, McVay pulling and pushing at him until they reached the front of the bridge. Water was pouring over jagged steel and there was no sign of the forward deck. McVay went through first, then clung to a bent section of coaming and gradually pulled him out.

'We'd have been better off using the hatch,' mumbled Slade, feeling his senses slipping away.

'That's right, bloody complain,' squawked McVay. 'You're such a disagreeable old bastard it wouldn't occur to you that we just might not have a blasted hatch.'

Slade grunted and passed out. The engineer glared at him and began to curse the weather, swimming on his back with his arms around the captain's chest. They were only just clear of the submerged deck when the *Tinkerbelle* rolled away from them and disappeared beneath the waves, air boiling around them like warm springs.

Panacero was sitting on a raft watching the German marauder head out to sea when he heard the unmistakable voice of McVay spluttering curses and calling Slade an insufferable bastard for not feeling like swimming. With spirits soaring he began to paddle towards them.

22

The crew of the *Tinkerbelle* toiled slowly up the hills towards Belle-Vue Mountain which rose one thousand two hundred feet above Fat Hogs Bay, urged on by Culpepper who knew it was vital that they find either caves or a sheltered ridge before the full force of the hurricane reached them. They were a dispirited group, trudging through thickets of willow and lime, forcing their way through the scrub of needle juniper and magnolia. They had heard the heavy guns of the marauder but were prevented from witnessing the duel by the adjoining tip of Beef Island and by the time they were high enough to look over it to the bay beyond the visibility was down to a few hundred yards and they could see nothing.

After half an hour they were exhausted and rested beneath a ridge, the wind howling around them, the sky an ugly purple lit every few seconds by garish lightning that flashed on the other side of the mountain. Pasqual and Torres had been helping Diana, concerned by her remoteness. She walked slowly, without interest, her eyes dull and listless. When they rested down below the ridge she crawled beneath a bush and sat hugging her knees. Pasqual brought her a drink from one of the canteens they had carried from the ship. She drank and passed the cup back to him, then stared off into the swirling wind.

After a while Mrs Hartford-Jones found her and crawled beneath the shelter beside her. Her trousers were stained with patches of red mud, her hair a tangled mass that she had finally tied with a strip of cloth torn from the tail of her shirt. Her face was streaked with dirt and her eyes hollow with weariness, but her voice was as caustic as ever.

'That man Slade has a lot to answer for,' she snapped bitterly.

Diana turned and gazed at her as though she were a total stranger. 'That man Slade is dead.'

'We don't know that,' she replied, considering her warily. 'In fact with a man like Captain Slade that is a rather foolish assumption.'

'Oh no.' Diana shook her head wildly, her lips white, tightly compressed. 'It wouldn't occur to him that it's not his war, that he hadn't got a chance against a marauder. He'd keep on going until there was nothing left of his ship, or of him!'

A tear rolled down her cheek and she wiped it quickly away. Mrs Hartford-Jones gazed at her in astonishment. It was beyond her comprehension that anyone, particularly a nice girl like Diana Curtis, could possess any of the finer feelings for a man like Slade. But the evidence was unmistakable.

'I'm sure you're wrong, my dear,' she said hesitantly. 'He may be stubborn and arrogant and totally irrational at times, but he's no fool.'

'You heard the guns,' cried Diana. 'You saw what they can do from a mile away.'

'Well I think you're quite wrong,' Mrs Hartford-Jones said firmly. 'If Captain Slade had died I would know. I'm very good at things like that. Why, when the *Cormorant* sank and we were all in the water, I knew Henry had gone. I didn't need to look for him. I just knew.'

Diana wiped a tear from the corner of her eye, nibbling uncertainly at her lip. 'Really?'

'Absolutely. He's probably cursing that dreadful Scotsman right now.'

Diana turned and gazed down the hillside as though expecting to see them. In the purple gloom the trees and bushes thrashed each other wildly, adding to the howling elements. Culpepper appeared, leaning against the wind, his face lined with exhaustion. He bent down, cupping his hands and shouting to them.

'We've found a cave over the ridge. We're going to be alright.'

'Well thank heavens for that,' said Mrs Hartford-Jones, then quickly mellowed her words. 'Of course I knew you would, Rodney. I've never known a man with such courage. And that poor arm.'

She reached for it, but Culpepper took her hand with his good arm and pulled her to her feet. She swayed against him, clinging around his waist, enjoying his confusion briefly before disengaging herself with a maidenly murmur of apology. The rest of the crew were on their feet, gathering up the canteens of water and packs of supplies. She felt depressed looking at them. They were a sorry bunch at the best of times, but out of their own environment they looked more like a pack of half-drowned rats looking for a local sewer. '*Oh God,*' she thought with a wave of hysteria, '*I hope it's a very big cave.*'

'You don't look at all well, Helen,' Culpepper said with concern.

She forced a smile. 'I'll be all right.'

Diana had left the shelter of the bush and was standing on a small knoll looking down towards the bay. Culpepper moved quickly to her, grasping her arm.

'We have to go up over the ridge,' he shouted.

She smiled sadly and shook her head. 'You go on.'

'Miss Curtis, we don't have much time.'

'I know.'

He looked towards Mrs Hartford-Jones, baffled by the girl's manner. The older woman came to them and gently turned her round.

'Come along, Diana. There's nothing you can do here.'

'I'm going back.'

They looked at her in horror. Culpepper opened and closed his mouth twice, then gestured wordlessly at the howling wind.

'That's out of the question,' said Mrs Hartford-Jones, her voice shrill and authoritative. 'You will kindly come with us.'

'No.' She was smiling again. 'I think you could be right. Lincoln might be down on the beach somewhere. If he is I'll find him.'

Culpepper was close to panic. Half a tree had just sailed over their heads and careered down the hill. 'Miss Curtis, we have to go. Please don't be difficult.'

'I'm sorry.' She looked genuinely upset, touched his arm and turned and ran down the slope.

'Come back, you stupid girl!' screamed Mrs Hartford-Jones.

But she had gone, the bushes closing behind her in the gloom. Culpepper couldn't really believe it had happened. He looked around helplessly. A deep moan was coming from the ridge above, sending a chill of fear through them. It seemed to vibrate in the ground beneath them, as though the forces of nature were rising up to meet the screaming sky. There was a sizzling flash of lightning that made them all jump, then a clap of thunder that rolled around them with such ferocity that some of the crew instinctively crossed themselves.

'We'd never find her,' shouted Mrs Hartford-Jones.

Culpepper nodded and turned, gesturing towards the ridge. They began to move, hanging on to each other, lashed by the bushes and needle sharp junipers. There was open ground on the ridge itself, giving way to a small depression that was thick with shrubs. As they started into it the full fury of the hurricane came over the high ridges of Belle Vue Mountain with an unearthly shriek of power. Lightning laced the sky and slopes around them, thunder rolled and was swallowed by the wind that was reaching a hundred and fifty miles an hour once it was free of the mountain. Bushes and trees, rocks and pebbles, a ten foot section of corrugated iron that had once been the roof of somebody's house, sailed past them in the howling gloom.

Somehow they struggled through the brush to the comparitive calm of the rocky cliff and staggered into the cave, collapsing on the sandy floor, shaking with fear at the cataclysmic forces they had witnessed.

Diana ran through a nightmare world of trees bending down to whip the earth around her. Rocks the size of cannonballs curved lazily through the air to explode into fragments against the trunks of trees. She had no real comprehension of the forces around her and consequently no fear for her own safety. She was concerned only with getting down the hillside to the beach, convinced that once she was there she would find Slade and everything else would be all right.

Within minutes of leaving the crew she was hopelessly lost, but as long as the slope went down she didn't care. Twice she lost her footing, falling and sliding until she was stopped by bushes. Junipers lashed her arms and face, opening a dozen cuts so that blood mingled with the rain that was now falling in razor-sharp sheets. At one point she ran out onto a ridge and the wind picked her up and whirled her out over the slope, hurling her into a clump of wild pineapple which broke her fall, depositing her on the other side with the scream still rising in her throat.

Although it had taken them half an hour to climb to the ridge, it took her only five minutes to slide and stumble down through the trees to the beach. She came out much further up the bay with Beef Island a hazy outline in the distance. Sand was being sucked from the beach in whirling spirals and the sea was a seething white cauldron as the wind howled across the surface producing strange writhing columns of water that danced over the waves before disintegrating into the atmosphere.

She clung to the trunk of a palm tree that was leaning out from a bank, finding a meagre shelter there as she took in the horrifying scene. Even as she felt the surge of terror a tree whirled end over end from the hillside above and smashed into the beach, shattering with the impact. The wind screamed and collected the pieces, flinging them out towards the sea.

With a choking cry of despair Diana realized that finding any one or any thing was hopeless. Any clues the beach might have held had long since been wiped clean by the wind, and when she looked at the bay her heart froze. Nothing could survive in that. Not even Lincoln Slade.

Boulders were beginning to crash down the hillside, one of them bouncing out over her head and thumping into the sand. She knew that she had to find a better shelter and began to work her way along the shoreline. Palm trees, bent almost double, provided a precarious series of holds and she staggered from one to the other, her brain numb with fear. The deafening shriek of the wind and the deep, vibrating rolls of thunder that seemed to shake the earth itself, gradually deadened her senses so that she moved by instinct rather than desire. She finally reached a break in the line of palms and saw beyond it a jumble of boulders.

Taking a deep breath she lunged across the open beach towards them, but the moment the full ferocity of the wind caught hold of her she knew she was lost. It picked her up bodily, whirling her round with flailing arms, then hurled her at the sand. All strength went from her and she rolled loosely, choking on sand, feeling herself tumbling over and over towards the sea. She was half-way across the beach, a bundle of arms and legs, when Panacero saw her from the rocks where they were sheltering. He ran with the wind, leaning back against it, missing her twice before he was able to grab her round the waist and press her down into the sand.

She gazed at him with bewildered eyes, barely conscious. There was no way they could speak, so he wrapped one arm around her waist and with the other began to claw at the sand, pulling them forward. She understood and weakly followed suit, the sand biting into their faces so that they were forced to shut their eyes and crawl blindly towards the rocks.

It took all their last reserves of strength to reach them,

but at the last moment McVay was waiting beside a huge boulder to pull them into shelter. Diana lay for a while, gasping and coughing, finally lifting her head and weakly mouthing one word. The engineer smiled and pointed towards a cluster of rocks that made a natural windbreak beside the boulder. Slade lay there, pale and unconscious, but clearly alive. She crawled towards him, felt his hand and touched his face, looked at the bloody wound the two men had bound with a shirt in an attempt to stop the bleeding, then with a sigh of relief lay down beside him.

The hurricane rolled down from the hillside for the best part of two hours, buffeting them with ferocious fury as though enraged by their ability to survive. They huddled around Slade, arms wrapped around their faces, unable to speak or move. The heat of the wind, flailing them relentlessly with sand and pebbles, dried out their mouths and throats until their lips cracked and bled. The lightning and thunder passed, moving on out to sea, and then the purple gloom became a dull red glow which in turn gave way to a pale yellow light as the howl of the wind subsided. Suddenly there was silence and blue sky overhead.

'We must move now,' Panacero told them. 'We are at the centre of the hurricane. When it starts again the wind will change and drive the sea across this beach.'

'But how can we?' Diana asked, looking helplessly at Slade.

'Mr McVay, if you will get two branches we can make a litter.'

The chief engineer nodded, getting to his feet. The beach was littered with everything from a fully grown palm tree to saplings by the score. He quickly found two of equal length and brought them back to the rocks. Diana went to the water's edge where the sea still seethed from the wind, and took off her shirt to soak it. When she returned to bathe Slade's burning face with the wet shirt, Panacero had removed both the captain's trousers and his own. He gave her an apologetic look and began to slide the saplings into the legs of the trousers, one pair over each end so that the waists met in the middle.

'That's very clever,' said Diana. 'It makes a perfect stretcher.'

McVay returned with some lengths of vine to lash across the poles and gazed at them both, chuckling. 'A fine pair, I must say. One in his underpants and the other in her . . .' He began to cackle again.

Diana finished bathing Slade's face and stood up, putting her shirt back on. 'It's not exactly unusual in these parts is it?' she enquired coolly. 'I gather the women don't bother to dress above the waist.' She paused, looking pointedly at the engineer's singed head. 'On the other hand, you look distinctly odd, Mr McVay.'

He glared at her, his cheeks reddening. 'That's a hell of a thing to say, Miss. A hell of a bloody thing!'

She beamed at him, buttoning her shirt. 'Then don't get personal.'

Slade recovered consciousness as they lifted him onto the stretcher, his eyes focusing on McVay who was holding his shoulders. 'What the hell are you trying to do now, McVay? I told you the ship is sinking.'

'It sunk hours ago you stupid bastard!'

He raised his head and saw Diana. 'What are you doing here?'

'Questions, always questions!' snapped McVay. 'If you must know we're going to carry you to higher ground. If you don't like it just say the word and we'll toss you back into the bloody sea!'

Slade lay back, his eyes closing as he murmured: 'I might have known, McVay. Pissed as usual!'

As they began to climb up the hill from the beach the sky turned blue and the sun came out. Panacero saw Diana's relieved expression and shook his head grimly. 'It won't last long. Five, maybe ten minutes, then it begins to get bad.'

The rain had made the slopes treacherous and their progress was frequently blocked by fallen trees. The clear blue sky quickly turned a dull copper and the wind began to whisper through the trees, coming from the north now as the opposite side of the revolving storm began to reach them. Diana moved ahead, pulling bushes aside and helping McVay over the most difficult stretches. The ridge they were making for seemed hopelessly far away and when the hurricane began to howl they were no more than fifty feet above the beach.

They struggled through a twilight world, each tree ahead their next goal, but at least this time the wind was behind and as it grew to its full fury they were being blown uphill. They found a ridge dominated by a massive Banyan tree, the roots of which grew down from its branches to form a natural barrier, and gratefully crawled into its shelter. In the bay below the waves were rising up into grey mountains that moved forward until there was no longer a beach, only a boiling sea that crashed against the hillside. The rain came again, lashing the slopes to produce a thousand cascades which quenched their thirsts but then threatened to wash them down to the sea.

When the hurricane finally passed it did so with an abruptness that was almost as unreal as the storm itself. One moment the elements raged like demented demons, the next there was a total stillness and the gloom gave way to a brilliant light as though a curtain had been drawn. In seconds the sky to the west was blue with a hot afternoon sun beating down upon them. They crawled out from beneath the tree, gazing in awe at the majestic wall of cloud that rose from the sea to tower above, twisting and writhing as though some gigantic cauldron was boiling within.

Slade was still unconscious, his breathing shallow and uneven. Diana felt a spasm of fear as she bathed his face with fresh water, alarmed at the hot dryness of his skin and depth of his coma. Panacero checked his pulse with grim features, then looked up the hill which was still running with water from the rain.

'I think we must find the others,' he announced. 'The

captain needs that wound dressed and they will have the medical kit.'

'I think it's that top ridge,' Diana told him, gazing up the ravaged hillside with worried eyes. 'But they don't know we're here. They might go on.'

'Then let's make a start.' McVay paused, patting her arm gently. 'Don't you worry, lass, we'll manage something.'

They began to traverse the hillside, moving steadily in spite of the treacherous conditions. The heat of the sun was bringing veils of mist off the saturated ground, the still air allowing it to form layers that hung before them, like cotton wool islands suspended on invisible threads. Even if someone above had tried to look down towards them they would have been completely hidden by the mist. Diana helped with one of the poles, the fear an icy lump in her throat as she watched Slade's waxen face roll from side to side.

They climbed over the edge of the ridge to find the rocky cliff extending away on either side. They were wondering which way to go when there was a shout and Felipe came running through the mist, his wizened features wreathed with smiles. His whoops of delight quickly brought the others, gathering around them with beaming faces. Culpepper arrived, his disbelief giving way to humility as he sank on his knees beside the captain and clasped his hands in prayer. They stood in respectful silence until Mrs Hartford-Jones pushed her way through the crowd, hugged Diana with tears in her eyes, then quickly set to work on Slade.

'I need a fire, hot water, the cleanest shirt you can get. When it's been boiled, tear it into strips and hang it up to dry.' She glared at McVay whilst men ran to carry out her instructions. 'I suppose your filthy hands have been all over the poor man.'

'Madam,' said McVay, 'it was our filthy hands that got him this far.'

'It's a miracle,' said Culpepper, raising his head. 'Only God could have brought you back.'

McVay looked as though he would have liked to argue the point but Torres asked about the *Tinkerbelle*, reminding them all so that their smiles vanished.

McVay sighed and shook his head. 'Gone, laddies. Gone for ever.'

Although many of them had expected as much the news was still hard to bear. Some sat around in dejected groups, others went to the edge of the ridge, gazing down at the bay as though half hoping that somehow it would be there. They were all conscious that something had ended, not just the ship and all it had meant to them, but a way of life that would never return. After a while they began to talk, quietly at first, about the way it had been. And as the stories refreshed their memories, so the laughter lifted their spirits.

Diana hovered over Slade, doing what she could, until Mrs Hartford-Jones lost her patience and told her to go into the cave. She went instead and sat beneath a tree where the warmth of the sun finally overcame the tensions and fear so that she drifted off to sleep.

Culpepper assembled the crew at three o'clock and told them that he was going to Roadtown, the only settlement on the island some three miles along the coast. Although he planned to return with food and what medical supplies he could obtain, the rest of the crew might just as well stay in Roadtown. McVay, Panacero and Pasqual offered to remain at the camp to help look after the captain, although since Mrs Hartford-Jones had moved him into the cave no one had been allowed anywhere near him.

Culpepper agreed, with some relief, and set off immediately with the rest of the crew along the ridge that would eventually curve around Mount Belle-Vue and drop down to the cotton fields that surrounded the small town. McVay and Panacero stretched out beneath the trees on ground already dry and wondered, pessimistically, if Culpepper would be considerate enough to bring back a jug or two of rum.

When Diana awoke the sun was falling behind the hills and the air was beginning to cool. She hurried into the cave where Mrs Hartford-Jones sat beside the still figure of Slade. She had dressed the wound, which had begun to bleed again, and the tell-tale stains on the bandage brought a gasp of alarm from the girl.

'There's nothing more we can do until Rodney gets back,' the older woman told her.

'He looks so weak, and now it's bleeding again . . .?'

'It's a bad wound, but fortunately the shrapnel missed his spleen. He's strong so it should heal quickly enough as long as infection doesn't set in.'

'And if it does?' Diana asked with huge eyes.

'I'm hoping that Rodney will be able to get sulphonamide tablets in Roadtown. He said there was a missionary who usually has a supply of medicine.'

'You mean he could die, don't you?'

'Diana, we can all die,' she said irritably. 'It so happens that Captain Slade is one of a breed of men who tend to ignore that fact. I suppose that gives him a better chance than most.'

It was about all the comfort she was able to give and after telling her what to do she left the cave which was now almost in darkness. Diana sat and listened to his shallow breathing, periodically wiping the perspiration from his face, and prayed that he would not develop a fever. Some hours later Culpepper returned with food and little else. The hurricane had wreaked havoc on Roadtown, flattening most of the buildings that tended to be thrown together beneath corrugated iron roofs. Only the old stone and adobe buildings around the harbour had survived, although even these had been extensively damaged. The missionary, an elderly English minister, had been busy treating a dozen injured islanders and his meagre supply of sulphonamide was only sufficient to treat a pregnant woman with a badly gashed arm and a man whose leg he had just amputated.

'The place is a shambles,' said Culpepper. 'I left the crew

pitching in to help the locals. Half of them are still in a state of shock. At least five people died.'

'Can we get supplies from another island?' Diana asked.

'Not until the ferry arrives from Puerto Rico, and nobody seems to know when that's likely to be.'

She nodded, biting her lip. Mrs Hartford-Jones bustled round the fire putting pieces of chicken and vegetables in a pot. McVay and Panacero helped, looking hopefully at the pack the first officer had brought. He watched them, fully aware of the reason for their interest.

'You'll find it at the bottom, underneath the flour and salt,' he said finally as McVay was beginning to give him disgusted looks. 'One jug.'

'Och, you're a fine man, Mister Culpepper,' the Scotsman said happily, retrieving the bottle.

Culpepper had news of the marauder. One of the islanders had seen it anchored in Trellis Bay, about a mile beyond Road Harbour, although at the time he had assumed it was a freighter sheltering from the storm. The coral reefs that protected the bay must have blunted the worst effects of the hurricane for when he saw the ship it was already preparing to leave.

'And good riddance too,' said Mrs Hartford-Jones, turning from the fire. 'Let's hope it keeps on going.'

By the time they had eaten there was a chill in the air and they gathered closer to the fire. Culpepper had brought a roll of blankets and they sat with them around their shoulders, reflecting on the day. Diana returned to Slade, enabling Culpepper to ask Mrs Hartford-Jones for a more realistic report on the captain's condition.

'If he regains consciousness and gets through the night, then he'll manage tomorrow.'

'You're a pessimistic soul, aren't you?' said McVay, his cheeks flushed happily from the jug he was sharing with Pasqual and Panacero. 'I suppose if he gets through tomorrow he just might manage the day after.'

She glared at him across the fire. 'You saw that

wound, Mr McVay. Most men would be dead already.'

'Aye, but the cap'n isn't most men. I'd say he'll be up and about in a week.'

'Then I'd say you're a fool!' she snapped. 'If infection sets in he's got no defences left.'

McVay rose to his feet and swayed unsteadily so that Panacero and Pasqual reached anxiously for the rum. He waved the jug at her, an incongruous figure with his half bald head and tattered clothes. 'You'll not bury Lincoln Slade here tonight, or tomorrow, or this week, and I'll not sit by and listen to you do it!'

With that he tottered off into the darkness from where there shortly came a satisfying gurgle. Panacero and Pasqual exchanged looks and slipped away towards the sound.

Culpepper considered her anxiously. 'Do you really think the Captain isn't going to recover?'

She looked into the fire as though expecting to find the answer there. After a moment she sighed and shook her head. 'No. Mr McVay is probably right. He's got the kind of will that fights off anything.'

He smiled and took her hand. 'With your help, Helen. Heaven knows what we'd have done without you.'

The words dissolved the lines of weariness and she leaned against him, squeezing his hand. 'Nonsense,' she said warmly. 'I haven't done much at all. Without your strength I couldn't have done even that.'

They sat and fed their dreams into the fire, watching them grow.

23

The sea was crimson, the sky a purple dome, and he was alone in a boat that was curiously transparent so that he could see far down into the burning depths. There were people everywhere; old men and young women, children with enormous eyes and gaping mouths, people he knew from a long time ago and everyone was screaming and yet there was no sound. He was standing alone in the bow of his crystal boat, watching them flounder in the foaming red sea, pushing the successful ones back so that they sank slowly beneath him with horrified eyes.

Beyond the ocean of people was the *Titanic*, rolling onto its side like some enormous black whale. A wound gaped open along its hull, spouting water and people and great columns of steam. He watched it with a curious sense of wonder, as though nothing that big was capable of sinking. And as it slipped beneath the crimson waves the sea of people began surging towards it, twisting around and around each other until they were all part of a vast whirlpool that sucked them into the depths as though they were attached to the ship by invisible umbilical cords.

He was able to watch them going down and down beneath him, their mouths frozen in silent screams, their accusing eyes locked on his until they became tiny pupils of light. He began to weep, calling after them, searching desperately for one last face. But he was alone in the sea. There was no one left.

The nightmare continued for hours and there was little that Diana could do except bathe his chest and face with damp cloths, holding him down when he writhed and moaned in anguish, soothing him when he cried out words she did not understand. But as the night wore on she began to understand the man, if not the events that tormented him.

At first it seemed to be no more than a feverish nightmare which related to the sinking of the *Tinkerbelle*, but gradually she realized that this was some other ship. At times he seemed to be telling people to get into boats, at other times telling them to keep away. There were clearly many people and somehow Slade was responsible for them. His agony was so real that it was as though she was there with him, hearing the pleas for help and Slade's repeated refusal. His anguish was in being unable to help and frequently he begged them to understand that there was nothing he could do.

Shortly after dawn, during a particularly tormented period, he opened his eyes and stared at her with contorted features. 'I can't take you,' he whispered. 'I just can't take any more.'

'I know,' she said gently. 'I understand.'

'You do?'

'Yes, of course. We all understand.'

His eyes closed and he went immediately to sleep, his breathing deep and even for the first time. She covered him with a blanket and turned to find McVay standing watching her. He smiled apologetically, his face gaunt in the grey light, and held out a mug that steamed and smelled of coffee. She took it gratefully.

'I'm thinking it's time you got some sleep, lassie,' he said gently.

She sipped the coffee, feeling the exhaustion rising in her like layers of cotton wool. 'I think I will. He should sleep now.'

'Thanks to you.'

She shook her head. 'There wasn't much I could do.'

'I just watched you do it. No one could have handled it better.' He considered her for a moment, his eyes curious. 'The captain's more of a man's man than a woman's.'

She flushed. 'Yes, Mr McVay, I had reached that conclusion.'

'You saw a side of him tonight that not many people know about.'

'Yes. All those terrible memories.' She hesitated, then asked him bluntly. 'Do you know?'

The engineer nodded, looking sadly at the sleeping captain. 'Aye, though he'd not thank me for telling you. It was a long time ago, 1912 to be precise. He was a junior officer, only a lad really on his first commission. He was in charge of a boat station on the night the ship went down. He watched more people drown than anyone before or since.'

'What ship?' she whispered.

'The biggest of them all,' he replied. 'The SS *Titanic*.'

After he had left she lay down beside Slade and gazed at him in the dim light. He was calm now, sleeping peacefully, and his skin was cool. For the first time she felt close to him, able to understand how he must have felt when he saw the marauder's victims. She fell asleep wondering what he would have been like without either of those experiences.

Mrs Hartford-Jones took over later in the morning, ordering the younger woman out of the cave with characteristic asperity whilst she changed the dressing. The wound was heavy with pus and an angry red around the edges, the purple bruising going up around the rib cage with enough swelling to convince her that further infection could be developing in the peritoneum.

She washed it with hot water and antiseptic, wishing there was more that she could do. She was binding it with clean strips of cloth when Slade opened his eyes. They were bright, feverish, focusing on her with difficulty.

'I had a feeling there was a barracuda about,' he said in a voice so weak it was barely more than a whisper.

'Let's not get personal, Captain.'

'You're getting pretty personal with me. What the hell are you using down there? Broken glass!'

'I'm doing the best I can.'

His eyes wandered away and for a moment she thought he was going to lose consciousness again, but he forced them back, somehow managing a crooked grin.

'You're a cold one, Mrs Hartford-Bloody-Jones. You've got hands like ice and a mouth like a steel trap.'

'I need them with a man like you around, Captain. Ice cold steel is about all you understand.'

He glared at her. 'You've got shitty eyes too!'

'That's through looking at you for too long!'

His head rolled and he made a monumental effort to raise it, colour coming back into his pale cheeks as his anger grew. 'I haven't liked you from the start.'

'It was mutual.'

'You're a shrewd old cow, though. I'll give you that. A shrewd old cow.'

'And you, Captain, are an arrogant old bastard with a mouth like a sewer. I wouldn't have you in my privy, let alone my sitting-room!'

His eyes bulged and he tried to lift a threatening hand. 'You're not talking to me like that!'

'Why not? You're on the way out, Captain.'

'Like hell I am!'

'You'll never get through tonight.'

'I'll get through it, Mrs Hartford-Bloody-Jones, make no mistake about that!'

'Balls!'

'What did you say?'

'I said balls, Captain!'

He glared at her, his face tight with fury. 'Listen to me you insufferable cow, I'll be here tomorrow. I'll be on my Goddamn feet tomorrow!'

'We shall see!' she snapped.

She left him staring furiously at the roof of the cave, pausing outside to wipe the tears from her eyes. She had hated doing it, but at least there was now some adrenalin in his veins. Perhaps enough to give him the strength he needed.

During the afternoon Torres arrived from Roadtown with fresh supplies and news that the island ferry was due in three days. It was on its inner run and could take them as far as Guadeloupe from where they could take a ship to Caracas. The news cheered them all, although it presented Culpepper with a dilemma. If Slade could not be moved in time to catch the ferry it would mean at least two more weeks on the island.

After a meal of fish cooked by Pasqual and Torres he walked along the ridge with Mrs Hartford-Jones, waiting until they were some distance from the camp before broaching the question. She considered it gravely, filled with doubt.

'I just don't know, Rodney. The infection looks worse, but it could change in a matter of hours.'

'But if we carried him down to Roadtown there would be more help, and if things got worse we could get him onto the ferry?'

'Moving him now could be fatal.'

'So you think we should wait?'

She nodded. 'The infection will either clear up or get worse. If it gets worse I think it will all be over before the ferry gets here.'

Culpepper looked shocked. 'So quickly?'

'The wound is too close to many vital organs. Even with sulphonamide it would be difficult, without it I fear he will have no chance.'

Culpepper gazed out across the darkening hillside to a sea turning to indigo as the sun set behind them. 'I can't believe he'll die,' he said. 'It just doesn't seem possible.'

'I know,' she agreed, then shivered although the air was still warm. 'But I have such an awful premonition.'

Slade's temperature began to rise again during the evening until, by midnight, he was in the grip of a raging fever. The two women bathed and nursed him, trickling fresh lime juice into his mouth, wrapping him in blankets when the shivers came. In his delirium he raved about the German marauder, the deaths of Jimmy and Susan Hardcastle, and at one point about Mrs Hartford-*Bloody*-Jones.

'I'll see you in the morning, you bitch,' he snarled, his eyes staring blindly past them. 'I'll be here.'

'What on earth does he mean?' Diana asked.

The older woman smiled wearily, changing the damp cloth on his forehead. 'It doesn't matter. Just as long as he does mean it.'

The fever left him shortly before dawn and they covered him with blankets, not sure whether he had fallen into a deep sleep or that coma which precedes death. Diana sat beside him with eyes hollowed by fear and exhaustion until Culpepper took her place and insisted that she get some sleep.

She went out and lay down beside Mrs Hartford-Jones in the lean-to they had erected, wrapping herself in a blanket and watching the dark blue sky grow golden in the east. When she finally slept the birds were already singing on the hillside and it was only total exhaustion that closed her ears to the medley of sound. Even the smell of cooking later in the morning failed to wake the women and as the sun moved high in the sky McVay and Panacero stretched blankets on poles to afford them better shade.

Culpepper was dozing beside Slade when the captain spoke and at first he thought he was delirious.

'A large gin with ice and angosturas, Mister Culpepper,' he said in a husky voice. 'And when you've managed that I'll have another.'

'We have no gin, Captain,' Culpepper replied wearily, noting with rising excitement that his eyes were clear. 'The best I can do is lime juice.'

'Shit!' said Slade. 'I might have known.'

'Do you know where you are?' he asked cautiously.

'Well of course I bloody-well know.'

'And you feel alright?'

'I feel like a drink, Culpepper, and if you don't do something about it I'll just have to get myself down to Road-town.'

Culpepper grinned with delight. 'You really are better.'

Slade glared at him. He quickly poured a cup of water and squeezed two limes into it, lifting his head and pouring it between his cracked lips. The captain grimaced with disgust, but drank it all down.

'We'll get some chicken broth heated up and there's fresh fruit. You just rest.'

'Never mind the bloody chicken,' replied Slade, his voice already stronger. 'Just get me a drink. That's a booze-type drink, Culpepper. Not one of your teetotal lemon and limes.'

'We'll find something,' the first officer said cheerfully and hurried from the cave.

Slade lay back, closing his eyes, feeling as though he had picked up a dozen lead weights during the night and the heaviest were on his eyelids. When he tried to move pain lanced around his side, but his head was clear and he was already regretting cancelling the chicken. There were foot-steps and he opened his eyes, focusing on the grinning faces of McVay, Panacero and Torres. They were looking at him as though he had just won first prize in a fancy dress ball.

'What the hell are you staring at?' he snapped.

McVay chuckled. 'Sounds like you're better, Cap'n.'

'Jesus, McVay!' he exclaimed as the engineer leaned for-ward. 'You look like a drunken commanche!'

'It'll grow,' he said sharply, his face reddening. 'And making insulting remarks won't make it grow any faster.'

Slade started to laugh and winced. McVay glanced back towards the mouth of the cave, then nodded to Torres who produced a jug of rum. They poured some into the cup and added a little water.

'We thought you might be feeling a wee bit fragile,' said McVay, lifting his head so that he could drink.

The rum sent waves of warmth through him and he closed his eyes, enjoying the sensations. The strong spirit took the weights off his limbs and made him feel pleasantly drowsy. He must have slept because the next time he opened his eyes they had gone and Diana was beside him, looking incredibly beautiful.

'God, but you're beautiful,' he said, intending the words to be mocking. Instead they came out with a sincerity that put high spots of colour in her cheeks. She bent and kissed him and he felt the wetness of tears.

'Don't ever frighten me like that again,' she said in a choking voice.

Her emotion embarrassed him. 'Hell I wasn't that bad.'

'You had Helen convinced.'

He grimaced at the thought. 'Wishful thinking.'

'She did more than anyone.'

'Yeah?' he glowered. 'That's really made my day.'

'I can see you're getting back to normal, Captain,' said Mrs Hartford-Jones, moving into view with a bowl of soup and a spoon. 'But then we can't have everything.'

She sat on the floor and whilst Diana lifted his head thrust a spoonful of soup at him. He swallowed it grudgingly, trying not to let the woman's manner irritate him. She behaved like a rather strict maiden aunt saddled with a precocious nephew.

'I gather you've been in charge of the nursing?'

'It helped to pass the time,' she replied crisply, poising another spoonful an inch from his nose. 'Even if you were rather trying.'

He gave her a crooked grin. 'You're lucky I couldn't talk.'

'You did little else, Captain.' She beamed at his discomfort. 'But I made a point of not listening.'

'Well I'm grateful,' he muttered.

'Pardon? I didn't quite hear?'

'I said I'm grateful!'

'Splendid. Now prove it by eating your soup nicely instead of making a face after every mouthful. Mr McVay cooked it specially.'

'McVay!' He shuddered. 'No wonder it tastes of diesel.'

She insisted that he finish the soup, then removed the bandages around his waist and examined the wound, clucking and nodding with a pleased expression. She put on a clean dressing, taping it lightly instead of using a bandage, and told him firmly to get more sleep.

'I've been doing nothing else,' he told her argumentatively.

'Suit yourself, Captain.' She rose to her feet. 'I was going to suggest that a small measure of rum might help.'

'I'll have that anyway.'

She gazed at him with eyes like cut glass. 'You're in no position to give orders, Captain. Kindly remember that.'

She left him grinding his teeth in fury. Diana, hiding her amusement, tucked the blanket around him and kissed him before getting to her feet.

'You deserve everything you get from Mrs Hartford-Bloody-Jones, as you were calling her. And if you'd seen her here last night you'd feel thoroughly ashamed of yourself.'

'She's still a barracuda,' he declared emphatically.

He slept for most of the day and in the evening ate his first solid meal of fish and fresh fruit. Culpepper and McVay spent half an hour with him before being ejected by Mrs Hartford-Jones, but they had time to tell him about the hurricane and the marauder. Although it had not been seen since, the shipping frequency was now carrying regular broadcasts warning everyone to be on the lookout for the German vessel. Culpepper believed that it could well have left the Caribbean to hunt in the Atlantic, but Slade disagreed. The *Tamerande* would be holed up somewhere carrying out repairs, then she would begin to kill again.

The following day he was able to walk, with the help of Culpepper and McVay, out onto the hillside. The sun was warm and he felt better by the hour, eating everything that Diana placed before him. During the afternoon the entire crew arrived from Roadtown, standing around with unaccustomed diffidence and repeatedly asking how he felt.

Felipe and Pasqual began to excavate a large barbecue pit and a surprising number of chickens began to appear from the sacks the men had brought with them.

'What's the celebration?' he asked McVay who had paused from supervising the construction of the chair they would use to carry him down to the coast the next day.

The engineer gave him a disgusted look. 'Have you forgotten what day it is, Cap'n?'

With something of a shock he realized that it was Christmas Eve. Diana explained later that, as they had to be in Roadtown tomorrow for the ferry, the crew had decided to have a party that night.

It began as darkness fell with chickens sizzling over the glowing pit and jugs of rum being passed from man to man. Pasqual had managed to find a bottle of gin in the town and this was presented to Slade on behalf of the crew. After the meal the serious business of drinking began and in spite of Culpepper's plea for moderation, the hills were soon alive with the sound of drunken singing.

Mrs Hartford-Jones sat in the shadows with Culpepper, apparently deaf to some of the more ribald verses. McVay managed to outdrink everyone else and went crashing off down the hillside howling Scottish war cries. He was not seen again until the following day when his white face and bloodshot eyes prompted Slade to suggest that he should be the one they carried down to Roadtown.

But long before the party reached its maudlin climax, when tearful toasts were drunk to the memory of the *Tinkerbelle*, Slade had been helped back to his bed in the cave. Diana refused to return to the party and he was still arguing with her when sleep came and ended his protests.

He awoke in that still hour that precedes dawn to find Diana asleep beside him and he lay watching her for a while, wondering at the way their lives had become enmeshed. She with all the optimism and romanticism of youth, he with all the cynicism and reality of age. The gulf between them was formidable and yet love, that mad alchemist, gave no heed to time or space or logic. The chemistry that worked between them was not bound by physical laws, it was the stuff of dreams.

Somehow she became aware of his gaze and her eyes opened, glowing with an inner light as she saw him. She smiled and gently touched his cheek, saying nothing.

'Go to sleep,' he told her gruffly.

'I am asleep,' she said. 'I'm dreaming that you're well and thinking about me.'

'You're delirious.'

'Yes.' She smiled and kissed him. 'So you're going to have to get well and do something about it.'

'It's ridiculous. It's just too bloody ridiculous.'

'It had to happen sooner or later.'

He glared at her. 'Do you know how old I am?'

'I don't care. I've worked it all out. Ten years with you is worth forty with anyone else.'

'Jesus, is that all I've got left!'

She laughed triumphantly. 'There. You see.'

'No I don't bloody-well see. What am I going to do when I get on my feet? Pick cotton? Plant tea?'

'Why not? You'd probably make a fortune.'

'You really think you've got the answers, don't you?'

She nodded and kissed him again. 'I love you, Lincoln Slade. In spite of your bad temper and nasty habits I love you and if you don't agree to marry me I'll tell the minister in Roadtown and the chief of police, or whatever it is they have there, that you had your evil way with me when I was a prisoner on your ship.'

'You rotten cow!'

The laughter gurgled in her throat and she nodded, unashamed. 'Take it or leave it, Captain.'

He gave her a baffled look. 'You're a hell of a difficult woman, Miss Curtis.'

'And you're a hell of a difficult man.'

Later, as she slept nestled in the crook of his arm, he stared into the darkness and tried to consider dispassionately the tantalising future she offered. It was more than he deserved, probably more than he could handle, and it would be easy to give way to images that ignored the harsh reality of life. There would come a time, he knew, when passion died and she would look into a distant sunset, dreaming dreams that did not include him.

He fell asleep wondering if he had the courage to face that day.

24

Whilst the crew of the *Tinkerbelle* were taking turns carrying Slade across the hills to Roadtown, the crew of the *Tamerande* were sitting down to a Christmas dinner of turkey stuffed with spicy sausage meat and the best selection of tinned vegetables the cooks could muster. Every man had two bottles of beer and a packet of cigarettes, a streamer that could only be thrown after they had drunk the health of the Fuhrer, and a personal message from the captain. Spirits were high for the maintenance crew had completed repairs to the hull the previous evening and the new plates had been given a coat of paint that morning. A new name had also been painted on the stern and bow so that the ship that swung gently at anchor behind the reef that sheltered Mosquito Island was now the *Azora*.

After dinner with the crew on the main mess deck, Captain Kroehner retired to the wardroom with the senior officers. After drinking the health of Grand Admiral Raeder the captain moved to a chart of the Virgin Islands and indicated the cluster of islands extending towards Puerto Rico.

'This will be our hunting ground for the next week, gentlemen. Freighters carrying sugar from the Windward Islands, rubber from Venezuela, cocoa and coffee from Colombia, they will all come this way heading for the Mona Passage into the Atlantic. Our task is to stop this traffic, to disrupt shipping in the area before we move on to the West Indies. There will be no more secrecy. We will now strike at every opportunity until the British are forced to send escort vessels to the Caribbean.'

'Do we exclude any flags, sir?' asked the chief gunnery officer.

Kroehner shook his head. 'None. Our intelligence people report that food and strategic materials are being shipped by all available means from the Caribbean to the Bahamas where they are transferred to British Merchant Navy vessels. From now on every ship we meet is a target. We are the wolf, gentlemen, as our executive officer will testify,' he paused for the laughter at his reference to Tellmann's christian name, then continued with grim emphasis. 'From now on we kill and keep on killing until the sheep no longer graze on these waters.'

When he sat down Wolf Tellmann rose to inform them that they would sail at midnight, heading out through Gorda Sound to put them south of Tortola by dawn.

'I expect our first kill to be the *Island Queen*, it is the only vessel that regularly calls at these islands and apart from the blow to morale its loss would cause, it is bound to be carrying supplies of fresh food.' He paused, smiling bleakly. 'Considering the amount consumed by the ship's company today we can hardly afford to let it pass!'

There was a burst of laughter and the gunnery officer rose, holding up his glass. 'Gentlemen. I give you the *Island Queen.*'

25

The *Island Queen* was a converted cargo carrier of some three thousand tonnes which eked out a precarious existence transporting people and produce among the crescent-shaped cluster of islands that made up the Lesser Antilles. Once a month, beginning at Puerto Rico, it made its way down to Trinidad carrying anything from a prize bull to an early crop of melons.

It was an ungainly vessel, sitting low in the water with a squat bridge and two tall, thin funnels that belched smoke from its wood-burning boiler. The after deck had been cut away so that up to four vehicles could descend a ramp into the long hold. There were two cabins beneath the bridge, but they were usually so hot and stuffy that only the most inexperienced passenger ever bothered to pay the extra fare. In the forecastle there was a small room with wooden benches and beyond it a tattered awning that provided minimal shade over further wooden seats.

The crew of ten came from Trinidad, where the ship was based, but the captain, Andre Rochelle, was French and had been born on Guadeloupe. He knew Slade well having met him on numerous occasions over the years and showed touching concern when he arrived on the quay in a bamboo litter carried by members of his crew. Rochelle immediately offered one of the cabins, grinning broadly when Slade told him what he could do with it. They settled for the only reclining deckchair on board and exclusive use of the forecastle saloon.

Slade insisted on walking up the gangway, surprising even himself by the ease with which he negotiated it.

Although he was still unsteady on his feet, his strength was returning rapidly and he felt that another week would see him back to normal. This had also been the view of the missionary, the Reverend Moreton, when they called at his mission on the way into Roadtown.

He was a small, cherubic man with a contented smile and the kind of patience that could accept the considerable damage to his mission as a minor setback which would soon be overcome. He served soft drinks and fresh fruit on the lawn in front of his bungalow, never once referring to the fact that half the roof was strewn across it. His wife was on a visit to a mission in Venezuela, but he assured Diana and Mrs Hartford-Jones that she would never forgive him if he failed to provide them with dresses and underclothes. After taking them into the house he led Slade to the clinic, a long stone building that had once been used for drying tobacco.

A dozen islanders occupied every bed in the ward, two of them still in comas. Others were making the best of broken legs or, in the case of one young man, no leg at all. The surgery was small, hot and smelled of antiseptic. Moreton helped Slade onto a couch and removed the dressing, shaking his head and clucking like a hen when he saw the extent of the wound.

'You're a lucky man, Captain. You must be closer to God than I thought.'

Slade grinned. 'Maybe he's got something special in mind for me.'

Moreton's eyes twinkled and he bobbed his head. 'Quite possibly, Captain. Quite possibly. We can certainly discount your recovery as being any kind of reward for past blessings.'

He cleaned the wound and painted it with iodine, then taped a clean dressing over it. Slade thanked him and sat up, putting on his shirt.

'You'll pass me fit to travel, then?'

'Only as far as Guadeloupe.' He gazed at him sternly. 'As

soon as you reach it you must go to see Father Giraud who has a mission there. I rather imagine he'll put you to bed for a few more days.'

'I'll consider it.'

'You'd be foolish not to, Captain. If that wound were to open you might not be so lucky the next time.'

As they walked slowly back to the lawn Slade asked about the marauder. The missionary pulled a face and shook his head. There had been no word of it for four days and they were all praying that it had left the Caribbean for good.

'It was last seen heading for Gorda Sound you know,' he added. 'That could mean it was going out into the Atlantic.'

'Or anchoring off one of those uninhabited islands.'

'I hope not,' he said fervently, then gave him a critical look. 'You'd do well to feel the same.'

Slade made a non-committal shrug, any further discussion being prevented by the approach of Diana who twirled before them in a long skirt and white cotton blouse. She thanked Moreton for the dress and promised to send it back when she reached Caracas, then took Slade's arm and pointed him towards a chair.

'Time for a rest, old man,' she said firmly. 'You have been on your feet for at least ten minutes.'

He started to protest, but changed his mind. His legs were beginning to feel as though the elastic bands were giving out. She sat him down and poured a glass of fresh orange juice, asking what the Reverend Moreton had said about the wound. He told her that it looked as though he would have to spend a few days at Guadeloupe, but the crew would probably head for Venezuela.

'That'll be sad,' she said. 'But I suppose there's nothing else for them to do.'

He nodded, his mouth bitter. The loss of the *Tinkerbelle* was only now becoming a reality. 'Anyone who gave me another ship would need his head examined.'

'Right,' she said, smiling at his scowl. 'In fact he would

probably qualify for automatic admission to the nearest mental institution. So that solves one problem.'

'It does?' he growled.

'It makes you available for social engagements. After Guadeloupe you're coming to see my uncle in Venezuela.'

'What uncle?'

'The one who sent me on the Caribbean cruise. You see, Lincoln Slade, there are quite a lot of things you don't know about me.'

'I was afraid to ask,' he said dryly.

'Uncle Walter is in tea. He has lots and lots of it, plantations everywhere. He sends it to my father in Boston, and he sells it.'

'Jesus! Don't tell me you're one of those rich Yankee daughters?'

She laughed gaily. 'I wasn't going to tell you, but then I remembered that Uncle Walter does send a lot of tea to Boston.'

'You'll be telling me next he started the tea party!'

'No. But he's very fond of me, and he's often threatened to buy his own ship.'

Slade's mouth dropped open. She leaned forward and kissed it, her eyes bright and happy as she rose to her feet. 'I'll get your porters ready, Captain. We don't want to miss that ferry.'

*   *   *

The *Island Queen* sailed out of Road Harbour in the late afternoon of Christmas Day, rounding the reef that sheltered the wide bay and heading west down the Sir Francis Drake Channel before turning south round St John Island. The ferry was only carrying three extra passengers, all Trinidadians who had embarked in Puerto Rico hoping to get home for Christmas. They soon joined the *Tinkerbelle*'s crew in their celebrations and by the time darkness fell they were singing creole songs and smelling happily of rum.

Culpepper and Mrs Hartford-Jones spent an hour with Slade, telling him that they planned to go straight on to Caracas from Guadeloupe. The first officer had decided that the least he could do was to help Helen settle her late husband's affairs, a task which Slade suspected would take him a great deal longer than he imagined.

Later Diana sat on the floor of the forecastle saloon, her head on his lap, content to listen to the creole songs and feel the ship move gently beneath them. The night was still and when the air cooled she rose and found a blanket, wrapping it around him. He was already asleep, his face deeply lined, his sunken cheeks making him look very old. She found herself wondering how long it would be before he always looked this way and was immediately ashamed of the thought. His spirit would never change and it was this that had moulded him, putting the gleam in his eye and the strength in his voice.

Sometime around midnight McVay and Panacero put their heads around the door, grinning stupidly until she told them to go away. She was dozing some time later when the spotlight swept the deck with a dazzling light, holding finally on the bridge. At first she thought it was a passing freighter flashing a welcome, but it stayed on too long and with a shiver of fear she realized that this was no friendly greeting.

'Attention *Island Queen*. You will heave to immediately and wait for our boats. Any attempt to use your radio will result in the immediate destruction of your bridge.'

The words, amplified by loudspeaker, boomed across the water. It was repeated again, the voice carrying an unmistakable German accent, and then to emphasise the instruction twin lines of tracers arced out of the darkness behind the spotlight and passed over the bow. A moment later Captain Rochelle sounded the ship's siren and blew off steam. The ship slowed rapidly, coming to a stop with the spotlight still holding on its bridge.

The *Tinkerbelle* crew lined the rails, their faces slack with disbelief, their brains bemused by alcohol so that many of them were convinced it was really part of some drunken hallucination. But soon they heard the sound of launches and out of the darkness came three boats, each carrying six men in dark grey battle fatigues.

They came on board with cool efficiency, short-handled Schmeissers forcing the men back from the rails. A young officer with clean-cut features and short blond hair snapped out orders in French and then English, telling everyone to stand in the centre of the deck with their hands clasped on their heads. Other men had moved to the bridge and the after cargo hold, returning shortly with the captain and the remaining members of the crew who seemed totally baffled by the development. Only Captain Rochelle seemed to understand the full implications of the Germans' seizure of his vessel and he stood alone in tight-lipped silence as they gathered crew and passengers together.

McVay was dragged shouting and cursing from the galley where he had been happily drinking himself into a stupor. He was followed by Torres and Santiano, both barely able to walk and peering owlishly at the Germans whenever they barked commands. Culpepper and Mrs Hartford-Jones were brought from the cabin they had been occupying, the first officer flushed with embarrassment and still trying surreptitiously to tuck his shirt back into his trousers. Demers sidled up to him, a note of awe in his voice.

'Christ, sir, did they catch you on the job?'

Culpepper glared at him, his cheeks burning. 'Of course not. We were . . . we were just relaxing.'

Demers nodded as though he didn't believe a word and gave Mrs Hartford-Jones a sympathetic look. The smile she gave him would have put Medusa to shame.

Diana awoke Slade when the Germans began to board, her mouth dry with fear as she realized what could happen if they found out who he was. He was in a deep sleep and had to be shaken roughly before he opened his eyes, but even as he began to frame a question he heard the clatter of feet on the deck and the harsh commands in German.

'Slade, don't say anything. We're just two people travelling from Tortola where you were injured in the hurricane.'

He smiled at the urgency in her voice. 'Is that what I think it is?'

She nodded, expecting them to burst in at any moment. 'The marauder. If they find out who you are they'll . . . they'll . . .' She made a helpless gesture, gazing at him beseechingly. 'Promise me you won't lose your temper.'

Later she realized that she had no clear idea of what his reaction would be, only that the last thing she expected him to do was laugh.

'It's beautiful,' he chuckled. 'I couldn't have arranged it better myself.'

He shook with laughter, wincing with pain but not caring. She watched with a bewildered expression, her tension giving way to anger as she saw that he really did find it amusing.

'It's not funny,' she snapped finally.

He nodded and chuckled again. The door behind them burst open and a squat, ugly man with hard eyes was pointing a sub-machine gun at her. She froze, feeling faint.

'Out on the deck, both of you.' He gestured with the gun. 'Do as I say, quickly!'

'Not a chance, Kraut,' drawled Slade.

The German swung the sub-machine gun towards him and cocked it with deliberate menace.

'Oh, please, Linc,' whispered Diana.

'You will stand up,' the German said sharply.

'No can do, Kraut. You'll need a stretcher to get me out of here.'

'It's true,' Diana said quickly. 'He's been hurt. Badly.'

She pulled the blanket off Slade and unfastened his shirt. The German moved closer, his eyes suspicious until he saw the dressing. He began to relax, easing his finger off the trigger.

'The fräulein will go out with the others.'

'She's not a fräulein you Goddamn Kraut!' snarled Slade.

'She's American, and just in case it's slipped your tiny little mind you're not at war with the USA . . . yet!'

'Will you shut up!' she said fiercely. 'I don't care what he calls me.'

'I care. No Kraut bastard·is going to start calling you a Goddamn fräulein!'

'If you say one more word, Linc, I'll . . . I'll hit you!' She showed him a small fist trying to look as though she meant it.

The German was getting nervous, his small eyes moving quickly from one to the other. He gestured with the Schmeisser again, but they ignored him.

'So hit me if it makes you feel any better,' said Slade, his eyes holding hers. 'You know I wouldn't have the strength to stop you.'

'Why are you always such an offensive, stubborn, arrogant . . .' She ran out of words, fuming.

'Bastard,' he supplied.

'Moron,' she snapped.

'You will go out on deck now,' insisted the German, a hint of desperation in his voice. 'If you refuse it will mean trouble.'

'Listen, Kraut, if I could get up on my knees the first thing I'd do would be to stick that popgun right up your teutonic ass!'

Diana was aware that Slade was making far too much of his injury and every time he stared at her there were signals in his eyes. Now that the initial shock of being captured was wearing off she was recognizing a new set of fears. Slade was up to something. From the moment he had opened his eyes and heard German voices there had been a purpose behind every word he had uttered. She gave him a beseeching look. He winked. Before she could express any further objection the barrel of the gun nudged her insistently in the ribs.

'Yes, alright, I'll go,' she said. 'But he can't be moved. Not without a stretcher.'

Slade gave her an approving nod. The German seemed relieved that at least she was willing to comply with his order. They moved to the door where she paused, looking back.

'You just relax, Linc,' she said, a note of warning in her voice. 'I want you to promise me that?'

'You worry too much,' he said laconically. 'I'm not going anywhere.'

She went out of the forecastle saloon to the main deck where everyone was gathered within a circle of guns. The huge bulk of the marauder loomed over them, bumping gently against the hull as mooring lines dropped to the deck. A moment later a rope ladder clattered down towards them and figures began to descend.

Diana moved through the milling group, joining Helen and Culpepper who greeted her with worried looks. She grimaced, nodding towards the saloon. 'He doesn't want them to think he can walk.'

Culpepper's face fell. 'Then he's up to something?'

'He's like a cat who just locked himself in with the mice.'

'What on earth can he do?' snapped Mrs Hartford-Jones. 'Apart from making everything worse for the rest of us!'

'He laughed,' said Diana in an empty voice. 'When he knew who they were he just sat there and laughed.'

The German officer faced them, holding up his hand for silence. 'You will please board our vessel now where you will be escorted to your quarters.' He held up his hand again as a murmur of protest began. 'It is necessary, but as long as you do what you are told no harm will come to any of you.'

'This is piracy,' Captain Rochelle said furiously. 'You have no right to detain my ship or my passengers.'

'The rules of war, Captain,' the German said smoothly. 'This vessel has a strategic value and we therefore intend to sink it. I suggest you comply with my order.'

'And if I don't?' he snapped.

'Then we shall sink you with it.'

The officer turned away and began issuing orders to the

men who had descended from the marauder. They moved off towards the rear cargo hold, returning a few minutes later with boxes of supplies. A winch clattered above and a cargo net descended from the darkness. The Germans began piling the supplies into the net.

'Will they hold us prisoner for long?' Diana asked.

Culpepper shook his head, watching the steady stream of supplies. 'I don't think so. They needed provisions, otherwise they would probably have put a torpedo in us.'

'I don't think I can take any more,' Mrs Hartford-Jones said suddenly. 'I thought we were going home and now it's all starting again.'

'It'll be alright,' Culpepper promised, taking her hand. 'They won't want us in their hair for very long.'

The German officer began to push through the crowd, his eyes on Culpepper. Mrs Hartford-Jones shuddered, clutching at him.

'You mustn't tell him who you are.'

Culpepper had no time to reply before the German reached them, his eyes going over his stained and crumpled uniform with thinly veiled distaste. 'Are you the first officer?'

Culpepper hesitated. Captain Rochelle, who had begun to move towards them once he realized where the German officer was heading, tried to catch his eye.

'I am a first officer,' Culpepper replied carefully.

Mrs Hartford-Jones paled and opened her mouth to speak. The German silenced her with a gesture, his eyes boring into Culpepper.

'On this vessel?'

Captain Rochelle reached them, speaking before Culpepper could answer. 'Well what do you think he is? A bus conductor?'

The German gazed at him coldly. 'Then why was he not on duty? Why does he not give orders to the crew?'

Rochelle gave him a condescending look and pointed to the splints around Culpepper's arm. 'I would have thought that was obvious, even to you. Mr Culpepper broke his arm during the hurricane and is unfit for normal duty.'

The officer gazed at Culpepper for a long moment, then turned and considered the sullen group of men who were watching the exchange. 'And these men, Captain? Are they all passengers from Tortola?'

Rochelle hesitated, his eyes going to the stocky West Indian who acted as both purser and mate. He was remembering that he had once had a bitter fight with the *Tinkerbelle*'s bosun over a girl on Montserrat. The mate, as though reading his mind, stepped forward.

'I deal with the passengers, not the captain. Most of the men took passage at Puerto Rico. They're going to Martinique, looking for work.'

'They look like seamen to me,' said the German.

The West Indian shrugged, as though any fool could see that. There was a clatter from the winch above and the cargo net began to rise up from the deck bulging with cases of supplies. Rochelle bristled, gesturing angrily towards it.

'I don't suppose you'll be paying for any of that.'

The officer smiled bleakly. 'The spoils of war, Captain.'

He turned and left them, speaking to the guards who began to move men towards the ladder.

'They can check your papers, Captain,' Culpepper said quietly.

'Not unless they're prepared to dive for them,' Rochelle replied. 'I threw everything over the side ten minutes ago.'

The cargo hoist returned a few minutes later with a stretcher and two German crewmen took it towards the forecastle saloon. Diana hung back with a worried expression until Helen and Culpepper urged her towards the ladder, telling her there was nothing she could do. Captain Rochelle helped her onto the swaying rungs, the German officer watching without expression until Culpepper helped Mrs Hartford-Jones onto the ladder and reached for it himself.

'You may use the hoist,' he said stiffly, 'the arm will make it difficult for you.'

Culpepper stepped back, watching until the women were safely over the side of the marauder, then crossed to the cargo net where Slade was already waiting on a stretcher. He gave the first officer a crooked grin, his grey eyes like cold slate as he glanced at the black hull beside him.

'I always knew I hadn't seen the last of this bastard,' he said as Culpepper squatted on the net beside him. 'It feels just like coming home.'

The net came up around them and they began to rise off the deck. Culpepper leaned down to him, his voice urgent. 'Linc, you're in no condition to do anything about it. None of us are. Just take it easy and they'll put us off on one of the small islands, probably in a matter of hours.'

Slade's smile put a shiver down his spine. 'You're missing the point, Culpepper. They're the ones who think I'm in no condition to do anything. Think about that!'

Culpepper groaned. 'I am thinking about it. It's called suicide.'

They cleared the side of the marauder and swung over the deck. Crewmen moved towards them. Slade winked and lay back, closing his eyes. 'Say a prayer for them, Culpepper. They're going to need it.'

26

Lieutenant Commander Tellmann lowered his binoculars and glanced towards the gunnery officer, nodding his head.

The man spoke quietly into his headset. 'Fire one!'

The officers on the bridge moved to the windows, looking across the dark stretch of water to the *Island Queen* that drifted, brilliantly lit, only five hundred yards away. They didn't have long to wait. The torpedo took the ferry amidships, blasting a massive hole into the engine room. The boiler exploded an instant later, blowing the bridge and foreward deck apart, and the vessel rolled slowly onto its side in a cloud of steam. It sank within minutes and the sea was dark again.

'Good shot,' Tellmann said mechanically.

'Thank you, sir,' replied the gunnery officer, looking pleased. 'I hope they're all that easy.'

The executive officer gazed at him for a moment with unreadable eyes, then nodded and moved towards the companionway. 'Yes,' he said dryly. 'It's a great help when they don't shoot back.'

After he had gone the gunnery officer glared defensively at the other officers on the bridge. 'Well what does he want now?'

'War,' replied the duty officer. 'I think he wants to feel we're at war.'

Tellmann tapped on the captain's door, knowing he would still be up but not sure whether he wanted to be disturbed. It was a moment before he heard movement, then the door opened and Kroehner told him to enter.

Only the desk lamp was lit, the ship's log open beside it. Kroehner crossed to the desk, sitting down and gesturing to a chair.

'I gather it sank immediately,' he said.

'An old ship, sir. It was a bit like using a sledge hammer to crack a walnut.'

'I suppose that's what we are,' the captain murmured. 'A sledge hammer surrounded by walnuts.'

'The *Island Queen* was necessary. There'll be demands for protection. The British will have to send something.'

'And then it will get interesting. Have you thought about putting the prisoners ashore?'

'We'll be off the island of Saba by noon, sir.'

Kroehner frowned. 'It's a bit small. It could be a long time before they're found.'

Tellmann said nothing. The captain went to the chart table and stared at it for a moment.

'How many are there?'

'Thirty-seven men, two women, sir.'

Kroehner's head came up sharply, his eyes narrowing. 'That's rather a lot, isn't it?'

Tellmann nodded. 'The boarding officer said they're mostly seamen looking for berths at Martinique.'

'Did he establish that from the ship's papers?'

'No, sir. The ferry captain destroyed them before we boarded. They say they took passage at Puerto Rico.'

They looked at each other silently for a moment, then the captain nodded slowly. 'You think we're carrying the crew of the *Tinkerbelle*?'

'It's more than likely, sir.'

'Where are they?'

'Forward mess deck. We can move them into number six hold if they're going to spend any length of time.'

'How many officers are there?'

'Only two, but they're from the *Island Queen*.'

Captain Kroehner prowled the cabin for a minute, pausing finally in front of Tellmann. 'I suppose Slade could have

240

gone down with his ship. That last salvo tore the bridge in half.

'The crew would know, but I doubt if they're in a mood to tell us.'

'Then we'll wait until they are. Forget about Saba. Have the intelligence officer work on them later in the day.'

Tellmann nodded and moved to the door. He was about to step out when he paused, glancing back. 'There is one man in sick bay, sir. A stomach wound. Quite bad from the sound of it.'

'Has he been examined?'

'Only by the orderly. The surgeon is off duty at the moment.'

Kroehner's voice cracked like a whip. 'No man on this ship is off duty, Tellmann. Get him up and tell him I want to know what kind of wound that man has. I also want to know his age and nationality.'

The executive officer stiffened, his cheeks burning. 'I was planning to see him myself, sir.'

The captain started to make a sharp retort, but changed his mind, softening his voice. 'I don't doubt that, Wolf. But let the surgeon do it. If that wound was caused by shrapnel it will tell us a great deal.'

27

Lincoln Slade lay in the antiseptic stillness of the sick bay and tried to control the savage emotions that had been urging him to act the moment the door had closed behind the orderly. It was a struggle he enjoyed, feeling the strength building in him together with the conviction that this moment had been ordained a long time ago – perhaps even as far back as the *Titanic*.

He gazed up at the white ceiling with its single night lamp glowing a greenish blue, feeling the ship breathe and pulse around him. In his mind he was creating every part of the vessel, feeling the spaces below the weather decks, the deep holds that would be crammed with torpedoes and shells, fuel and provisions. There would be three mess decks with crew's quarters below them; a wardroom beneath the bridge surrounded by senior officers' quarters. Above them would be the radio, gunnery and navigation cabins. Then aft, beneath the deckhouse with its heavy guns, would be the main holds and workshops and below them the engine room and fuel bunkers.

His own position was forward, clear of the crew's quarters and busier areas of the ship. He had to be close to the hold where they had kept the Heinkel and that meant the torpedoes would be nearby. He went over it all again and came to the same conclusion, his spirits soaring as he realized how vulnerable they were. There were footsteps outside the door and he closed his eyes, hearing the door open and close. The room brightened through his eyelids and he let himself move restlessly, turning his head away from the light before opening his eyes.

A tall man in his late thirties was gazing at him with a slightly irritable expression. He wore a long white coat with enough ribbons of rank on the epaulettes to suggest that he was the senior surgeon. He pulled the sheet back and opened Slade's shirt, frowning at the dressing.

'How long since this happened?' he asked.

'Five days,' replied Slade.

'Have you been treated by a doctor?'

'The missionary on Tortola.'

He nodded, touching the area around the dressing and watching his face. 'I shall take a look at it. Do you think you can walk across to the examination table?'

He indicated the table beside the instrument cases. A large lamp hung above it and against the wall was a wash basin and sterilisation cabinet. Slade nodded, easing his legs off the bunk and leaning on the doctor's arm as though he barely had the strength to stand.

'Do we have to do this now?' he complained, moving slowly to the table with the doctor's help. 'It's been a hell of a night.'

'I apologise,' the doctor said stiffly. 'I am simply following the captain's orders.'

Slade reached the table and supported himself against it as the doctor turned to the instrument case and took out a kidney basin and a pair of forceps. From a drawer he took a pair of rubber gloves, removing them from the sealed cellophane wrapper before turning back to Slade.

'It won't take a moment. On the table please.'

Slade grinned. 'That's true, doc!'

Even as the surgeon's eyes widened at the sudden assurance in his voice, Slade's right fist was whipping at him, taking him high up along the jaw before he even had time to drop the kidney basin. The metal bowl and instruments clattered across the floor as Slade caught his body and dragged it back across the room to the bunk. He paused there, waiting for any reaction to the noise. When he was satisfied that it had not been heard he stripped off the surgeon's white coat and put him into the bunk, covering him with the sheet so that only the top of his head showed.

Donning the coat, he let himself out of the sick bay and stood in the dimly lit corridor, getting his bearings whilst listening for movement. The ship was still, only the distant thump of the engines sounding through the walls. He began moving forward, walking casually as though he knew where he was going. They had taken Culpepper further along this corridor so that meant they were holding everyone in this area. The corridor turned left, a sign in German telling him nothing at all. He went with it, turning right almost immediately. Ahead was a seaman with a stocky Schmeisser hanging from his shoulder. He was leaning against the wall beside double steel doors that were locked. Slade strolled towards him, hands in the pockets of his white coat, praying that the dim light would confuse the guard for a few seconds more.

The German straightened as he saw him coming towards him, stifling a yawn as he came to attention. The white coat was all that registered so that Slade was almost up to him before he realized that the surgeon's trousers were a dirty grey and wrinkled instead of the crisp white he would have expected. With a vague feeling of alarm he stepped away from the wall, reaching for the weapon at his side. And then he saw the eyes, gleaming with purpose, and a face he had never seen before.

Slade lunged across the last few feet separating them, his left hand grasping the barrel of the gun the man was trying to raise across his body, his stiffened right hand slashing up into his throat to cut off the cry of alarm. The German was stocky and strong, striking him an agonising blow in the stomach even though he was gasping from the blow to his throat. Pain seared up into Slade's chest, as though a white hot knife had plunged into his wound. He let go of the gun, clamping his hand to his side, but somehow found the strength to bring up his knee into the man's groin and hit him hard behind the ear as he instinctively doubled up.

Waves of nausea beat at him and he clutched the handle of the door, forcing the pain into the back of his mind, refusing to give way to the weakness that was turning his legs to rubber. He had no idea how long it was before he was able to stand up straight, but had the guard not been unconscious he would have been helpless. When he was finally able to take his hand from his side he found it red with blood. He cursed and wiped it on the German's tunic, then searched him quickly. He took the Luger from his waist holster together with the Schmeisser, a spare clip of ammunition and a cigarette lighter he found in his breast pocket. Using the guard's keys, he unlocked the doors and stepped into the dimly lit mess, finding Culpepper and McVay gazing at him with grimly expectant features.

'It could only be you,' Culpepper said tonelessly. 'I don't suppose you've given much thought to what the outcome of all this will be?'

'Only the end bit,' growled Slade. 'That's the part where I sink the bastard!'

*   *   *

Wolf Tellmann checked the bridge at 2 am before dropping into the wardroom for a coffee, undecided whether or not to turn in for the night. Two of the younger officers were nodding sleepily over cups of coffee, straightening when they saw him. He recognized one of them as the officer who had led the boarding party and, after pouring a coffee, went over and sat beside him.

'Quite a useful night, sir,' he said politely.

'The supplies will come in handy. I don't suppose we'll have that many opportunities to raid a ship's stores before sending it down.'

The young German smiled and nodded, then tried to think of something else to say. Tellmann sipped his coffee, feeling the tiredness pulling at the corners of his mind, clouding his train of thought so that for a moment he forgot what it was he had wanted to say. He took a cigarette out and lit it, stifling a yawn.

'The man you brought aboard on a stretcher? Did you get a chance to talk to him?'

The officer shook his head. 'No, sir.'

Tellmann allowed himself the yawn and leaned back, closing his eyes. 'I just wondered if he was American.'

'Oh yes, sir. A real tough character too.'

Tellmann snapped awake. 'How do you know?'

Muller was in charge of him, sir. He was saying that he was as awkward as they come, called him every kind of name and didn't seem to care if he did anything about it.'

'How old would he be?'

'Oh . . . middle age. Somewhere in his fifties.'

Tellmann got to his feet and put his cup down, wondering whether he should wake the captain. He decided against it, moving towards the door, surprised at how uneasy he felt.

'Get on to the duty officer and tell him I want a guard in the sick bay right away. I'm going there now.'

He left them gazing at each other in astonishment. The young officer whistled softly and started towards the bridge phone.

'He didn't like that at all, did he? Not one little bit.'

*   *   *

Diana was gazing furiously at Slade with tears on her cheeks, but whether they were there out of anger or concern he could not tell. He was leaning against the wall of the mess beside the door, trying to look casual whilst keeping his arm over the spreading crimson stain from his wound. Culpepper and Captain Rochelle were gathering everyone at the door, watching the corridor beyond.

'None of it makes sense any more, Slade,' she said tearfully. 'You've been as close to being dead as anyone can be, but still you go on.'

'A few more minutes is all I need,' he said calmly. 'Then it'll be finished.'

'But it isn't your war!' she cried, raising her fists as though she wanted to punctuate each word with a blow. 'I won't let you fight it any more.'

He took her by the wrists, feeling the determination in her and wishing it would always be there for him. 'Listen to me, Diana. I should have died a long time ago, but instead I found all kinds of reasons to watch others die instead. The *Titanic* was my ship, just as much as if I'd been its captain, and yet I managed to persuade myself that it wasn't, that I could survive whilst innocent people were drowning.'

She started to protest but he shook her, stilling the words. 'You have to understand that when I saw what this ship had done I couldn't step aside again. It had to be stopped and no matter what it did to me or Tommy or Susan and Jimmy Hardcastle, I knew I would have my chance. Maybe you love me, maybe I love you, but this isn't the time to remind each other of that.'

The strength ran out of her eyes in warm tears and she leaned against him, her lips brushing his cheek with such tenderness his heart ached. 'Promise me you'll try to get away,' she whispered. 'At least promise me that?'

He nodded, not trusting himself to say the words. Helen Hartford-Jones took her gently by the arm, her eyes unaccountably bright as she gazed at him for a brief moment, then took Diana towards the others at the door.

Culpepper was pale and grim. 'We're close to the midships boat deck. If we're not spotted we can get into the shadow of one of the boats.'

'Do that,' Slade ordered. 'As soon as I start the fire all hell will break loose. If I do my job right nobody will try to stop you. They'll be too busy getting off themselves.'

Culpepper's glance dropped to the widening stain over his side. 'You won't get far like that. Let me go.'

'Not a chance.' He smiled, gripping the man's good arm. 'Just get them off, Culp. And say a prayer for me.'

They went quickly out of the room and along the corridor towards the companionway which went up to the boat deck. Slade waited until they were out of sight, then turned towards the hatch leading to the lower decks. McVay stepped out of the shadows, his eyes glittering, ready for an argument.

'I don't need you,' snapped Slade.

'You've got me so don't waste time arguing, you stubborn Yankee bastard!'

Slade grinned and handed him the Luger. They went through the hatch and down a steel ladder to a gantry that ran along the side of the forward hold. Below were stacks of cases and drums of fuel that rose in black tiers from the darkness. They ran to a dogged hatch which McVay opened, stepping through into the next hold. There were lights on and below two mechanics were working on one of the ship's launches, glancing up as they heard the clatter of feet although unable to see who it was.

At the far end of the hold drums of fuel were stacked against the bulkhead and from the red warning signs Slade knew that beyond it lay the ship's arsenal. This was where the Heinkel had been kept so the drums must contain aviation spirit. He grinned at McVay and indicated the ladder leading down from the gantry.

'You first. I'll cover you.'

McVay nodded, climbing over the rail and starting down. Slade leaned out so that the two men below could see him in the light. He tapped the Schmeisser against steel.

'Either of you two speak English?'

They gazed up at him incredulously. One of them began to shake his head, then changed his mind. 'Ja. Ein sprecken small English.'

'Sprecken Schmeisser?' Slade asked with chilling menace.

They nodded, looking at each other with bewildered expressions. As McVay reached the floor of the hold he took the Luger from his pocket, pointing it at them.

Tellmann entered the sick bay and gazed at the figure in the bunk with a deep sense of relief. He had no clear idea of what he had expected to find, but the mere presence of Lincoln Slade on the ship was enough to put a shiver down his spine. The American had shown such remorseless courage that the last place for him to be was alone in the sick bay.

He moved towards the figure, wondering whether he should wake him before the surgeon arrived. He glanced at his watch, suddenly aware that he should be there already. As he stepped towards the bunk his foot hit something metallic that spun across the room and came to rest against the wall. It was a pair of forceps and close by lay a kidney basin.

He lunged at the bunk, pulling the sheet away, knowing already what he would find. The surgeon was breathing shallowly, but still unconscious. With a bitter curse he crossed to the wall phone and turned the handle viciously, the bridge responding immediately.

'Sound the alarm,' he snarled. 'Get a squad of armed men to the forward mess deck immediately. Seal all watertight doors and put guards in every hold. And do it fast!'

He slammed the phone down and ran from the sick bay, heading for the mess deck. He slowed to a stop as he turned the corner, staring at the open doors and unconscious guard with bitter features. Slade, he said savagely, the name beating in his brain like a gong. Almost in answer the ship's alarm began to sound, clamouring along the corridors like the bells of doom.

*   *   *

McVay and Slade were working on opposite sides of the hold, unscrewing the caps from ten gallon drums and tipping them onto their sides. The German mechanics had started to protest with horrified voices, but the Schmeisser presented an even greater threat and they made no attempt to interfere. When the alarm gongs sounded they had ten drums pouring fuel over the floor of the hold.

'Right. Get them up top,' Slade said, grabbing a rag and soaking it in the spirit. 'I'll follow.'

The Germans needed no encouragement. They ran for the ladder and began climbing rapidly to the overhead gantry. McVay followed, watching anxiously as Slade pulled himself slowly from rung to rung. Blood was dripping steadily from his side, running down his leg so that he left bloody footprints wherever he went, but his eyes showed no pain—only triumph. McVay was pulling himself onto the gantry, turning to reach down for Slade, when three armed men came through the bulkhead hatch from the next hold. They knelt and opened fire immediately, a bullet taking the Scotsman in the arm and knocking him round so that he had to grab the rail, dropping his gun.

The two mechanics shouted urgently and ran towards them, forcing the men to hold their fire until they were past and through the hatch. The few vital seconds were enough for Slade to reach the edge of the gantry and lean onto it, firing a long burst which took the Germans by surprise. Two died instantly and the third, badly wounded in the stomach, only just managed to stagger back through the hatch. A moment later it slammed shut and from the clang of steel they knew that those on the other side had dogged it.

'What the hell did you let them shoot you for?' Slade asked irritably.

'What kind of question is that?' yelled McVay, trying to tie a filthy handkerchief round his arm. 'You're bleeding all over the place like a stuck pig yourself!'

'You put that on and you'll get gangrene,' said Slade. He took off the white coat and ripped a piece from the back, tying it tightly above the hole that was pumping out a steady stream of blood. It slowed to a trickle and he grunted, turning to look around the hold.

'So how do we get out of here?'

'There's got to be a service hatch, but they're probably waiting up there for us by now.'

Slade nodded and looked towards the hatch leading into the arsenal. 'Do you feel like a bit of a gamble?'

The engineer gave him a disgusted look. 'Would it make any difference if I said no!'

Slade grinned and shook his head. They went along the gantry to the door covered with red warning symbols and unfastened the clamps, going through to an extension of the gantry. They looked down with bulging eyes.

'Jesus!' said Slade.

'You mad Yankee bastard,' whispered McVay. 'If that lot goes up they'll be picking bits of us up in China!'

The hold below contained row after row of torpedoes that gleamed dully in the dim light. Beyond them, stacked in racks like bottles of vintage wine, were hundreds of shells and bombs and cases of ammunition that rose in grey tiers along every wall. The air smelled of oil and the resin-like tang of wax that sealed each case of ammunition.

'Think of the ships they can sink with all of that,' murmured Slade. 'Think of all the poor bastards that'll never know what hit them.'

They looked at each other, then Slade took the petrol-soaked rag from his pocket and moved to the hatch. McVay winced, but went with him, holding the steel door as Slade lit the rag and tossed it through. They slammed the hatch and bolted it, feeling the concussion through the bulkhead as the high octane fuel ignited in one sizzling blast and blew the top of the hold straight out of the deck on a pillar of flame.

*　　*　　*

Tellmann was on the boat deck confronting the dejected group of prisoners who were being held at gunpoint by a dozen crewmen. Culpepper faced him with drawn features, pointing out that neither he nor his charges could be held responsible for any action taken by Slade.

'Never mind that,' snapped Tellmann. 'Where is Slade and what does he intend to do?'

At that moment the deck shook and beyond them the forward hold erupted in flames. They crouched instinctively, the heat beating at them. Tellmann straightened, his face gaunt, his eyes filling with fury as he watched the inferno turn night into day. The crewman nearest to him gestured nervously with his gun.

'Sir? Do I keep them here?'

Tellmann gazed at Culpepper, his mouth pinched. The two women beside the officer watched with hollow eyes, expecting the worst. He took a deep breath, fighting the savage emotions, and nodded his head. 'Of course. Three short blasts will be the signal to abandon ship. If that happens they will be allowed to take this lifeboat.'

Culpepper looked at him in surprise. 'Thank you, sir.'

'But not Slade!' Tellmann added harshly. 'If Slade appears, kill him!'

*   *   *

Slade pulled McVay up through the narrow hatch in the bow, hidden from the bridge by billowing clouds of black smoke. The flames lit up the entire ship, showing the rushing figures of the crew as they ran to their boat stations. Others were trying to approach the blaze with water hoses, but it was impossible to get near.

'You want to jump?' asked Slade.

'Of course I don't want to jump,' the engineer said irritably. 'With one arm I'd be worse than useless.'

'Then if we're going to run for it now's the time. It's not going to get any cooler.'

They ran, shielding their faces from the flames, jumping over burning wreckage and feeling their skin scorch as the heat from the blazing hold beat at them like a blast furnace.

They were lunging into the worst of the flames when a sheet of water jetted across the deck as one of the fire fighting teams tried to direct it into the hold, looking at the pair in astonishment as they ran out of the smoke.

'Head for the boat deck and make sure that Culpepper gets off,' shouted Slade, angling towards a stocky German who was beginning to realize who they were and reaching for the pistol at his side.

McVay watched Slade bowl the man over and head for the bridge before taking the companionway to the boat deck below. There was pandemonium on the deck as seamen dashed towards boat stations putting on life jackets, others hauling the stacked rafts to the rails.

No one paid any attention to the Scotsman as he pushed his way towards a group midway along the deck. He could make out Culpepper and the women, but his spirits fell when he saw that they were being guarded by armed crewmen. He had almost reached them when the clamour of fire bells stopped and there was a moment of deathly silence, then the ship's siren sounded three short blasts.

The boat stations came alive with activity as orders were shouted and the lifeboats began to swing out on their davits, lowering down to hang level with the deck. In the confusion he slipped between Panacero and Santiano, winking at them, and moved up to Culpepper. Diana grabbed his hand, her eyes huge and afraid. He forced a smile.

'He's alright. He'll find his own way off.'

Culpepper turned, hearing his voice. 'They'll kill him if they can,' he said quietly.

McVay shrugged. 'They keep trying.'

The guards seemed to be uncertain about what they should do, so Culpepper made up their minds for them by shouting instructions to get into the lifeboat. One of the Germans stepped forward, looking worried, his gun waving indecisively as they began to climb into the boat.

'You heard what your officer said,' Culpepper reminded him. 'Three blasts is abandon ship.'

The guard sighed and shook his head, turning to his companions and shrugging as though it didn't matter any more. They moved towards the next boat station, leaving Culpepper and Captain Rochelle to supervise their own boat and lower it away.

Tellmann found the captain alone on the bridge, staring off into the billowing smoke that obscured most of the forward deck. The flames were shooting forty feet above the ship, fed in incandescent flashes as fresh drums of fuel exploded. The glow of the fire etched the lines of defeat deeper into his face giving it a coppery cast, like some classical mask from a Greek tragedy.

'Cypher bag over the side, sir?' he asked quietly, holding up the weighted canvas bag which he had filled with the contents of the ship's safe.

'If you please, Mr Tellmann,' he replied.

He went out onto the wing of the bridge, coughing in the acrid smoke, and flung the bag out into the night. When he returned the Captain had not moved from the window.

'I think we should take to the boats, sir.'

Kroehner turned, nodding heavily. 'Yes, it won't take long now.' He paused, gazing at his executive officer with haunted eyes. 'I'll stay for a while and jump from the stern.'

Tellmann didn't like it and opened his mouth to protest. The captain stopped him with a firm gesture. 'That's an order. You are to leave now.'

Tellmann hesitated, his face tormented, then turned abruptly and left the bridge. Kroehner smiled, almost wistfully, and gazed into the deeper shadows beyond the green glow of the helm compass. There was a whisper of movement, then a figure stepped forward into the dim light, a Schmeisser held steadily in bloody hands.

'A good officer, Captain. He does what he's told.'

'Part of our tradition, Captain Slade.'

He watched him move slowly, painfully, past the compass and telegraph, reaching for the command chair. His face was chalk white, the skin stretched tight as though all the tissue and fibre of his body had been consumed in the struggle to live. But his eyes were ferocious, like grey smoke obscuring a brilliant light. The dark sheen of blood covered his left side from the waist to the knee and when he sank into the chair the breath left him in a slow, agonized wheeze.

'It is not necessary to die,' Kroehner said gently. 'You have your victory.'

'Not yet,' said Slade.

There was silence between them until a concussion shook the deck and another fountain of fire soared into the sky. The captain watched it for a moment, then looked at Slade, shaking his head as though he still found it difficult to believe.

'Was it that easy, Captain? A ship like this . . . with a match?'

Slade's eyes gleamed and he nodded. 'A hell of a way to go, Captain. But then it was the very least I could do.'

'Why?' whispered Kroehner.

'Bodies. Old women and little girls, boys in pyjamas and young men blown up like obscene balloons. They didn't even know you'd started your filthy war until you blasted their liner out of the sea.'

Kroehner's shoulders sagged and he gazed at his hands for a long moment. Behind him there was another explosion and blazing oil soared into the crimson sky in a golden curtain. It rained fire, running down the armour-plated glass like rivulets of wrath.

'Ah yes, the liner,' murmured the captain.

'You bastard,' said Slade.

'No, Captain, not a bastard. Just a merchantman like you fighting a war his country chose to start. An officer of the Kriegsmarine out of duty, not conviction, and a captain of this ship because it was mine in more peaceful times.' He gazed at him with anguished eyes. 'When the mist cleared and I saw that liner my own private nightmare began. It made no difference that I had believed it was another ship, a tanker we had been following. It made no difference that my direct orders from the Seekriegsleitung were to sink any ship in these waters. All that mattered was that I gave the order to fire.'

Slade looked at him with a baffled expression. 'What the fuck are you saying?'

'I'm saying it was an accident, but once that accident had happened it was my responsibility. Just as you, on the *Titanic*, could not see the iceberg, you still had to live with the consequences for the rest of your life.'

They gazed at each other with brooding eyes, Slade trying to relate the humble man before him with the image in his own mind which had driven him so relentlessly. With sudden insight he realized that the bodies in the sea had bridged time itself and it was his own ghost he had been fighting. All the wasted years, the tortured nights, the alcohol that dulled the pain. All of that would be erased, vindicated, if he could only have gone back and done the right thing. And so he had, but in a different way and in a different time.

'Oh, shit!' he said.

And the deck trembled beneath them, as fragile as a leaf, and the air shimmered as though a great bell had rung. But neither of them heard the sound. Like a scarlet flower the ship beneath them burst apart and erupted into the sky.

The light lit up the sea for a mile in every direction and the air screamed over the boats where the survivors huddled, watching in awe as the ball of fire rose up towards the heavens.

And then the darkness came and there was peace once more.